SEASONS
FOR CHANGE

What Reviewers Say
About KC Richardson's Work

A Call Away

"…the romance between both characters was nice and gave me all the feels by the end. I really think this is the kind of novel you take on holiday and read by the pool. I look forward to seeing what's coming up next for KC Richardson."—*Les Reveur*

New Beginnings

"Pure and simple, this is a sweet slow-burn romance. It's cozy and warm. At its heart, *New Beginnings* by KC Richardson is a story about soul mates that fall in love. …If you're looking for a sweet romance, the kind of romance that you can curl-up with as a fire crackles in your fireplace, then this could be your book. It's a simple love story that leaves you feeling good."—*Lesbian Review*

Courageous Love

"Richardson aptly captures the myriad emotions and sometimes irrational thought processes of a young woman with a possibly fatal disease, as well as the torment inherent in the idea of losing another loved one to the same illness. This sensitively told and realistically plotted story will grab readers by the heartstrings and not let them go."—*Publishers Weekly*

"Take one happy and well-centered ER nurse add one handsome Cop and the scene is set for a happy ever after. But throw in a life-threatening disease and KC Richardson ramps up the angst. …This is a great storyline and felt very well done. While there is a heavy dose of angst, it's justified and well handled."—*Lesbian Reading Room*

"[A]n enjoyable read that doesn't shy away from the realities of dealing with a life-threatening illness."—*Rainbow Book Reviews*

Visit us at www.boldstrokesbooks.com

By the Author

New Beginnings

Courageous Love

A Call Away

Taking a Shot at Love

Seasons for Change

SEASONS FOR CHANGE

by

KC Richardson

2021

SEASONS FOR CHANGE

ISBN 13: 978-1-63555-882-1

This Trade Paperback Original Is Published By
Bold Strokes Books, Inc.
P.O. Box 249
Valley Falls, NY 12185

First Edition: July 2021

CREDITS
Editor: Cindy Cresap
Production Design: Susan Ramundo
Cover Design By Tammy Seidick

Acknowledgments

A huge thank you goes to Radclyffe, Sandy Lowe, and everyone at Bold Strokes Books involved in helping produce outstanding books. Special thanks go to my editor, Cindy Cresap, who always teaches me something new. Editing is my favorite part of writing because I always learn something new, and in Cindy, I have a patient teacher.

Thank you to my fantastic beta readers, Inger, Dawn, April, and Rebecca. Because of your insight, I was able to turn in a pretty decent first draft.

This book is set in a special place for me: Lake Tahoe. I grew up there, made amazing friends that I'm proud to say are still part of my life. For me, there is no more beautiful place than Tahoe. The clean air, crystal clear water of the lake, the scents of the pine trees and earth, and the tranquility that the area offers. I'm always at peace when I'm there, and I'm proud to call Lake Tahoe my home. Tahoe Strong.

Finally, I want to thank you, the readers, for your continued support in my writing endeavors by buying my books, leaving reviews, and sending me messages on Facebook, Twitter, and email. You inspire me to keep writing, and I hope you enjoy reading this book as much as I enjoyed writing it.

Dedication

For my wife, always.

For my parents. Thank you for moving us
to Lake Tahoe in our early childhood and enabling
us to have the most amazing adventures.

Chapter One

Summer

"Order up!"

Shawn Evans handed back the change to the customer, wishing them a good day. She saw that all the servers were busy taking orders, so she grabbed the plates and headed to table seven. The smell of bacon, biscuits, and gravy made her stomach growl.

"Who had the short stack?" She placed the plate of pancakes with a melting dollop of butter sitting on top in front of the younger woman who raised her hand. She placed the other plate in front of the man sitting across from her. "Can I get you two anything else?"

"No, this looks great," the man exclaimed, his eyes widening almost as big as the plate of eggs, bacon, sausage, biscuits, and gravy. The "Black Bear Special" was a big seller ever since the diner had been featured on a popular food channel. Who would've thought that her small diner in Small Town, USA, would always have a line of people waiting to get inside, even at the ungodly hour of six a.m. when they opened?

Shawn returned to the cash register to ring up the next paying customer while their table was being cleared and cleaned for the next group. The sound of silverware clinking against plates, ceramic coffee cups being placed on the Formica tables, and the low hum of conversations being held over breakfast was like music to her ears. Not bad for a former art director of an advertising agency. Shawn was having the time of her life running her diner. The "regulars" had become her friends even though they rarely hung out together outside of the restaurant. Maybe they'd see each other at the market or post office, where they'd chat for a few minutes before getting on with their day. She considered them her friends because they were the ones that were loyal, coming in for breakfast or lunch often more than once a week. The diner didn't serve dinner; it never had even when Shawn's grandfather owned and ran it. "You can't have any fun if you're working your tail off day and night, Shawny. When would we go fishing?" Shawn could hear her grandfather's deep baritone voice in her ear when she had the nerve to suggest he could charge higher prices for dinners. She'd been in her senior year in college when she'd taken a business class to have under her belt.

"But, Grandad, if you served dinner like some steak or seafood, maybe got a beer and wine license, you could make a killing."

"That's not why I run this place, Shawny. There are plenty of places the locals and tourists can go for dinner, but not many places have the ambience we have for breakfast and lunch. We serve the best tasting coffee lakeside, and nobody can beat our breakfast specials."

In honor of her grandad, Shawn had abided by his wishes. The restaurant closed its doors at three p.m. Shawn headed home and got ready for whatever adventure she was in the mood for. On the west shore of Lake Tahoe in the late summer, there were plenty to choose from. Until then, she had to finish her workday and help out in whatever way she could. She grabbed four laminated menus that had their breakfast dishes on one side and lunch on the other, called out for the Jenkins group, and led them to their table.

"Your server will be right with you. I hope you enjoy your meal." She headed back to the register and called out the next group. Despite her knowledge for advertising, Ray's Diner was known strictly by word of mouth. The spot on the popular show from the Food Network also helped. It was that way, every day, and what truly surprised her was how energized she got as she drove home. She had the windows down in her Subaru, and she breathed in the fresh mountain air. The smell of pine, vanilla, and hot asphalt made her smile. She had a fifteen-minute drive from the diner to her cabin, and she'd take that time to take deep breaths and decompress.

Shawn turned right on Mountain Way that would lead to her place deep enough in the woods that she didn't have another residence closer than five hundred yards, but close enough where she could see the lake over and through the trees. Her grandparents built the cabin themselves over fifty years ago. She and her parents would drive the two hours northeast of Sacramento, where she grew up, and spend the weekends or holidays, and for Shawn, she spent the summers there. The house was filled with happy memories that made her smile. Memories of helping her grandfather stack firewood, going fishing with him, exploring the woods on her mountain bike, and learning to cook with her grandmother. Occasionally, she'd get emotional being alone in the house, missing her grandparents fiercely. She'd like to think that they were still there with her, looking down on her from heaven, with love and pride in their eyes.

After Shawn turned off the ignition, she immediately loaded up her kayak and paddle on the roof rack then opened the door to her Lab mix rescue impatiently waiting for her to arrive home. The amber-colored dog whined and barked and wagged his tail furiously, turning in circles, welcoming her home and making her laugh. She placed her bag on the floor and squatted down to give her doggo some love.

"Hey, Jameson. Yes, I know, I missed you too, but I have a fun outing planned for us. Do you want to go kayaking today?" The word "go" made his ears perk up and he tilted his head. He followed her into her bedroom where she changed into board shorts and a tank top. She pulled her and Jameson's life vests out of the guest room closet, and she laughed when he started excitedly turning in circles again. "Okay, let's go."

Jameson beat Shawn to the door and darted out to the car when she opened it. She grabbed his leash off the hook next to the door and followed him, almost as excited as he was. She opened the rear lift gate, and he jumped in as she threw the life vests in the back seat.

One of the many nice things about living where she did was that she had her own private dock that had a locked gate so no tourists could use it. Her grandfather had purchased it when it became available just a couple of years after they moved there. Once she got Jameson into his life vest and she opened the gate, he started running to the end of the dock. She stuck two fingers in her mouth and whistled sharply, causing Jameson to stop and look back. She commanded him to stay until she got her kayak in the water. She held on until Jameson got in, then she slid in behind him, and she started paddling out into the deep blue water. The sun sparkled on the tiny ripples that looked like shiny diamonds glinting off the lake, and Shawn's heart filled with joy. To be out on this magnificent day with her constant companion in what Shawn felt was the most beautiful place on earth warmed her to the core.

The water was calm with just a slight breeze ruffling her hair that did nothing to cool the late afternoon heat. Her skin glistened with sweat after just ten minutes of paddling. They stayed out on the water for a couple of hours, occasionally stopping to take in the scenery around them. The lake was outlined with rock formations and tall, mature pine trees. She had run into one of her buddies who was stand-up paddle boarding, and she promised to go mountain biking with him the following week. The time on the water had given her new life, and a slight sunburn despite having applied plenty of sunscreen. Once they arrived home, Jameson peed on almost every tree on her property, remarking his territory while Shawn unloaded her kayak and hung up the life vests to dry. After they ate their respective dinners, Jameson jumped on the couch and laid his head on Shawn's lap while she sipped a beer and read her book. Life was good.

Morgan Campbell; her best friend, Jane; and Jane's wife, Annie, had arrived to their rental cabin late the night before, much later than they had anticipated. Between her work meeting running late, her argument with her girlfriend over her having to work and not being able to go with them to the mountains, and Friday night traffic, it was well after eleven p.m. when they arrived. Morgan had been looking forward to this long weekend with her girlfriend, Jessica, and reconnecting. They had both been working so much lately that it felt to Morgan like they were drifting apart. Now she was going to be the third wheel to Jane and Annie, although they'd never make her feel like that.

She had tossed and turned once she got into bed, still stewing over the fact Jessica waited until Morgan got home to tell her. She didn't understand why Jess hadn't called her or texted her earlier in the day to drop her little bombshell. Now, in the early morning and empty bed, Morgan felt more sad than angry. She wanted to shake it off and try to make the most of this weekend. She knew Jane and Annie would improve her mood with whatever they had planned for the day.

By the time she'd showered and dressed, the smell of coffee lured her to the kitchen where she found Jane and Annie wrapped in each others arms. Morgan felt a tinge of jealousy, imagining that she could be cuddling with Jess. She quickly shook it off and cleared her throat.

"Good morning, sleepyhead."

"Good morning, ladies. Any coffee left for me?" Morgan smiled as she picked up a mug off the counter. She knew there'd be more than enough for her, and if Annie made it, she knew it would be delicious.

"Just one cup though because we want to have breakfast at a diner that Jane saw on the Food Network. It's just down the road a bit, then we thought we could walk around town and visit the shops. How does that sound?"

Morgan sighed with pleasure as the first sip of hot coffee hit her lips. "That sounds good. What's the weather supposed to be like?"

"Gorgeous. Mid to high seventies during the day." Early September weather in Lake Tahoe could be unpredictable. One day it could be hot, the next day it could be snowing. There was a saying she'd heard about Lake Tahoe once—there were two seasons in Tahoe, winter and July.

Morgan considered the sweater she had on, and she decided to wear a tank top underneath in case she got warm. "Let me go change really quick and we can go."

Morgan met Jane and Annie back in the kitchen a few minutes later, and they left the cabin. As Jane drove, Morgan sat in the back seat and marveled at the tall pine trees that inhabited the area. Farther down the road from their cabin, the lake came into view and Morgan gasped.

"You okay back there?" Annie asked as she turned her head toward the back seat.

"Yes, but I'm always amazed by the beauty of the lake."

"You've been here before though."

Morgan thought about her occasional trips with Jessica to Lake Tahoe, but this one was different. "Yes, but we always go to the South Shore so Jess can gamble, and we usually end up staying at a casino. It's so crowded near Stateline, so it's not like this area." Morgan was trying to find the words to describe it. She felt serene, at peace with the scarcity of houses and cabins. There was so much…space. "Not that South Shore isn't beautiful, but the main thoroughfare is lined with motels, stores, restaurants, and it feels like it's more geared for the tourists. It's busy there."

Jane looked at Morgan through the rearview mirror. "I get what you're saying, and I agree. The west shore of the lake is all about the locals. It's a different vibe here, more laid-back and friendly. No messing around with city slickers."

Annie cuffed Jane on the arm and laughed. "We're city slickers."

Morgan laughed. "I know what you mean, Jane. So, tell me about this restaurant we're going to."

Jane put her left blinker on and turned into a small-ish driveway. "No time. We're here."

They got out of the car to the sound of rushing water. The Truckee River was a stone's throw from where they stood. Annie threw her arms around Morgan and gave her a tiny squeeze. "Wanna go river rafting?"

Morgan ducked out from under Annie's hold and turned away. "Oh, no. You're not getting me on a raft." Jane laughed as she held the door open for Morgan and Annie. The diner was packed, and people stood waiting to be seated. Morgan was impressed with the eatery. The entire front of it had floor to ceiling windows, giving every diner a partially tree-obstructed view of the lake.

"Good morning. Welcome to Ray's Diner. How many?"

Morgan felt her mouth go dry when she heard the deep timbre of the voice that belonged to the butch behind the register. She smiled at Morgan as she waited for her answer.

"Um, three of us. How long is the wait?" Jane took over since Morgan's voice seemed to be gone.

"Just about twenty minutes. I promise, it'll be worth it." She smiled as she looked at Morgan.

I just bet it would.

"Great. Is it okay if we wait outside?"

"Sure. Can I get a name?"

Annie nudged Morgan, and she faltered forward.

"Morgan."

"Hi, Morgan. I'm Shawn. I'll come get you when your table is ready."

Annie grabbed Morgan's arm and pulled her outside to Jane's laughter. Morgan was feeling suddenly warm, and she felt the heat flash to her face. She also felt a little lightheaded, but that could have been from the altitude. Morgan accepted that reasoning.

"Oh my God. Did I just do that?" Morgan grabbed Annie's arms and she felt her eyes bulge. "Please tell me I just did not do that. Tell me I didn't go speechless and make a total ass out of myself."

Annie and Jane were laughing hard enough to bring tears to their eyes. "Morgan, sweetie, you have drool on your chin," Jane said, which made them laugh harder, and made Morgan want to jump in the deepest hole she could find. She covered her face with her hands and shook her head, feeling the heat on her face.

"No, no, no. We can't go back in there. Jane, tell her we changed our minds."

Jane continued to laugh. "Not a chance. I've never seen you behave that way. Normally, you're cool as a cucumber, but she sure did a number on you."

"I can't believe I behaved that way. I have a girlfriend, for Christ's sake."

"Yes, who should be here with you right now."

Morgan didn't miss the irritation in Jane's voice. "Look, I already know you don't like her, but she is my girlfriend."

Jane hugged Morgan and she slowly relaxed into her arms. "I'm sorry, but you're my best friend, and I just don't think she deserves you. Now, we're here for a long weekend, and I really want us to have a great time."

Morgan gave Jane one more squeeze and stepped back. "I want that too."

The door to the diner opened, and a large group exited and walked toward the river. A few minutes later, Shawn opened the door and smiled at them.

"Morgan, your table is ready."

They followed Shawn to the table, Morgan finding it difficult to keep her eyes off Shawn's backside. Shawn held the chair out for Morgan. Just that tiny move made Morgan feel giddy, and she thanked her. Shawn handed them their menus and told them their server would be right with them. As Shawn headed back to the register, Morgan felt her gaze lingering once again on Shawn's ass that filled out her jeans in the best possible way. She caught Annie and Jane staring at her, and she used the menu to fan herself. Annie and Jane laughed, and Morgan joined them.

"Just because I'm taken doesn't mean I'm dead. That is one good-looking woman, right there."

Throughout the meal, Morgan stole quick glances of Shawn. She always had a smile on her face when she interacted with the customers. She even gave a few hugs as the patrons left, and it made Morgan wish she could get to know her. She liked Shawn's style and easygoing interaction with people. Once they'd finished breakfast, they sat back in their chairs and collectively sighed.

"That was the best breakfast ever."

Annie nodded in agreement with Jane.

Morgan patted her stomach, feeling like it was going to explode. "I ate too much."

Jane chuckled. "You had oatmeal."

"I know, but did you see the size of that bowl, not to mention the sides that came with it? Not all of us can eat like a lumberjack."

Jane shrugged. "What can I say? The fresh mountain air makes me hungry."

"Speaking of fresh mountain air, let's go walk off this food coma before we slip too deep." Annie picked up the check the server had dropped off at the table, and they walked to the register.

"So, how was everything?" Shawn asked as she rang up the charges.

"The Black Bear Special was just as amazing as it looked on the television show," Jane exclaimed.

"You saw that, did ya? Imagine my shock when they wanted to do a segment on my little establishment."

"Well, I think I can speak for all of us that this was probably the best breakfast we've ever had. But tell me one thing. Why is it called the Black Bear?"

Shawn raised her arms and snarled like a bear standing on its hand legs, then lowered her voice into a near growl. "Because it's just enough food to fill me up." She lowered her arms and chuckled, making some of the diners laugh along with her.

"You tell 'em, Yogi," one of the diners yelled out.

Morgan stood off to the side, content to let Jane do all the talking and observe the diner owner who she found attractive. She usually wasn't so shy, but she just couldn't come up with any words for the woman behind the register that wouldn't make her sound like a schoolgirl, which was exactly how she felt when Shawn smiled at her. Shawn was dressed in a plain black T-shirt and light blue jeans. Her tanned skin that covered well-toned muscles had Morgan thinking all kinds of nasty thoughts. Morgan's fingers itched to run through Shawn's dark, short, thick hair, and Morgan could see Shawn had been living a great life as evidenced by the laugh lines around her eyes.

"How about you, Morgan? Did you enjoy your oatmeal?" The hopeful look on Shawn's face urged Morgan to not let her down.

"It was delicious. I'd love to eat here again." Jesus. Could Morgan sound more juvenile? However, the look of satisfaction on Shawn's face pleased Morgan, and she wished that she could see that look on Jess' face once in a while.

"So, are you ladies here for vacation? I don't recall seeing you before."

Morgan continued to stare, but she found the courage to finally answer. "Yes, here for the holiday weekend."

Shawn looked Morgan up and down, and she felt like she was being undressed with Shawn's eyes.

"Too bad." Shawn looked disappointed, and Morgan wondered what that was about. "Thanks for coming in, ladies. I hope you have a great stay."

They left the diner and Morgan felt like she could finally breathe again.

"Morgan has a girlfriend," Annie sang.

"Shut it, Annie." They all laughed again as they meandered their way into town to do some shopping. Morgan wondered what the next few days would hold, and if she'd see Shawn again. Not that she would do anything. She wasn't a cheater, and she wouldn't start now. Still, it was fun to have a little fantasy.

The following night, Morgan's phone rang, and she frowned when she saw the name on the caller ID. She was hoping it would be Jess, as she hadn't returned any of Morgan's texts or the one message she left.

"Hey, Steve, what's going on?" He was the senior member on their team in the outside sales department for the medical manufacturing company she worked for.

"Oh, Morgan. Thank God. I need you to come back early from your trip. My wife just went into labor, and I'm supposed to have a big meeting with the new client in a couple of days. You're the only one I trust to do the presentation."

"Steve, I'm on vacation. I rode up with my friends so I don't have a car."

"Please, Morgan. You know I wouldn't ask if I didn't have to. The baby wasn't due for another two weeks. Rescheduling is out because the Orthopedics chief I'm supposed to be meeting with is scheduled to leave the country on Wednesday."

Morgan heard the anxiety in his voice, and she wasn't sure if it was because his wife was about to have a baby, or because this meeting was so important. She knew it had the potential to be a huge account, supplying the orthopedics surgery department with new instruments.

She let out a huge breath. "Okay. Email me the presentation and PowerPoint, as well as contact info. I'll be there."

"Morgan, you're the fucking best. I'll never forget this."

Morgan laughed. "I know you won't because I won't let you. Go have your baby and I'll call you after the meeting. Good luck, and give Maria my best."

Morgan hung up and looked out her bedroom window into the dark forest and sighed. She was going to have to break the news to Annie and Jane. Damn, and she was having such a great time, but at least she was only missing out on a couple of days left on her trip.

CHAPTER TWO

Thanks for dropping me off at the car rental, guys. I'm sorry I have to leave early."

"We are too. Are you sure you don't want us to drive you? It's only a two-hour trip."

"No, you stay here and enjoy the rest of your time. We'll get together soon. Love you, guys."

"We love you, too," Jane said as they hugged good-bye.

Annie was next. "You drive carefully and text us when you get home so we know you arrived safe."

Morgan waved before she stepped through the door. A short time later, she was in her rental car headed home. She used the time to think back on her too-short trip to the lake. She'd truly enjoyed herself with her friends exploring the small towns that dotted the west and north shores of the lake. They'd bought some crafts at a little outdoor market, they took a walk on a path along the Truckee River, and had spent some time at the beach. Morgan had truly relaxed in the two full days she'd spent there, so much so that her anger and sadness toward Jessica had dissipated.

She felt the corners of her mouth tug as she thought of Shawn from Ray's Diner. She was taller than Morgan by a good three or four inches, and she had a sturdy build to her—not that she considered Shawn to be overweight, but kind of brawny and athletic. Her short, dark brown hair looked thick and sat just above the collar of her T-shirt. She had the mountain woman look to her. And her eyes. Oh, those eyes that were the color of whiskey, and made Morgan feel a little drunk when she looked into them.

Morgan spent the rest of the drive making up stories about Shawn—what her house looked like, what activities she liked to do. She wondered if she liked to play around or if she was relationship material. Morgan would bet a year's salary that she was fantastic in bed and knew how to please a woman. Damn, she and Jessica needed to have sex soon and get their relationship back on track. Maybe they could start tonight. They could order dinner in, have some wine, and get reconnected.

Once she'd arrived in Sacramento, Morgan drove straight to her office to look over Steve's email and get prepped for tomorrow's meeting. That way, there'd be no distractions, and she'd be able to enjoy her night with Jess. She shot off a quick text to Jane to let her know she'd arrived safe and told them to have fun.

Morgan had spent a good four hours reviewing all of the notes Steve had emailed her, and she did some research on the doctor she'd be meeting with. She had no intention of adding anything to Steve's notes and presentation, but she also didn't want to get caught with her skirt around her ankles. She wanted to be as prepared as she could be to answer any questions Dr. Molinari might have. Satisfied she was as prepared as she was going to be, she turned off her computer and locked her office.

While driving home, butterflies started moving around in her stomach as she anticipated surprising Jess by being home two days early. Her excitement increased as she pulled into their driveway next to Jess's Acura. Morgan's car was parked in the garage already. She unlocked the front door, expecting Jess to be in the living room, but it was empty, as was the kitchen. As she walked down the hallway, she peeked into Jess's home office, not wanting to startle her. Empty. *I wonder if she's taking a nap.* She opened the door to their bedroom where she found Jess—with another woman sitting on her face, Jess's hands on the other woman's hips. The bag that dropped from Morgan's hand caused a loud thud. Jess and her floozy looked her way, and Morgan grabbed the doorway to steady herself. Her pulse raced with fury and she felt like her legs were about to give way. She never once considered coming home to find her girlfriend cheating on her.

"Morgan, I can explain," Jess started as she used her sheet—HER sheet—to wipe the woman's juices off her mouth.

Nausea and rage rumbled like an inferno through Morgan's body. "Pack your shit and get the fuck out of my house. Now!" Morgan turned and quickly made her way to the kitchen. She pulled down a glass from her cupboard and fumbled while removing the cork from the bottle of whiskey she saved for special occasions, and she took a healthy swallow. This was an occasion, all right. She poured another finger, which went down her throat easier than the first time, leaving a slight burn down to her stomach.

She heard the front door slam then she poured another finger that she intended on sipping. She turned to find Jess standing there in ripped jeans, a V-neck T-shirt, and barefoot. She had her nerve standing before Morgan. Any other time, Morgan would've found that look sexy as fuck, but now all she wanted to do was throw up.

"I didn't expect you back so soon."

Morgan had a sour taste in her mouth as she replayed the betrayal she'd walked in on just five minutes ago. She was speechless.

"It didn't mean anything, Morgan. She's just a woman I met the other night. Baby, she doesn't mean anything."

Morgan's entire body shook as she felt the explosion coming like a volcano ready to erupt. She locked her knees to prevent herself from falling to the floor due to the sudden weakness in her legs.

"No, Jess, obviously, I don't mean anything to you, otherwise you never would've cheated on me. Seriously? You bring another woman into our house?" Morgan slapped her hand against her chest. "MY house and fuck her in our bed?" Morgan was screaming, but she would not give Jess the satisfaction of seeing her cry. "Pack a bag and get the hell out of my house. I'll call you when you can pick up the rest of your shit."

Jess took a step toward Morgan, and she put her hands up to stop Jess from advancing. "I swear, Jess, if you don't get out of here in five minutes, I'll throw all your shit on the front lawn and set it on fire. Go! Now!"

Jess turned around and headed back down the hall. What the hell did she just walk into? Three years of her life, their relationship destroyed, over a one-night stand, or one-weekend stand. Did Jess have so little respect for Morgan? Maybe that explained their drifting apart, their lack of sex. Had she been cheating all along? Morgan pinched the bridge of her nose, forcing herself to take deep breaths despite feeling like her chest was being squeezed. She clinched her fists and pounded them into her thigh muscles, wishing it was Jess's face instead. She wanted Jess to hurt as much as she did at that moment. Jess came back out to the living room with her suitcase and looked at Morgan.

"I'm going now."

Morgan finished off her whiskey and raised an eyebrow. "Bye."

When Jess closed the door behind her, Morgan hurled the glass at the door, and it shattered into a thousand pieces. Morgan crumpled to the floor and buried her face in her hands. She'd expected the tears to start as soon as Jess walked out the door, but maybe she was too shocked to cry. Instead, her whole body trembled. She wrapped her arms around herself as tight as she could and started rocking back and forth in an effort to calm down.

Morgan didn't know how long she'd been sitting on the floor, but her house was almost dark. It was time to get herself together and do what needed to be done. She stood and went to her bedroom where she stripped off the sheets, blanket, and comforter, and she took them outside to throw in the trash. She grabbed a box of trash bags and started stuffing them with everything that belonged to Jess—clothes, shoes, toiletries, makeup. She picked up Jess's jewelry box, took out the TAG Heuer watch Morgan had given her for her birthday and stomped on it over and over, rendering it useless. She threw the jewelry box into one of the garbage bags, tied it up, and took it out to the garage. She went into Jess's office, and loaded up more garbage bags with her books, computer, and knickknacks. She sat in her chair and went through the desk drawers to make sure nothing of hers was there. In the middle drawer on the right, she'd found letters written to Jess that weren't from Morgan. The author of said letters explicitly explained how sexy she found Jess, and what she couldn't wait to do to her when Jess's girlfriend left town. "I know you're planning on breaking up with her for me, but I can hardly wait until we're together for real." *Met her at a bar, my ass.*

There were only three letters, but they weren't signed, only an initial, D. Morgan ripped the letters in half and threw them in one of the bags. Framed pictures of Morgan and Jess throughout the house went in a different bag that would go into the trash can outside. By midnight, the whole house had been cleared of everything that belonged to Jess. Tomorrow, she'd have to order a new mattress and have the old one hauled away. In the meantime, Morgan would be sleeping in the guest room. She crawled into bed utterly exhausted, feeling completely numb, though she'd be surprised if any sleep came her way.

She tried putting Jess out of her mind by thinking about the presentation she had to give tomorrow. Thankfully, it was scheduled for mid-morning. She'd have enough time to make herself presentable, slap on her marketing personality, then after she met with Dr. Molinari, she'd take the next couple of days off. She was technically still supposed to be on vacation, so she was going to be busy. She had a mattress to buy, locks to change, and a house to be scrubbed clean of any remnants of her cheating girlfriend.

Two days later, Morgan's mattress was delivered, the locksmith had been out, and Morgan had texted Jess to let her know she could come by sometime that day to pick up her shit that was already packed up and sitting in front of the garage. Morgan had told her not to bother knocking or trying her key, Morgan had no interest in seeing or talking to her.

By the time Annie and Jane arrived with pizza, wine, and beer, the bags were no longer in front of the garage, much to Morgan's relief. She still hadn't cried—maybe she was still in shock, but the moment Jane threw her arms around Morgan and held her tight, Morgan had completely lost it. The tears fell and fell hard. Morgan saw Annie take the pizza into the kitchen, probably trying to give Morgan and Jane some privacy, but maybe she felt a little uncomfortable. As loving as Annie was to Jane, she never had been one to show her emotions to anyone but Jane.

When the tears slowed, Morgan released Jane and went in search of tissue. By the time she returned, the pizza had been plated, and the drinks were poured. They sat at the table, but Morgan had no appetite.

She lifted her wine glass and took a healthy swallow. She had no problem drinking, but except for the night she discovered Jess was a cheater, she hadn't overindulged.

"Tell us everything," Annie commanded, and Morgan could see the fire in her eyes. She knew Annie and Jane never were crazy about Jess, but they tolerated her for Morgan's sake.

Morgan went into full detail from the time she discovered them in bed to the time she went to sleep. Recounting the story reignited the rage inside her. She slammed her fist onto the table, making the wine slosh in the glass.

"I just don't get it. Why wasn't I enough for her? I have a great job, I'm not bad to look at—"

Jane and Annie both said she was gorgeous and quite the catch.

"Sure, we'd grown apart over the past few months, but I thought we could reconnect. It's bad enough to cheat on me, but to do it in my house, in my fucking bed. That's inexcusable!"

Jane and Annie remained silent as Morgan purged through her tirade. Morgan covered her eyes with her hands and took a deep breath. "I'm a good person. I try to help others however and whenever I can. Why can't I find a girlfriend who is the same? I just don't get it."

Jane laid her hand on Morgan's arm and she looked at Jane. "You are a wonderful person. Just like most of us, you've had some good relationships and some bad ones. But your 'one' is out there. There is a woman who is waiting for you to find her. She's going to be kind, considerate of your feelings, and worship the ground you walk on."

Annie refilled Morgan's and Jane's glasses with wine and grabbed another beer for herself. Morgan thanked her before taking a sip.

"God, I sound so pathetic. Pity party for one, please."

"Hey, you're allowed some time to wallow. It's only been a couple of days after being together for three years. You just need some time."

Annie had been pretty quiet the entire time, allowing Jane to do all the talking. Annie looked at Jane then Morgan. "You want me to go kick her ass? I will, ya know. I'll kick her ass all the way into next week then back again."

The seriousness on Annie's face and tone of her voice set Morgan into a fit of laughter, followed by Jane while Annie just sat there grinning like Morgan's protector. The thing that Morgan found so amusing was Annie was smaller than Morgan, and although Morgan considered Annie a soft butch and had an intensity about her, she really was a softie at heart.

"I love you both so much. Thank you for being here with me tonight. I know you didn't like Jess, so you must be relieved that it's over."

Annie found her voice and continued to talk. "Look, just because we didn't like her, we'd never wish for this kind of pain on you. Are we sorry she's gone? Fuck, no, but we are sorry she hurt you. Karma has a way of being a bitch and Jess will get what she rightfully deserves. Now, stop picking at your pizza and eat a slice. If you do, then I'll let you have more wine."

Morgan smiled and reached her hands out to hold Jane's and Annie's. "You two are the best, just in case I don't say it enough."

"We love you, too. Now eat."

CHAPTER THREE

Shawn brought the plate of greens topped with grilled chicken to the table where Paige was sitting alone. She was a fairly new resident of the west shore, having moved to the lake last spring. She'd seen her around on her bike while riding through town and stand-up paddle boarding while Shawn had been out kayaking. Shawn didn't know a lot about her other than she opened an ice cream shop not too far from the diner. Paige came in occasionally, and Shawn had caught her looking at her more than a few times. They'd had a few pleasant exchanges about the food or weather, but nothing overtly flirty. Shawn found Paige attractive, but there hadn't been a huge pull for her to ask her out. She knew from her best friend, Marcy, that Paige was gay, but she hadn't seen her spend time with anyone.

"This looks great, Shawn. So do you." Paige held Shawn's gaze. The lower octave in Paige's voice let Shawn know that she may have been flirting, however Shawn wasn't sure if she wanted to return the gesture. Plus, this was new for them. Shawn had thought Paige might be shy, but she wasn't being that shy now.

"Enjoy your lunch. Let us know if you need anything else."

Shawn went back to work, taking and picking up orders. They were short-staffed today, which played a part in Shawn not encouraging further flirting from Paige. She didn't know why it made her uncomfortable. She usually had no trouble flirting with vacationers so it shouldn't be any different with Paige. The difference was that Paige was a local now, and if things didn't work out, it might make things uncomfortable between them. With tourists, Shawn could have some fun and move on. She was getting ahead of herself though. Paige hadn't said anything about being attracted to Shawn. That wasn't entirely true—it was mostly nonverbal. First the glances, then some harmless touching. Hell, who was she trying to fool? She knew exactly what Paige wanted. Maybe it was time to get into the game. After all, that's what she really wanted was to actually be in a relationship with a woman who could be more than a fling.

Shawn had decided then and there that she'd cast a line to see if Paige wanted to get caught. As if on cue, Paige got up from her chair and headed toward Shawn to pay her bill. Shawn took the time to openly appraise the soft sway of her hips and her tanned, toned legs that were probably the byproduct of her active lifestyle. The fringed denim cutoffs were just long enough to cover the lower swell of her bottom. Paige smiled, obviously pleased that Shawn was checking her out. Shawn had placed her hand on the counter next to the register and leaned in, trying her best to look cool.

"So, were you satisfied?"

"Almost." The coy smile Paige gave her made Shawn's insides flutter a little bit. Flirtation always got Shawn a little hot.

"Almost? What can I do to make your experience better?" Shawn leaned a little closer, and Paige mirrored the move.

"You can finally ask me out." Paige's eyes darkened with desire, and Shawn wondered if hers did the same.

"You'd say yes if I did?"

Paige handed over her cash to pay her bill but held on tight when Shawn went to take it. "Why don't you come by the ice cream shop when you get off work, and I'll let you know."

"Do you have pistachio ice cream?

Paige bit her bottom lip and nodded.

"Then I'll see you soon." Shawn's gaze followed Paige out the door until she was out of sight. She looked behind her and caught Shorty and Melvin, her chefs, watching her. They both gave her a thumbs-up, which made her laugh.

"Get back to work."

Later that afternoon, Shawn walked down the street toward town, toward Paige. Shawn tried to rid her nerves by shaking her hands out. It was a gorgeous day. The sky was deep blue, the sun was shining but making its way over the western mountain range. The lake was calm, and the birds were chirping. There was no reason to be nervous. It was fun flirting with Paige earlier, but she still wasn't too sure about dating her. Well, technically, it would only be one date. Paige might think Shawn was a dud and realize it was a mistake. That was why it was easier having flings with the tourists. If they didn't click, it didn't matter as she'd more than likely never see them again. The little bell on the door chimed as Shawn entered the shop. She immediately saw Paige behind the glass casing that held large containers of ice cream. Paige looked up from scooping and smiled brilliantly at Shawn.

Paige wasn't the type of woman Shawn was normally attracted to. Paige was more of a tomboy/athletic type whereas Shawn was mostly attracted to femmes. Shawn's memory flashed back to the blond-haired, blue-eyed beauty who had breakfast at her diner the week prior. She couldn't remember her name, but she thought it had started with an M. A lost opportunity with that one, but Paige was there, standing in front of her, waving her up to the counter.

"Hey, you! I was wondering if you were going to come by."

"I told you I would. When I make a promise, I keep it."

The look in Paige's eyes spoke loud and clear about future promises and caused Shawn to avert her stare. "So, what's good?"

"Well, you said you wanted pistachio. Do you want a cone, a sundae, maybe a little whipped cream?"

Shawn had the urge to fan herself. Was it hot in there? She wanted to continue the flirting, but no comeback came to her. "I think I'll have a cone. I might go for a ride later, so I don't want to feel bogged down."

"Right. Maybe later for the whipped cream?" Paige winked at her, and Shawn could feel the heat rise in her face.

Paige scooped an extra-large portion of the pale green ice cream on a sugar cone and handed it to Shawn refusing her money. "So, are you going to ask me out, or what?"

Damn, this woman did not beat around the bush. She certainly seemed to know what she wanted and wasn't afraid to ask for it.

"I mean, unless you're seeing someone, but I thought I'd heard you were single, and it just so happens I'm single. We could go out, get to know each other. Who knows? You might just like me."

Shawn took a lick of her ice cream, trying to buy a little time. She still wasn't sure if it was such a good idea to date Paige. Maybe there'd be a connection once they got to know each other better. That was the purpose of dating, right? She mentally nodded, coming to a decision.

"Paige, may I take you to dinner?"

"Why, Shawn, that was so sudden. I'll have to think about it."

"Whaaa?"

Paige laughed and Shawn decided she liked that sound.

"Gotcha. I would love to have dinner with you. Does Saturday work?"

"I don't know, Paige. I mean, making me work for it, and all." Shawn smiled to let her know she was kidding.

"I promise that I'm worth it."

Jesus. Shawn liked her confidence. The more she talked with Paige, the more she thought that maybe she would like to get to know her better. She handed her phone to Paige and asked her to put in her number. When Paige handed it back, Shawn looked at the contact information. Paige Jackson.

"Okay, Paige Jackson, I'll call you with a time. Thanks for the ice cream."

"No, Shawn, thank you. I look forward to Saturday night."

Shawn waved as she walked out the door and headed back to her car. *I have a date!*

Shawn picked up Paige Saturday night for dinner at a local steak and seafood restaurant. Shawn had worn pressed khakis with a black button-down shirt. Paige had dressed similarly except her shirt was a shade of green that brought out the color in her eyes. Paige had worn some light makeup, and Shawn had to admit that she cleaned up well. Maybe tonight might be the start of something nice. They followed the hostess to their table and took their seats.

"I'm glad we're finally doing this." Paige raised her water glass to Shawn and they clinked them together.

"Me too. So, tell me about yourself. Where did you live before you moved up here?"

"I lived in Southern California. I liked it, but when I came up here a couple of years ago for vacation, this placed called to me, and I knew I had to live here. Once my girlfriend and I broke up, there wasn't much keeping me from moving up here. I felt like I needed a change."

"I hear ya. My grandparents lived here, and even though I lived in Sacramento growing up, I always felt like this was home."

They spent the rest of their meal discussing family, hobbies, and work. Shawn had to admit she was having a really nice time. When Shawn took Paige home, she walked her to her door.

"I had a really great time tonight."

Shawn smiled when Paige stepped closer. She placed her hands on Paige's hips and brought her even closer. "I did too." Shawn leaned down and kissed Paige softly on her lips. Paige put her arms around Shawn's shoulders and pulled her toward her. Paige's kiss had more heat, and when she whimpered, Shawn pulled away.

"Do you want to come in?"

Shawn shook her head. "Not tonight. I have to get home so I can let my dog out, but maybe we could go out again?"

Paige smiled. "I'd like that."

"Good night, Paige. I'll talk to you soon."

During her drive home, Shawn reflected on her evening with Paige. They'd had nice conversation, some laughs, really good food, and the good-night kiss had been pleasant. Shawn cringed when she thought of that word to describe their first kiss. It wasn't toe curling, no fireworks, but pleasant. Maybe it was first date, first kiss jitters that prevented the toe curling. Hopefully, the next kiss they'd share would be more than pleasant.

When Paige asked Shawn to come in, she surprised herself by saying no. With a non-local, she wouldn't have hesitated, but if she was going to give this dating thing a shot, she didn't want to muddle things up by jumping into bed too soon with Paige. She wanted a chance to get to know her better, and after tonight, Shawn thought they were off to a good start.

❖

After a few dinner dates, some time spent on the water kayaking, and hiking part of the Tahoe Rim Trail, Shawn liked Paige. They got along great, had a lot in common, but there still hadn't been a huge spark when they kissed and touched each other. Shawn kept trying to force her feelings to change, which was why Shawn hadn't rushed into sleeping with Paige. She wanted there to be more between them. Paige certainly wanted more. She'd been up front with Shawn about taking their relationship to the next level, and she certainly wasn't making it easy for Shawn to say no.

Shawn and Paige had dinner at the steakhouse where they'd had their first date. Paige looked especially lovely that night, her hair had a slight curl to it, she wore a little more makeup, and her light cashmere sweater hugged her full breasts and trim waist. Shawn had to force herself to keep her eyes up during dinner and not let them linger too long on Paige's breasts. At some point during their dinner, Shawn felt Paige's stockinged foot inch her way up Shawn's pant leg, and she let out a surprised yelp. Paige looked at Shawn like she was ready to devour her. She traced her bottom lip that shone with gloss with her index finger and gave Shawn a slow wink. Shawn shifted in her chair, now fully aware of the wetness pooled in her boxer briefs and the seam of her pants rubbing against her hardened clit. Shawn raised her hand to get the waiter's attention and asked for the check. Even though Shawn had been getting to know Paige better and didn't want things between them clouded with lust, she was only human. Paige pulled her shoulders back, thrusting her chest forward, and that was all she wrote.

During the drive back to Paige's house, she kept moving her hand up and down Shawn's tightening thigh, exploring higher with each stroke, raking her nails against the thin material covering Shawn's legs. Shawn shivered as her body craved to be touched by Paige's hands. They'd spent the next few hours teasing and pleasing each other. Shawn had come a few times that night, but it left her feeling empty inside. She would have to look into what that meant later. She had to try to dress without waking Paige. She sat on the edge of the bed while she tied her shoes and felt arms wrap around her waist.

"Where are you going, lover?"

Shawn startled and touched Paige's hand that was rubbing small circles on Shawn's stomach.

"I have to get home to Jameson, then I have to get up early for work tomorrow."

"Can't you stay with me?"

"Sorry, I can't tonight." Shawn turned her head and kissed Paige's forehead. "Go back to sleep, and I'll call you soon."

Shawn entered the near-dark house, save for the lamp in the corner, and she was greeted by Jameson. He whined and turned in circles as Shawn gave him pats.

"I know, buddy, I'm sorry for being out so late. I'll try not to let it happen again." She took Jameson out back so he could go to the bathroom. He ran back in the house and down the hall to her bedroom as she locked up and turned off the hall light. By the time she walked in her room, Jameson was on his bed in the corner, curled up in a ball and snoring. She was always amazed at how quickly he could fall asleep. Unless he was faking. Shawn chuckled to herself as she brushed her teeth before getting into bed. She needed to explore why she felt so empty after having sex with Paige, but that would have to wait. Her alarm would wake her before too long. Luckily, she had the same skill as her dog, and within minutes of closing her eyes, she was fast asleep.

CHAPTER FOUR

Fall

Shawn had arrived home late afternoon after she ran some errands after work. Jameson, as always, was there to greet her at the door. She grabbed his leash after she changed into her hiking boots, and they took off for their walk. Now that winter was getting closer, they didn't have much light left. Tahoe had received its first snowfall in mid-October, but the days were warm enough that it melted by the next day. Since then, they'd accumulated a few more inches. Shawn could see that the tops of the mountains were still dusted in white patches. The air was crisp and the crunch of dried pine needles under her feet was the only sound on the near desolate road.

Shawn loved taking that route because there were very few homes and cabins that far away from the lake, and she didn't have to worry about traffic. She did have bears to worry about so she always brought her bear spray, but thankfully, she'd never had to use it. With Jameson's heightened sense of hearing and smell, he always alerted her to any possible danger by refusing to go any farther. He would just stop and head back to the safety of home, and Shawn knew to follow.

Shawn thought about Paige during her walk, the silence of nature allowing her to focus on her feelings. They had made tentative plans to hang out that night, but Shawn just wasn't feeling it. She wanted to be alone tonight, hanging out with Jameson, watching a scary Halloween movie on the TV. They'd been dating for almost a couple of months now, had slept together a handful of times, and

Shawn's feelings for Paige weren't deepening. She felt like a total ass and wondered if it had to do with her. She'd had relationships that were fulfilling before, but she just wasn't feeling it with Paige. Shawn wanted to be in a relationship, but at what cost? It wasn't fair to either one to continue something when they weren't on the same page. Paige hadn't said those three important words, but Shawn felt like she wanted to. Shawn, on the other hand, had no desire or need to say them. She'd never tell a woman she loved her unless it was the absolute truth.

They had reached the final little outlet of paved road when the sun finally ducked behind the mountain. The temperature seemed to have dropped at least ten degrees, causing Shawn and Jameson to walk a little faster back down the road. By the time they were almost home, it was pitch-dark. She was nearly blinded when a car with their high beams came upon them. Shawn threw her arm up to shade her eyes against the intrusion. She didn't recognize the car as one of her neighbors. The car that passed was a sedan, and she knew all her friends and neighbors had all-wheel drive for the winters. Must be a tourist staying in the cabin a little way up. The area was a hidden jewel because most tourists wanted to be on the south shore where there was more night life and the casinos. The south shore was always busy and crowded, whereas her part of the lake only got really busy in the summer and winter.

Shawn took the leash off Jameson once they'd walked into the house. She rubbed her hands together and blew into them, trying to warm them up. She loaded a few pieces of firewood on top of the kindling in her fireplace and struck a match. Once she was confident the fire would hold, she went to the kitchen to get dinner started. Shawn enjoyed cooking for herself, but she wasn't nearly good enough at it to help cook at the diner. She left that to Shorty and Melvin. They were hired by Shawn's grandad a few years before he passed, and they'd become like family to her, like the crazy uncles you couldn't wait to see during the holidays because you knew it was going to be a great time with lots of laughs.

Overall, she had seven employees, and in the summer, she hired a couple more servers to work the patio, but they were usually college kids who wanted to stay at the lake for a few months. After dinner,

Shawn and Jameson sat in the living room on the couch in front of the fireplace. She picked up her book and read while stroking her fingers over Jameson's neck. She loved these quiet moments at home. A self-described introvert, she had to come out of her shell while she was at work, talking with customers and her staff. The quiet nights at home allowed for her to recharge so she could be "on" again the following day.

If she was being honest with herself, the only thing she didn't like about living in such a small town was the lack of female companionship. She had dated a few women who lived near here, but there was no real attraction for her. She preferred the femme types—long hair, makeup, stylish clothes. She had realized her attraction to that type when she worked in advertising. Dressing up for dinner meetings with clients, seeing a woman with long hair, button-down blouses that teased a hint of cleavage, tight pencil skirts, and high, high heels that showed off a woman's shapely smooth legs. Shawn had to laugh because that was the exact opposite of herself, and most of the women who lived at the lake. Heels and skirts just didn't work well in the mountains, but Shawn liked what she liked. She also could appreciate a femme woman in jeans and flannel shirts, but she really did love looking at women in skirts. Sometimes she'd find a willing visitor to spend a night or two with, but she knew that those nights would end with the woman returning home off the mountain. She never let her walls down around those trysts because why bother? It wasn't like they were going to stay. She got in, pleasured them, and got out. Simple, no fuss, no muss. Now that she was getting older, she thought more of settling down. She had friends here, a successful business, and she felt like her grandfather was with her in her cabin, *his* cabin.

Shawn could see Paige was getting more serious about their relationship and her feelings just by the little things she did. She'd stop by the diner to say hi, she'd cook her dinner occasionally, and just last night while in bed, Paige suggested they go away for a long weekend. Although Shawn enjoyed her company, she knew her feelings for Paige were not very strong. Still no fireworks, the sex was good, and they were compatible in most areas, but Shawn had yet to feel the warm and fuzzies. She'd talked about her lack of feelings with one of her friends, and Marcy told her to give it a little more time. The same thing had happened between them a few years back when they had tried dating, but they'd realized that they were better off as friends.

Jameson barked and jumped off the couch, running toward the front door. Shawn's heart practically beat out of her chest at Jameson's disturbance. A knock at the front door caused Shawn to frown. Today was Halloween, but in the years she'd lived here, she'd never had a trick-or-treater, mostly because hardly any kids lived close to her. She looked through the peephole and saw a woman standing on her front porch with her arms wrapped tightly around herself. Shawn grabbed Jameson by the collar and held him back, although he would only be accused of profusely licking the woman, maybe putting his nose in her crotch, but he certainly was the least aggressive dog she'd ever seen.

Shawn opened the door and felt like she knew the woman standing on the porch, but she couldn't place from where. She was stunning. Shorter than Shawn by a good three to four inches, curly blond hair that caressed her shoulders, and blue eyes the color of the Tahoe sky in mid-July.

"Can I help you?

"Yes, I'm sorry to bother you, but I'm renting a cabin up the road, and I can't get the heater to turn on. I called the owner, but he wasn't answering. I was wondering if you could help me figure it out."

"Sure, let me get my jacket. You want to come in?"

Shawn pulled Jameson back so she could open the door a little more and let the woman in. Where had she seen her before? She looked so familiar. "Sorry about the excited dog. We usually don't get many visitors, so he's always ready to see a new face."

"He's beautiful. Can I pet him?"

"Of course. This is Jameson, and I'm Shawn."

"I remember. Ray's Diner, right?"

"Uh, yeah." Damn, was she a customer? Shawn definitely would've remembered if she was a regular.

"I'm Morgan Campbell. Two of my friends and I were up here a couple of months ago, and we ate there. The food was delicious."

The light bulb went off in Shawn's head as she remembered Morgan. "Right. Good to see you again." Shawn remembered that day when Morgan came into the diner with her two friends. She felt an immediate attraction to Morgan, more so when Shawn caught her glancing her way every so often. Shawn wasn't the arrogant type, but she couldn't help feel that Morgan had been attracted to her as well. Unfortunately, she didn't see her again once they left the diner that morning. Morgan had been her lost opportunity, and here she was now, standing in her house.

"Same. I love your dog's name. That happens to be my favorite whiskey." Morgan winked and Shawn felt herself warm all over.

"So, let me get my coat and we can go have a look. Jameson, you gotta stay, buddy." Shawn heard him whine when she closed the door. She shook her head. "Don't let him fool you into thinking he never goes anywhere. Once I get home from work, he's at my side for the rest of the day."

"He seems like a good dog."

Shawn nodded. "The best."

Morgan hit the unlock button on her fob and got in the driver's side. Shawn slid into the front seat and let out a low whistle. "Nice car." Shawn ran her hand along the dash then felt the leather of the seats, soft and supple. She admired the Audi sedan, but she didn't see too many of them in the mountains. The drive took less than a minute to get to Morgan's rental, and she followed her inside. Morgan led her to the heater and Shawn flipped open the panel.

"Yep, the pilot is out." Shawn looked around and saw a container of long matches sitting on the mantel of the fireplace that was surrounded by large stones of river rock. She got the pilot lit and turned up the heat. "That ought to do it. Need anything else while I'm here?"

The sadness and loneliness in Morgan's eyes didn't escape Shawn's notice, and it almost made her want to take Morgan into her arms and tell her everything would be okay.

Morgan smiled, but it didn't reach her eyes. "No, I think everything else is fine. Can I pay you?"

"Oh, no. Don't worry about it."

"Well, let me take you back home."

"Actually, I'll just walk since it's just down the street. Enjoy your time here and let me know if you need anything else." Morgan's melancholy made Shawn want to stay, offer her ear if she wanted to talk, but Morgan was a stranger, and Shawn felt like her company might not be wanted.

Morgan walked Shawn to the door and offered her hand. Shawn took it and held it while looking into Morgan's eyes, trying to figure out what she was thinking, but Morgan broke the hold and wrapped her arms around herself again, as if protecting herself from past hurts.

"Well, good night, then." Shawn took a deep breath of the crisp night air. The initial burn from the cold and altitude always made her feel so alive.

Shawn wondered what Morgan's story was. She seemed nice enough but also closed off. Morgan didn't mention if she was by herself or with someone who was coming up later, but why would she? It certainly wasn't Shawn's business. It'd be best to put the image of Morgan to the back of her mind.

Morgan was grateful for Shawn's help, but she was even more grateful that she left. Morgan had escaped up to the mountains to be alone and work on herself. Once the shock of seeing Jess in their bed with another woman wore off, Morgan ended up down the rabbit hole. She wasn't sleeping, she wasn't able to concentrate, and she was snapping at anyone who looked at her sideways. She'd managed to hold her shit together for the meeting she covered for Steve. In fact, she poured out her charm and knowledge and ended up helping the company get his business. She thought she'd perfected her facade until Steve called her into his office a couple of weeks ago.

He said he hadn't been the only one to notice the change in her behavior, and he asked if he could help her. When Morgan told him the gist of her breakup, Steve sympathized with her. Annie and Jane had recommended that she could take some time away, and Steve had agreed it would be a good idea. He'd agreed to take over for her until she came back, since she'd helped him out with the Molinari meeting.

Morgan had used that first week staying home, redecorating, repainting the walls, trying to make her house look different from when Jess lived with her. But at night when she crawled into bed, her thoughts kept replaying the affair over and over, like it was on a loop. Her restless nights and fitful sleep were the primary reasons Morgan had decided to rent the cabin in Lake Tahoe. It wouldn't make her forget, but at least she wouldn't be in the same house where it all went down.

This stay would be a whole new experience for her. Morgan had always lived in big cities with night life and too many activities to choose from. She didn't know anything about mountain life, and Morgan wondered if she'd be able to quiet her mind in this quiet town. Hell, she couldn't even figure out how to get the heater on. She hoped she wouldn't need to ask Shawn for too much help while she was here. Even though Shawn seemed nice, Morgan didn't need Shawn's good looks to cloud her judgment or her objective.

Morgan had been in this cabin once before when she came up with Jane and Annie a couple of months ago, but they were so busy, and she ended up having to leave early, that she didn't have a chance to get a good look around. She went through the cabinets in the kitchen and noted they were fully stocked with dishes, cups, silverware, and cooking utensils. She had brought a few essentials with her—coffee, protein bars, and wine. She would need to venture out tomorrow to find a grocery store to stock up on food for a while. She didn't want to be spending her time in restaurants, and the less people she had to deal with, the better.

The cabin was cute with two bedrooms, two bathrooms, and a couch that sat in front of the fireplace. Behind the couch was the kitchen, and off to the side was the dining table. It was one great room with windows on the three outer walls. The cabin had what Morgan would call a mountain motif. There were two skis crossed on the wall above the fireplace, two snowshoes that hung on the wall above the kitchen table, and knotty pine paneling on every wall. The cabin had a little, okay, a lot too much wood for Morgan's tastes, but it would have to do.

She poured herself a glass of wine and sat on the couch, looking at the unlit fireplace. She'd have to figure out how to light it tomorrow.

It would be relaxing to sit there every night with a glass of wine, maybe a good book, and look to escape reality for a while.

Tomorrow, in the light of day, she'd look around outside the cabin and maybe explore the forest that surrounded her. In the light of day, maybe she could get her head on straight and find a way to move on.

Chapter Five

Shawn's alarm buzzed just as her dream was getting good. She couldn't see the woman in her dream, but they were splashing around in a natural pool that was formed by a waterfall. The woman wrapped her legs around Shawn's waist, and they had just started kissing when the damn alarm went off. Even in her dream, she could feel the butterflies in her stomach and the fireworks that were shooting off during the kiss. That had been missing when she kissed Paige, despite trying her hardest to get there. Jameson was on his bed in the corner of Shawn's bedroom, and he couldn't even spare the energy to lift his head. The early mornings were the only thing she didn't like about owning a diner, but at least it gave her the opportunity to see the sunrise, and Lake Tahoe had some spectacular ones.

She went to the kitchen to pour herself some coffee then took it with her into the bathroom. Her mornings were always the same. She got her coffee, took a shower, then drank it as she finished getting ready. She let Jameson out to do his business, filled his bowl with breakfast, and unlocked the doggie door so he could get into the backyard during the day if he needed to.

It was still dark outside when Shawn kissed Jameson good-bye on the top of his head, and she left for work. The location of the diner couldn't have been better situated. Only a short drive from her house and right across the street from the lake on the main road that traveled from North to South Tahoe. The view of the lake was one of the big draws of the restaurant, along with the food Melvin and Shorty cooked up. They and Gina, the prep cook who also was one of their servers, greeted Shawn when she came in through the back door. They were busy getting ready for the breakfast crowd that would arrive shortly.

Twenty minutes later, as she unlocked the front door, a line of about ten people deep came through and were shown to their tables. Shawn knew most of them—the regulars—who came in before getting on with their day. Shawn filled four mugs of coffee and brought them to the table in the corner.

"Here ya go, fellas."

"Thanks, Shawny. How's life treating you these days?"

"You know me, Jack. I'm living the dream."

"Yeah, but do you have a lady friend yet?" The gleam in Jack's eyes told Shawn that he asked with only the best intentions while the other three guys laughed. They were all family friends of her grandparents, and to them, that made her family to them as well. They all liked to jab at each other, but it was good-natured and always entertaining.

"I have a lot of lady friends, Jack, but if you have someone in mind, let me know. Most of the ladies here like the fellas."

Jack scratched the gray stubble on his chin like he was scanning his mental Rolodex. "Hmm, let me think about it and I'll get back to you."

Shawn laughed and patted him on the shoulder. "You do that. Kerrie will be right over to get your order." Shawn shook her head as she headed back to the register. She loved those old guys. They were always looking out for her, and in return, she did the same for them. It wasn't a secret that Shawn and Paige were dating, but given that she wasn't sure if she was going to break things off with her, she didn't feel the need to drop that information in Jack's lap. Shawn couldn't recall ever introducing a love interest to her grandfathers, but then again, none of them lasted more than a week or two. There was something about her relationship with Paige that made her not want to introduce her to her surrogate family yet.

A few hours later, Morgan came through the door and just the sight of her gave Shawn a little jolt of pleasure. She was dressed in a green cable-knit sweater, black jeans, and tennis shoes. Her hair was pulled into a ponytail, and she had a light application of makeup.

Although she was dressed casually, Shawn had a feeling in her real life, Morgan dressed in heels and skirts, just the type of look she looked for in a woman. She could almost picture her now, and there was a slight tremor in her belly when she imagined what Morgan would look like dressed up. But as beautiful as Morgan was, she looked tired and worn. Shawn could see it in her eyes.

"Hey there. You want some breakfast?"

"God, yes. And all the coffee."

Shawn chuckled and showed Morgan to her table. She handed her a menu and retrieved her coffee. "Do you need an IV for your caffeine, or will a mug be okay?"

"I'll try the cup for now, but I reserve the right to ask for IV in the future."

Shawn smiled, and for some reason, she felt happy. She liked Morgan's sense of humor, something she hadn't been privy to the night before. Maybe she'd been stressed or tired, but she liked this Morgan much more.

"Was your cabin warm enough last night?"

"Yes, thanks again for helping me out. By the way, where is the nearest grocery store? My protein bars will only take me so far."

"Yeah, that's not much to go on. Just take a left out of the driveway and drive straight through the next light. You can't miss it."

"Thanks."

Shawn wanted to talk more, find out where she was from, what her story was, but she had a business to run. Besides, Morgan might not even be up for talking. Would she want the company? Was she even gay? Shawn could only hope, not that that had stopped her before from hooking up with a tourist. But that was something Shawn was looking to change anyway. She was getting tired of the hookups. If she wanted to have something different, she was going to have to change her prowling ways. She wanted stability, a commitment, a partner to share her life with. She wouldn't find that if she didn't get a chance to know a woman to see if they were compatible out of bed. Not that sexual compatibility wasn't important, but she wanted more. Hopefully, she'd find that one day.

❖

Morgan enjoyed her breakfast, but she enjoyed sneaking glances of Shawn more. The ruggedness of Shawn did things—delicious things—to Morgan's insides. She was in no emotional state to start anything new with a woman, but Shawn could definitely give her fantasy material. Morgan liked the way Shawn was dressed—dark blue jeans, a gray waffle Henley under a blue and gray flannel shirt. It looked like maybe Shawn showered, didn't bother combing her hair, except maybe with her fingers, then threw on her clothes. But damn, if that look didn't work for her.

Morgan took the opportunity to look at the other diners, eating their food and conversing with their companions. She also enjoyed the view of the lake from her table. There was a low murmur of the conversations, interrupted every so often from the kitchen window that an order was up. The smell of coffee, bacon, sausage, and other food was pleasant, and it made Morgan glad she'd stopped in for breakfast.

There was more about Shawn that made Morgan feel warm inside. The way she carried herself, confident and sure. The way she interacted with customers and the smile she gave them showed her appreciation for dining at her establishment. As much as Morgan wanted to know more about Shawn, she came to the mountains for a reason. She hadn't been herself since catching Jess in bed with that other woman, whose name she still didn't know. Just thinking about that turned her stomach sour, and she pushed her plate away.

Morgan had been irritable, short-tempered, and she hadn't been sleeping well since that discovery. Discovering Jess cheating on her did damage to her self-esteem. She questioned her ability to be a good judge of character, and to be the type of partner where the other wouldn't want to stray. Morgan could read all the self-help books that were available, but she knew deep down inside, she had to be alone with herself and her thoughts to do some reflection.

She placed her napkin on her plate, gathered her purse, and took the check up to Shawn. The closer she got, the quicker her pulse raced. Morgan wished she had more control over her heart rate when she was in close proximity to Shawn. Morgan felt the smile Shawn gave her was just for her, and Morgan felt herself blush like she was a shy schoolgirl with a crush.

"I hope everything was to your liking, Morgan."

Morgan caught herself speechless, looking to Shawn's warm brown eyes, so she just nodded and handed over her credit card. What was it about Shawn that caused an inability to string a few words together?

"Look, since we're neighbors for the time being, if you need anything, here's my number." Shawn handed Morgan the slip of paper with her phone number on it, along with her receipt. The gesture should've surprised her, but Shawn seemed like the type of person who would do what she could to help someone who needed it.

"Thank you. That's very kind, but hopefully I won't need it."

Morgan could've been mistaken, but she thought she saw maybe disappointment flash across Shawn's face. She tucked the phone number in her wallet for safekeeping, and she said good-bye. The only thing Morgan knew about Shawn was her job, her dog, and she was really, really easy on the eyes. She needed to get away from Shawn and get to work on herself.

When Morgan arrived back to the cabin that would be her home for the next couple of weeks, she put away the food and drinks she'd bought that should last her for at least a week. She stood in the kitchen, contemplated what she was going to fix for dinner, and looked around the cabin. She wasn't used to not having anything to do, and she wasn't quite ready to sit down with her thoughts just yet.

It was just before noon and there was a chill in the air, but manageable with just a light jacket. She decided that she would go explore the area around her cabin and maybe the neighborhood so she could get her bearings. She pocketed her keys after locking the door and set out on her exploration. She walked around to the back of the cabin and took in a deep breath of the mountain air. She was pleased to find a vinyl woodshed up against the back wall of the cabin, and it was fully stocked with firewood. Looked like she'd be able to have a fire tonight after all, and the thought of sitting in front of a fire with a glass of wine and her book pleased her to no end.

She continued her journey into the forest behind the cabin. She didn't have the bravery to travel too far. She was a novice to the mountains and unfamiliar with her surroundings. No, she would walk only as far as her view of the cabin. The only sounds came from the crunch of dried pine needles beneath her boots and the birds in the trees. She looked up to the sky, and it appeared the tops of the pine trees ended where the sky began. A slight breeze flew up and the rustle of the leaves added to the mountain symphony. Morgan closed her eyes, took another deep breath, and she felt a little bit of the world's weight release from her shoulders.

She headed back to the cabin, made a few trips to the woodshed, and stacked the firewood on the hearth. It was only four p.m., but she stood in the middle of the living room, trying to come up with an idea of what to do. She went into the kitchen and pulled most of the vegetables that she'd bought earlier from the refrigerator and started chopping. She threw them into a stock pot along with some chicken, broth, and seasonings for the soup she could have for the next two or three days. She put a lid over the pot but stopped from turning on the stove.

She was feeling restless and needed to expel more energy, so she left the cabin again, this time heading down the road to the lake. She spotted only one other house besides Shawn's. In the daylight, she was able to see Shawn's house better. It was adorable. It was a two-story cabin that was surrounded by huge pine trees, with a driveway big enough to hold four cars. The cabin was brown with green shutters and stairs that led to a small front porch. It had loads of character. Morgan had only seen the entryway that opened into the large living room, but the log cabin feel suited Shawn, in Morgan's opinion.

Morgan continued down the road that was dotted with A-frame houses and cabins set back amongst the trees, and it was easy for her to see what drew others to this place. She finally reached the lake and stood on the beach looking out on the water. The lake looked calm, mostly empty with the exception of a few boaters and kayakers. She tucked her hands into the pockets of her jeans and enjoyed the quiet for a while. Maybe this was where she should come to do some self-reflection rather than staying inside her cabin. It would be a shame to waste this beautiful scenery for the next couple of weeks. It didn't take long for the temperature to drop, and she had an uphill climb back to the cabin that would take longer for her to reach than it did to get to the lake. Once she got back to the cabin, it was almost five o'clock, and she decided to light a fire and turn on the stove to cook her soup.

Morgan had never had a fireplace so she wasn't exactly sure how to light it. Jane and Annie's fireplace just had a switch that she turned on, and poof, there was a flame. She rummaged through the kitchen drawers, looking for a lighter or matches, but she came up empty. She ran her fingers over her hair, placed her other hand on her hip, and blew out a breath. She dug Shawn's phone number out of her wallet, and she thought about calling her, but her pride stopped her. Shawn would think Morgan was completely useless, and she didn't want anyone thinking that, but especially her hunky temporary neighbor. She scanned the fireplace, then the mantel. She recalled Shawn pulling a long match from the container the night before. She took the top off the tall circular container to find long matches. Pay dirt! Morgan took one out and struck it on the bottom until it lit, and she placed it onto the logs. It didn't take long for the flame to burn out. She tried it again with the same results. Morgan let out an aggravated groan, then she put her ego aside and called Shawn.

"Hello."

The voice on the other end sounded gruff and Morgan was tempted to hang up, but she really wanted a fire, and damned if she didn't know how to get it lit.

"Um, hi. It's Morgan. From up the street?"

"Hey, what's going on?"

"Well, I'm sorry to bother you again, but I'm trying to light a fire in the fireplace and it keeps going out. Could you help me, please?"

"Sure. I'll be up in a few minutes."

Shawn hung up and laced up her boots. She thought she was in for the rest of the night, and honestly, she wasn't in the mood to be around anyone. A group had come into the diner about half an hour before closing, and they took their sweet time figuring out what to order, then they took longer to eat because they were talking and laughing. Shawn couldn't begrudge them their good time, but when they finally left, it was an hour after closing. She thought she'd still have a little time to go for a bike ride, but Murphy's Law told her to hold its beer. On the way home, she got a flat tire, and by the time she returned home, it was too late. She'd just taken off her boots when Morgan called. Now she had to put them back on and go help the city girl light a damn fire. Shawn shook her sour mood off, grabbed her flashlight, and started her walk up the street while she grumbled the entire five minutes it took to get there. By the time she knocked, some of her ire had dissipated, and she put on a cheery smile that she didn't feel.

Morgan opened the door, and Shawn's pissy attitude fell straight away. Morgan was gorgeous with her ponytail messier than it was that morning when she came in for breakfast. She held a glass of red wine and looked entirely too sexy to be real.

"Thanks for coming. I hate to admit this, but I've never lit a fire before, and I'm obviously no good at it."

"It's okay. Let me take a look." Shawn walked over to the fireplace and noticed only one log and two remnants of matches. "Um, okay. I see what the problem is. First, you need some kindling to start the fire, but you also need a couple of logs in there. I'll be right back."

Shawn went outside and collected some twigs, small branches, and dried pine needles, and brought them inside.

"You see this lever here?" Morgan came closer and bent over next to Shawn. She caught a whiff of Morgan's perfume, and she felt a little light-headed. The scent was faint and smelled a little like vanilla, a little like gardenia. Sweet, but subtle. Shawn cleared her throat. "This is the flue, and it needs to be open, otherwise the fire will smoke you out of the cabin." Shawn pulled the lever to the open position. "Now, the kindling goes on the bottom of the grate. Newspaper works, but you can also use these." Shawn placed the kindling in the fireplace then a couple of more logs to the one that was in there. She lit the match and moved it around to make sure the fire caught, and she replaced the screen.

"There you go. If you want to keep the fire going for a while, place another log on once the flame gets lower."

By now, the fire caught and Shawn could already feel the heat. Or maybe it was the warmth from standing so close to Morgan. She needed to get out of there and free from the intoxicating spell Morgan seemed to have placed on Shawn.

"You good? Need anything else?"

"No, but would you like to stay for dinner as a thank you?"

"I appreciate it, but I gotta get back and feed Jameson. I just got home when you called."

"Rain check then?"

Shawn didn't answer, not wanting to commit herself to anything regarding Morgan. Already, she had a major crush on her, and she knew nothing would come out of it. Nothing ever did when she hooked up with tourists. No, the best thing for Shawn would be to put as much distance between her and Morgan as possible. Shawn didn't want to be promiscuous anymore. She'd been that way out of need, not want. Well, that wasn't exactly true. She fooled around with visitors to the lake because there just weren't enough gay women in the area to offer much of a pool to choose from. Not to mention, she was dating Paige. That was the whole point of dating one woman—hoping they fell in love and would spend the rest of their lives together. Besides, Shawn wasn't the type to go looking elsewhere if she was dating someone.

"Take care, and maybe I'll see you around."

Yes, friendly but noncommittal. Shawn was pleased with herself. She turned on the flashlight as she headed home even though the almost full moon provided enough light. Shawn had no idea why Morgan came to the mountains alone, but it was none of her business. She didn't seem like the type of woman who would be helpless, but considering Shawn had to come to her rescue twice in as many days, maybe Morgan was a little more helpless than she seemed. Or maybe she was a princess who was used to other people doing everything for her. It would certainly be easier for Shawn to get Morgan off her mind if that was the case. Regardless, she was back home and was in for the night. She fed Jameson, grabbed a beer from the fridge, and started making her own dinner. Hopefully, tonight would be the last Shawn would see of Morgan, but she highly doubted it.

When Shawn closed the door, Morgan leaned close and banged her head on the door. Flue? Kindling? More than one log? Morgan was in over her head with this whole mountain trip. It seemed like a good idea initially. She'd have time to herself, could see the sights, and work on reconstructing her heart after Jess broke it.

Morgan gulped the rest of her wine before refilling her glass. She sat on the couch and watched the fire roar before her. The warm orange glow was almost enough to put Morgan in a trance. She thought back to that dreadful day. The shock of seeing Jess in bed with that bitch shocked her enough to not break down in front of her. She could almost still smell the sex that had emanated from their bedroom, the shock that showed on Jess's face, the "oh, shit" look from her lover.

Morgan had considered taking everything Jess owned and building a bonfire with her belongings in her front yard that night. Her hand shook as she brought the wine glass to her mouth. They had spent three years of their lives together, two of them cohabitating. The beginning of their relationship had been filled with romance—candlelit dinners, weekend getaways, hours spent in bed, only leaving to get water or snacks to replenish their energy so they could continue their lovemaking.

When Jess had moved in with Morgan, the romance started to fade. Morgan chalked it up to the stress of living together, but they would still make time for vacations, and they would spend that time reconnecting. Then Jess started working long hours and sex had become almost nonexistent. Morgan had recommended couple's counseling, but Jess said they didn't need it, that they just had to work harder on their relationship. The problem was, Morgan felt like she was the one doing all the work. Morgan would treat Jess to dinner, or bring her flowers, or try to spend time talking with her with no reciprocation.

Morgan wiped a tear that had escaped. Why hadn't she seen it sooner? Jess had probably been cheating on her for quite some time. Of course, she had no proof other than the love letters she'd found in Jess's desk the night Morgan kicked her out, but the nonexistent intimacy in their last year together was probably a sign that should've thumped Morgan on the head. Not once during their time together did Morgan ever consider cheating, or breaking up with Jess for that matter. Had she noticed other women? Sure. She wasn't dead. But even when offered on the rare occasion, Morgan would walk away and go home to Jess.

Morgan removed her sweater. Whether it was the fire or the wine making her warm didn't matter. She went into the kitchen to dish up her soup. She sliced the French bread and buttered it liberally. The steam and the smell of the seasonings from the soup wafted under her nose and made her mouth water.

She stood at the butcher block island counter and dipped her bread in the soup. She took a bite and wiped the drippings off her chin with her napkin. Once she had finished her meal and washed the dishes, she put her sweater back on and stepped outside on the front porch with her glass of wine. The smoky smell from the chimney comforted her somewhat. She looked to the clear night sky and marveled at the quantity and clarity of stars. She couldn't ever remember the stars being so vivid, but then again, she was a city girl, and the city lights took the brightness from the stars.

Morgan could've stayed out there all night, but the chill in the air drove her back inside. She removed her sweater again and draped it over a dining chair. The flame had died down, but it was warm enough that she didn't feel she needed to add another log. She took the poker that Shawn had pointed out, and she stoked the logs, just as Shawn had shown her. Morgan thought about her rugged neighbor, and if she hadn't been so broken, Shawn would be someone Morgan would want to know better. The couch cushion let out a whoosh when Morgan sat down, and she let out a heavy sigh. She didn't know much about Shawn other than she worked in a diner and she had a dog. *Don't forget she's handy to have around.* She seemed pleasant enough, but also kind of quiet. And she didn't appear to want to spend any extra time with Morgan.

She didn't need to think about Shawn anymore. She chugged the rest of her wine, placed the glass on the side table, and tried to quiet her mind. It was time to start working on Morgan Campbell.

CHAPTER SIX

Shawn went into the diner at her regular time, but once the breakfast rush was over, she took her car to the local garage to have a new tire put on. The owner of the garage talked her into replacing all four tires since they were starting to wear thin. Winter would be upon them soon, and she'd need the snow tires in better condition. The smell of rubber and oil drove her to take a walk in the fresh air since Al assured her it would take an hour or so. No use in going back to work for such a short time especially since this was her "slow time" of the year. The summer tourists had all but disappeared, and the snow bunnies wouldn't be in full swing until the Thanksgiving holiday that was still a few weeks away. They were still pretty busy, but it was mostly the locals that came in now.

Shawn considered going by Paige's ice cream shop, but something made her turn and walk in the opposite direction. She entered a shop that mostly catered to tourists. There were knickknacks, apparel, and wood-carved bears that were so popular with the locals and tourists.

"Hey, Shawn. What brings you in?"

"Hey, Marcy. I'm getting my tires changed at Al's so I figured I'd do a little window shopping. You been out riding lately?" Shawn and Marcy sometimes mountain biked together or went hiking. She was an ex-girlfriend but also one of her best friends up at the lake, and the one who urged Shawn to give dating Paige a little more time to see if more feelings appeared. Marcy was one of the few single lesbians that lived in town full-time, but unlike Shawn, Marcy was more of a granola girl. She liked flowy, hippie style dresses that she wore with

Teva sandals in the summer, and tights and Ugg boots in the winter. She was also vegan whereas Shawn was a meat and potatoes type of person, and Marcy didn't eat anything that wasn't organic. She had a great sense of humor even if she was a bit flighty.

"No, I've been busy with the shop. The girl who was helping me met a guy from San Francisco, and she decided to move to the city to be closer. You know of anyone looking for a job?"

"No, but I'll keep my ear to the ground. Let me know if you get some free time and want to ride. I'm just gonna take a look around."

"Sounds good. Let me know if you need anything."

Shawn gave a wave and went about her perusing. She looked at some hats and some work done by local artists, both paintings and prints. Some of them really caught the beauty of the Tahoe sunrises and sunsets with a mixture of shades of purple, orange, and yellow. She picked up a book titled *A City Girl's Guide to Mountain Living*. Her mind went to Morgan, and she had to chuckle. She scanned the table of contents and knew immediately she'd buy it for Morgan. Everything from starting a fire, winter driving, hiking with the right equipment, and what to do if you come across a wild animal, including bears, coyotes, and mountain lions. The more she read, the more she realized that there was actually good information in the book. She picked out a magnet with a picture of Emerald Bay, and she took both items up to Marcy.

Shawn laughed when Marcy held up the book and raised an eyebrow. "There's a lady staying in the cabin up the street from my house, and I've already had to get her heater lit and start a fire for her."

Marcy's body shook with laughter. "There are so many things I can say about that. So. Many. Things."

Shawn felt her face warm and knew she'd never live that down. "What I meant was—"

Marcy held up her hand to stop Shawn from digging herself further into innuendo. "I know exactly what you meant, Casanova. Does Shawny have a crush?"

There weren't too many people other than her grandfather who she'd allow to call her Shawny, but since Marcy was her best friend and didn't have a mean bone in her body, Shawn let her get away with it.

"No, you know I'm seeing Paige. I'm just trying to help her out so she stops calling on me to save the day." Shawn bit the inside of her cheek, anticipating Marcy's next comeback.

"Uh-huh. How old do you think she is?"

Shawn shrugged. "Maybe about my age, give or take a couple of years."

"Is she pretty?"

"I mean, she's not bad to look at." Shawn rubbed the back of her neck. That was the understatement of the year. Shawn could spend her days and nights looking at Morgan and not miss another thing.

Marcy looked like she might slap Shawn upside her head. "So why wouldn't you want her to call you if she needed help? Are you nuts?"

"Marcy, look, she's a tourist, okay? Besides, hi, remember Paige? The girl I'm dating? You know I'm trying to settle down with just one person. I really don't have a desire to continue being promiscuous."

"I know, but you said you didn't reciprocate her feelings. Maybe it's time to send ole Paige packing. Maybe see if your new neighbor is the one to set your loins on fire."

"Oh, my God, you did not just say that. Marce, she's a tourist. She won't be sticking around. I want to be with someone I can see a future with. Sure, it's not Paige, but it won't be with the neighbor either." Shawn needed to stop procrastinating and break up with Paige. She just didn't want to hurt her. She needed to find the courage to talk to her. She'd considered just acting like an asshole so Paige would break up with her, but Shawn wasn't an asshole and she'd feel like an even bigger one if she behaved that way. Possibly the biggest asshole of all the assholes.

"Are you sure about that? How much do you know about her?"

"I know she doesn't know how to start a fire or light a pilot light."

"Besides that, Lumber Jane. Is she psychotic?"

"What? No!"

"Well, she has that going for her. Look, you're not getting any younger, and it seems like you're wasting time with Paige since you aren't feeling it with her. Even if nothing comes out of your time with the neighbor, you might even make another friend. Or, and hear me out, she might just end up rocking your world."

"Jesus. Just ring up my things so I can leave you and your crazy ideas."

"You still love me, right?" Marcy looked at her with puppy dog eyes even though they were half covered with her wavy bangs.

"I do, and I appreciate you looking out for me, but I'm not interested in just sex. I want a relationship, a partner I can grow old with. I won't get that from Morgan."

"Ooh, her name is Morgan? I love that name. Very sexy. Morgan and Shawn." Marcy looked like she was rolling the names around on her tongue. "Your names sound good together. I wonder what her sign is and if it's compatible with yours."

"Stop. It's not going to happen. Can you just ring up my stuff please?"

"Fine." Marcy's bottom lip jutted out like a pouting three-year-old.

Shawn leaned over the counter and gave Marcy a kiss on the cheek. "Love you. Let's go riding soon before winter comes."

"Love you too. Tell Morgan to come by my shop."

"Hell, no!" Shawn laughed as she left the store. She looked at her watch and she still had thirty minutes before her car would be done. She ducked into her favorite sandwich shop that was in the next building over from Marcy's.

"Hey, Shawn. What're you doing out and about?"

"Hi, Chris. Al's putting new tires on my car so I thought I'd walk around a bit. I just came from Marcy's then decided to come over to my favorite sandwich shop and get some lunch."

"It's good to see you. Want your usual?"

"Yeah, that sounds good. Wrap it up to go, will ya? The day's too pretty to be inside when I don't have to."

"I hear that. A storm is supposed to be coming early next week so enjoy it while you can."

"Thanks, Chris." Shawn took her sandwich and soda and walked down the sidewalk until she came across the beach access. She hopped up on the stone covered retaining wall and unwrapped her sandwich. A sign it was off-season, there weren't too many people on the beach. The sky was the color of sapphires, as was the lake. One thing that always amazed her was that the lake was a microcosm of the sky because of the clarity of the water. Shawn found it was easiest for her to get lost in thought when she could sit by the water and listen to the tiny waves lap up on the beach.

Shawn thought about what Marcy had said while she ate her lunch. Yes, it was true she didn't feel romantic feelings for Paige, and the sooner she broke it off with her the better. It wasn't right to lead her on knowing that she wouldn't feel more for her. But she also was at the point where meaningless hookups didn't appeal to her either. Besides the fact that Shawn had no idea if Morgan was even interested in women, the fact remained that she wasn't a local. Starting something with Morgan didn't feel right to her knowing it would end when Morgan left. Shawn could never move off the mountain to follow anyone. She shouldn't say never. She'd never fallen in love with someone hard enough that she would follow them anywhere. Even as a child, though, spending her summers at the lake with her family, she knew that was where she'd end up. It took her a while to get back to Tahoe full-time, but now that she was there, she didn't ever want to leave.

There was something magical about Lake Tahoe. Maybe it was the clean air. Maybe it was the clear water. Maybe it was the laid-back lifestyle of living in the mountains. But no matter how busy she was at the diner, Shawn always felt at peace. She'd continued her grandfather's legacy, and she'd made some really good friends. This small community watched out for each other, and it would be really hard to find that family atmosphere anywhere else.

Her thoughts went to Morgan as she took a drink of her soda to wash down her sandwich. She couldn't deny her initial physical attraction to Morgan, but she hadn't spent any significant time with her to see if there was anything more. Shawn was too busy to spend any time with her, that is, even if Morgan wanted to spend time with Shawn. Maybe she could invite her for a hike, or a kayak trip out on the lake. According to Chris, she might not be able to go kayaking much longer if a storm was heading their way.

Shawn crumpled up her wrapper and dumped that and her empty cup into the trash can as she made her way back to the garage to pick up her car. Shawn had decided she would drop off the book at Morgan's cabin before she went home. Maybe she'd appreciate an invitation to explore the outdoors of Lake Tahoe. That might be asking for trouble, spending more time with Morgan. Hell, she might not want to do anything with Shawn anyways. Shawn drove by Paige's ice cream shop and felt a twinge of guilt that she'd had no desire to see Paige today. She would have to call her later to see if they could get together and talk. Marcy was right. The sooner Shawn broke it off, the sooner they could both move on.

Shawn stopped by the diner to see if they needed her, but by the look of the parking lot, they probably weren't busy. She spoke to Shorty, and after he assured Shawn they didn't need her, she drove home. There was still plenty of daylight, and the weather was warm enough, so she decided she'd take Jameson on a hike. There was a nice trail that started up the street, one that only the people in her neighborhood knew about since it was pretty much made by them. The hike led to a small pond that was surrounded by wild grass and aspen trees. To Shawn, that was her happy place.

She packed a small backpack with some just-in-case essentials—waterproof matches, compass, first aid kit, a space blanket, some protein bars, and water. She grabbed her bear spray and attached it to her belt. The black bears up in Tahoe typically weren't aggressive, but it was always better to be safe than sorry. Shawn leashed Jameson's harness and started toward Morgan's cabin. The Steller's jays were squawking from the trees, and the whisper of the wind rustled the pine needles. A pair of squirrels bravely crossed before them and scampered up a pine tree, but Jameson knew better than to give chase. He'd chased after a skunk a couple of years ago and got sprayed. Ever since, he'd left the wildlife alone.

She climbed up the wooden stairs to the front deck of Morgan's cabin and knocked on the door. Morgan's eyes grew wide when she opened the door.

"Hey, sorry to bother you, but I got you something and I wanted to drop it off."

Morgan opened the bag and laughed when she saw the book. She pulled out the magnet next and smiled. "Thank you. That was very sweet of you to think about me."

If only Morgan knew how much Shawn thought about her in the past couple of days. Shawn looked down at her feet and shrugged, now feeling embarrassed by her gifts. Morgan was probably the type of woman who was used to the finer things in life, and here Shawn was giving her a book and a magnet. Geez.

"You want to come in for a bit?"

"Oh, no. I have Jameson and we're about to take a little hike." The frown on Morgan's face made Shawn ask the next question. "Would you like to go with us? We'll only be gone for two or three hours."

"Really? I'd love that!" The smile on Morgan's face made Shawn really glad she asked her. "Come on in. Let me change."

Morgan had been in lounging-type clothes, but she returned from her room wearing loose-fitting jeans, a zippered hoodie, and hiking boots that looked and smelled like they just came out of the box.

"Uh, are those new?" Shawn pointed at Morgan's boots. Her feet would be full of blisters by the time they finished their hike.

"Kind of." The blush that colored Morgan's cheeks was adorable. "I wore them around the house for a week before I came up here. They're clean but broken in."

"Excellent. You ready?"

Morgan grabbed her keys and slid them into her front pocket after she locked the door. Shawn chuckled.

"What's funny?"

Shawn shook her head. "Nothing. We just don't normally lock our doors around here, at least not during the day. We only lock the doors at night or if we're going away. There's no one around except for the ten or so people who live in the neighborhood. We all look out for each other."

"Well, I live in Sacramento near downtown. I lock the doors even when I'm home. Unfortunately, there are a lot of homeless people down there. A few politicians too, which I think I'm more afraid of."

Shawn laughed. "I used to live in Citrus Heights so I know exactly what you're talking about. That was another lifetime ago, and a totally different world from here."

They walked easily on the road that would lead them to the trail.

"Did you work in a restaurant in Sacramento?"

"No, nothing like that. I used to work in advertising, but I got sick of the office politics and I needed a change." Shawn didn't want to go into exactly what caused her to leave. Even though she'd been in Tahoe for ten years, the fact that the woman who was not only her colleague, but also her lover, betrayed her for her own corporate ladder-climbing still stung. She shoved that memory to a back corner in her mind. What good was it dwelling on the past since she couldn't change it? Besides, she loved where she ended up. If she had stayed in advertising, she might have been burned out by now. It wasn't unusual for her to put in over fifty hours a week. The money was good, but she never had time for fun or relaxation.

They reached the self-made trailhead and started their trek deeper into the forest. Sunlight streamed through the trees providing them plenty of light to see but kept the temperature cooler.

"This is an interesting hiking trail." Morgan glanced at Shawn with a smirk.

"That's because it's not technically a hiking trail. Some of the residents around here made the trail themselves. You won't find any forest rangers around here. Just us and nature at its finest. Besides, it's easier to hide the bodies if no one knows where to look." Shawn winked and Morgan cuffed her on the arm.

"That's not funny. I've seen plenty of slasher films that involve crazy guys like Jason and Michael. The people always get knocked off in the woods."

"I promise to protect you if we run into anyone I don't know."

"Going from advertising to working in a diner is quite a drastic change."

"True, however, I own that diner. My grandfather, Ray, started it in the early seventies, and he left it to me when he died. My home used to be my grandparents'. They built it themselves and we would come up to spend time with them often. When he died, I had our two chefs run the place since they'd been with my grandad for a while. They still pretty much run the place, and I just try to stay out of the way," Shawn said with a laugh.

"Well, you're obviously doing something right. It seems like it's pretty busy, and the food there is delicious."

"Thanks. I appreciate it. What do you do for work?"

"Outside sales for a medical device company. We manufacture joint replacement prostheses and surgical tools. I love my job, but it's stressful and busy."

Shawn and Morgan exited the canopy of Jeffrey pine trees into the view of a medium-sized pond surrounded by tall wild grass that was so bright green, the blades nearly shined. The field was rimmed by quaking aspens, their golden leaves quivering with the light breeze.

"Here we are."

"Wow." The look of wonder that engulfed Morgan's face was a sight to see. Shawn had been here too many times to count, but she continued to be in awe of the splendid beauty this hike had to offer. It was even more special to see Morgan experience it for the first time.

"Shawn, am I dreaming? Is this for real? Maybe I was killed by a serial killer and this is heaven."

Shawn laughed at Morgan's sense of humor. "It's heaven all right, but right here on earth."

"I can't believe a place this stunning actually exists. There are no words that can do this justice."

Shawn followed Morgan as she moved closer to the pond until they were standing on the bank. "I don't get stressed out often, but when I do, this is what I think of as my happy place. If the weather doesn't allow me to hike it, I have a large portrait of it in my bedroom that I can look at."

Morgan took out her phone and started taking pictures. Shawn took a few steps back to give Morgan some room. She unclipped Jameson's leash and told him to stay close. Shawn took that opportunity to study Morgan. She certainly looked more relaxed now than she did just a couple of days ago. Morgan was an attractive woman, even with the worry lines etched into her forehead. Shawn had a desire to smooth them out with her thumb and ask Morgan why she was worried. She also seemed sad, but Shawn didn't know how to go about asking her about it.

Jameson walked into the pond and slowly stepped into it until he started swimming. Morgan laughed, and Jameson became the new subject of her photographs. The dog swam across the pond a few times before he got out and shook the water off him and onto Morgan. Shawn quietly called Jameson and clipped his leash back on.

"Morgan, look behind you but move slowly and be quiet." The fear in Morgan's eyes was hard to miss. "It's okay, just do it. I promise it's not a serial killer." Shawn stood close to Morgan and could feel her tremble. She pointed to a mama bear and her two cubs walking across the meadow, and Morgan gasped as she grabbed Shawn's arm with a death grip.

Shawn kept her voice low so as not to disturb the bears. "Don't worry. They're far enough away that they won't bother us."

"Easy for you to say," Morgan whispered anxiously.

"Once they go into the trees, we'll head back. Do you want to take pictures?"

"I can't. My hands are shaking too bad."

Shawn took Morgan's phone, zoomed in, and took some shots. She switched to video when the bear siblings started to wrestle with each other. Shawn snuck a peak at Morgan whose eyes were wide and her lower jaw dropped. Morgan obviously did not believe what she was seeing. Black bears were commonplace in Tahoe, but as far as bears went, they were pretty docile as long as they were left alone. They got into trouble occasionally if trash wasn't properly disposed of in bear-proof trash cans, or if people tried to get too close to the cubs.

The bears had disappeared into the trees, and Shawn took Morgan's hand. "Come on, let's go." Shawn's heart was pounding, and she wasn't sure if it was because of the bears or Morgan's hand in hers. Morgan's hand was warm, and Shawn could feel herself warming up. They headed back to the trail, and Morgan's breathing was loud, so Shawn stopped them.

"Are you okay?"

"Shawn, we could've been mauled. How are you not freaking out?"

She chuckled and squeezed Morgan's hand before letting go. She immediately missed the contact, but she wanted to pull out a bottle of water for Morgan. "Here, drink this and try to slow your breathing before you hyperventilate. I'm used to seeing the bears around, but I still get a little nervous."

They started walking again, and Morgan grabbed Shawn's hand and held tight until they got back to the road. As they made their way toward Morgan's cabin, Shawn gave her a brief Bear 101 lesson.

"Listen, they won't bother you as long as you leave them alone and give them a wide berth. They're around people all the time, and mostly they're just looking for food. Make sure you throw your trash in the bear cans, don't leave food in your car, and don't cook with your windows or doors open unless you want company for dinner."

Morgan unlocked the door and invited Shawn inside. Jameson was mostly dry by the time they arrived, but Shawn told him to lie down right inside the door.

"What do you mean don't leave food in cars? Surely they can't get in."

Shawn laughed when Jameson let out a loud huff as if he was saying, "Trust me, lady, don't chance it."

"They break into cars and even know how to open the car doors if they're unlocked. Take a look at the video I shot for you."

Morgan pulled the phone out of her pocket and unlocked the screen. As the video started rolling, Morgan was amazed at the slow, lumbering gait of the mama bear, and she laughed when she saw the cubs chase and wrestle each other. Morgan was too freaked out at the time to truly appreciate how special that moment was, but she was grateful that Shawn had the inclination to take the video.

She looked at the other pictures she had taken of the meadow and pond, and they were good, but they couldn't do the reality of it justice. The vibrancy of the greens of the wild grass and pine needles, the golden yellows of the aspen trees, and the rich blue of the sky. Even if Morgan hadn't taken any pictures, she knew she'd never forget that place.

"I can't thank you enough for inviting me with you today, Shawn."

"I'm glad you could go with us. So, I never asked. How long will you be staying?"

Morgan looked upward and scrunched her nose, trying to think how long she'd been there already. "About another week and a half. I got here Saturday night. What day is today?"

Shawn laughed. "It's Tuesday. Hey, I get it. Time is easily distorted when you're here. When I came up here for the summers when I was a kid, it seemed like the days would last forever, but before I knew it, my summer break was over and I had to go back to school."

"Yes, that's exactly it. I haven't done much since I've been here, but just like that, three days have passed."

Shawn stuck her hands in her pants pockets and rocked back on her heels. "So, what do you have planned for the rest of your time?"

Was it Morgan's imagination, or did Shawn seem suddenly nervous around her? "Well, I'm supposed to be working on myself, sort of self-reflection, but I'm having a difficult time trying to quiet my mind."

Shawn looked confused, but Morgan knew how she felt. She was still confused how her personal life had blown up in front of her face. "It's a long story that I'd rather not get into now."

"No, no, that's fine. I just wanted to offer my services to you."

Morgan smirked and raised her eyebrow in suspicion, but she was amused at the look of mortification on Shawn's face.

"That's not what I meant." Shawn ran her hand down her flushed face and blew out a loud breath. "What I meant to say before I stuck my foot in my mouth is that the diner closes at three, and I usually do something after work, so if you'd like to join me, I'd like to invite you."

"What kind of things are you talking about?" Morgan so wanted this conversation to go in an innocent flirty direction. Morgan could think of all kinds of activities she'd like to do with Shawn if she had her head screwed on right. But maybe she could split her time. Until Shawn got off work, Morgan could work on herself, then in the afternoon, she could enjoy her time with Shawn.

"We could go hiking again, kayaking, ride bikes, or go for a drive so you can see more scenic spots of the lake and mountains."

"That sounds magical. Are you sure you don't have better things to do than hanging out with me?"

"Sure, I'm sure." Shawn's grin and the sparkle in her eyes almost made Morgan swoon. She hadn't noticed the shallow dimples that adorned both of her cheeks, but there they were and they just added to her good looks. There were certainly worse ways to spend her time over the next week and a half.

CHAPTER SEVEN

Have you kayaked before?" Shawn had called Morgan after the breakfast rush, but the prospect of seeing Morgan later had her so excited she'd forgotten her telephone manners.

"Excuse me?"

"I'm sorry. Hi, Morgan, it's Shawn. How would you like to go kayaking when I get off work today?"

The soft laugh that came over the line did things to Shawn's insides. Good, wonderful, wild things, and she couldn't remember when she'd been so affected by another woman. Which was crazy since she hardly knew Morgan, but there was something about her that made Shawn want to know more. She really needed to talk to Paige because while she and Morgan were just becoming friends, it wasn't right to string Paige along. Even if romance didn't come with Morgan, she knew that she didn't have feelings for Paige. She'd never had the reaction with Paige that she'd had when she'd held Morgan's hand yesterday on their hike. She made a mental note to call Paige that night and talk to her.

"Uh, isn't it a little too cold to be out on the water?"

"Heck, no. It's gorgeous out today. We should enjoy the sunny weather while we can because we're expecting snow in a few days."

"Yes, I'd heard that. Sure, let's go kayaking, but you should know that I've never done it before. Is it difficult?"

"No, it's easy. I have a tandem kayak so we can ride together. I'll load it up when I get home, then swing by your place around three thirty. Would that be okay?"

"Yes, and, Shawn? Thank you. I'm looking forward to this."

"Me too. See you soon."

Shawn returned to the register after she hung up with Morgan.

"Hey, boss. What's got you showing your teeth?"

Shawn hadn't realized she'd been smiling when she came out front, but Kerrie, one of her servers who had been with her for the past three years, stood before her with her hands on her hips, daring Shawn to lie.

"I don't know what you're talking about, Kerrie. I'm just happy. Is that a crime?"

"You're always in a good mood, but there's something different, a lightness to you. Is it Paige?"

"Uh." Shit. Everybody who worked in the diner knew Shawn and Paige had been seeing each other, so how was she going to explain this without looking like a player? Marcy was really the only person in her life who knew of Shawn's flings in the past. That wasn't something she wanted the townspeople to know about her, so she was always discreet when she fooled around. No PDAs, no romantic dates. "Not exactly. A friend and I are going kayaking today after work." That's it. Keep it simple. She wasn't doing anything wrong. She was just hanging out with a friend. A new friend. A beautiful new friend who made her insides quiver.

"There's more. What aren't you telling me?"

"Nothing. Okay, maybe something. There's a woman who is staying in the cabin around the corner from my house and we're going kayaking."

"Shawn, what are you doing?"

Shawn looked around, hoping she'd get out of this conversation by helping customers, but there were only a few tables that were taken, and the people were in the middle of eating. She lowered her voice.

"I'm not doing anything wrong. Morgan is here alone, and she looks like she could use a friend. Look, don't say anything because I don't want it getting back to Paige before I talk to her, but I'm going to break up with her. She's a nice lady, but I'm not feeling any connection with her. I kept wanting to, I swear I did. I haven't broken up yet because I don't want to hurt her, but I know I'm not doing her any favors by staying with her."

"And you're feeling a connection with Morgan?"

"I don't know. We've only met four days ago, but that's beside the point. Even if Morgan wasn't here, I'd still break up with Paige. Like I said, I like her, and I'm hoping we can remain friends, but the romantic feelings aren't there. Believe me, I've tried."

"You be careful, Shawn. I don't want you getting hurt or getting too far ahead of yourself with this other woman."

Shawn would be offended if she didn't like Kerrie so much, and she knew she was just looking out for her. Kerrie was about twenty years older than Shawn and acted more like a mother figure, or older aunt, so Shawn couldn't be upset with her.

"It's not like that. I know she's not sticking around, but she seems kind of lost and sad, and I'm only offering her friendship." Shawn held up her hand to quiet Kerrie's next remark. "Just my friendship. You don't need to worry about me."

Kerrie softly patted Shawn's cheek. "I'll always worry about you, Shawn. All of us here," she swept her hand around the diner, "we're all family, so that's what we do."

"Thanks. Now get back to work and stop wasting time." Shawn smiled to let Kerrie know she was kidding, and she rang up the customers who had saved her from further discussion.

Shawn raced home after work and got everything loaded up for her date with Morgan. Wait. It wasn't a date. Shawn was just trying to be Morgan's friend while she was in town. It wasn't like she was taking her out to dinner or hoping for a good night kiss. Even if it was offered, Shawn wouldn't allow it while she was still dating Paige. She'd never been a cheater and she wasn't about to start now. Going kayaking with Morgan was all about showing her the beauty of her town and how to relax. Shawn loved kayaking because it enabled her to forget everything while she rhythmically paddled and glided across the water. There was no better place to do that than on Lake Tahoe.

Morgan opened the door and Shawn's mind went numb. Morgan stood before her wearing a green-and-blue bikini top with matching boardshorts that came to mid-thigh. Her hair was up in a bun, exposing her slender neck that made Shawn's mouth water just with the thought of tasting her skin.

"I'm ready!" Morgan's smile was so bright, it added to her beauty.

Oh, God. I'm so not ready to look at the back of her for the next couple of hours. Shawn took a deep breath to calm her racing heart. "You look great." Shawn looked Morgan over, and she felt her heart race faster. So much for taking the deep breath. A lot of good that did. Shawn quickly considered diving in the cold lake just to cool down her overheated body. "Okay, let's go. Do you have on sunscreen? It doesn't take long to get sunburned up here."

"I brought it with me. I applied it to most of my body, but I'll need you to put it on my back."

Shawn gulped loudly. She'd considered telling her she wouldn't need it on her back due to the life vest, but that would have been stupid on her part. Besides, better safe than sorry. She agreed to the arduous task. Difficult work, but someone had to do it. Her fingers twitched at the idea of rubbing lotion into Morgan's smooth skin. Jesus. Morgan wasn't making things easy for Shawn, although why would she? She had no idea of the affect she had on Shawn or that she was dating someone for the time being.

"Look how cute you are, Jameson, with your own life vest." Jameson wagged his tail and tried to get in the front seat with Morgan before Shawn told him to get back. "I can't believe he's going with us."

"He loves it, actually. He sits in front of me and he stays completely still."

"I've been looking forward to this all day." Morgan reached over and placed her hand on Shawn's arm, making the skin beneath tingle. "And you were right. The weather is perfect."

Shawn lifted her chin and pulled her shoulders back, quite pleased with herself for suggesting this outing to Morgan. They arrived at her private dock, and Morgan helped her get the kayak off the roof rack. Morgan handed Shawn the bottle of sunscreen and turned her back to her. Good Lord in heaven, this was going to be torture. Morgan had no idea of the thoughts running through Shawn's head as she rubbed the sunscreen into Morgan's smooth white skin that was splattered with freckles and a faint tan line that looked to be from a one-piece. She cleared her throat and was grateful for the sunglasses that covered her eyes. They didn't hide her face, but at least Shawn could keep her eyes on Morgan without making it look too obvious.

"Normally, I take this to the end of the dock, but I think it'll be easier for you to get in if we're on the beach." Shawn quickly instructed Morgan on how to paddle and where she would sit. Her tandem kayak was a sit-on-top so Jameson could come with her. There was a flat area between the front and back seat where Jameson would sit, and once Morgan got in place, Shawn laid a towel down where Jameson would stay. She pushed them out in the water, then got in, careful not to capsize them.

"Okay, you ready?"

Morgan looked over her shoulder back at Shawn. "As I'll ever be."

"Okay, start paddling."

They started off slow, letting Morgan get the hang of paddling and get into a rhythm, which she quickly did. The small waves in the water added a little rocking to the kayak, but the farther out from shore they got the water became smoother, like glass. They veered right and paddled along the shore, Shawn pointing out to Morgan places of interest. During the paddle, Shawn gave Morgan a brief history of Lake Tahoe, stories she'd learned from her grandad when they'd take his rowboat out on the lake to go fishing.

The stories about the discoverer, the Washoe and Paiute Indian tribes that had settled there before any white man, the Donner Party, and even Tahoe Tessie, the lake monster that resembled the Loch Ness Monster according to folklore. Grandad would tell her those stories while their lines were in the water. One outing, Shawn had paid such rapt attention that she lost her pole when she hadn't noticed she'd had a bite on the line. Shawn had been around ten years old, and Grandad joked that maybe it was Tessie who'd taken her rod. The kayak had rocked side to side with Morgan's laughter.

"I can just picture you at that age, eyes wide and mouth open when your grandad told you it might have been Tahoe Tessie that stole your fishing pole."

"That sounds about right. I think I scooted closer to him so he could protect me from her. At the same time, I was afraid that he'd be mad that I lost the pole."

"Was he?"

"Nah. The next day when he came home from the diner, he presented me with a new one, then we went out fishing again. That time, I made sure to keep a strong hold on it. I ended up catching three trout that day, big enough to bring home to Grandma to cook for dinner."

"It sounds like you two were really close."

"Yeah, we were. I'll have to tell you more stories about him later." Shawn could now talk about her grandad without getting tears in her eyes, but that wasn't the case for about the first two years after he died. Now, it just reminded Shawn that she was keeping his memory alive when she retold his stories.

They paddled into shore and disembarked. Morgan had a little trouble getting out so Shawn came to her rescue. She grabbed Morgan's hands and pulled her up. Morgan had lost her balance with the force and landed pressed up against Shawn's body. She gripped Morgan's waist to keep her upright. Thank Tahoe Tessie they'd had their life vests on. The thought of Morgan's breasts pressed up against hers made Shawn's nipples hard and wetness pool in her lower region.

"I'm sorry—"

"Are you—"

They both spoke at the same time, and Morgan stepped back and stuttered as she apologized.

"Sometimes I don't know my own strength. You sure you're okay?"

"Yes. Thank you so much for today. It was so fun hearing your stories, and I'd like to hear more. Are you available to have dinner with me tonight?"

Now it was Shawn's turn to stutter. "Uh, no. I already have plans, but I appreciate the offer. Maybe another time?"

"Of course. Let me know when you're free."

Shawn would be free after she talked to Paige and broke it off with her. It wasn't a conversation she looked forward to having, but she'd put it off long enough. It was time to cut the line. They loaded up the kayak after putting Jameson in the car, and they drove the two minutes up the road to Morgan's cabin. She placed her hand on Shawn's forearm, and her muscles twitched under Morgan's fingers.

"Thanks again, Shawn. See you soon?"

"Yep. I'll call you. Have a good night."

Shawn pulled away when Morgan went inside. "Well, doggo, I'm in a world of trouble with that one. There's something about her that gets my insides all jumbled. I guess I can't put off talking to Paige any longer, huh, buddy?"

Jameson licked her cheek, and she wiped his slobber off. "I love you too, buddy."

After Shawn showered and redressed, she texted Paige to see if they could get together later. Paige had texted back and said she was free after she closed her ice cream shop at nine p.m. Great, Shawn had a few hours to kill before she'd go break it off with Paige. She went over in her head about what she'd say tonight. Neither one had discussed their feelings for each other, but Shawn had enjoyed hanging out with Paige, and she'd hoped they could remain friends. The town was too small not to run into each other on occasion. Shawn had been lucky that she and Marcy were able to remain friends after they broke up, and now Marcy was her best friend. Maybe she and Paige could go that route.

Shawn had jumped in her truck about twenty minutes prior to Paige closing. Shawn paced the sidewalk near the shop, her heart racing and her nerves frazzled. She didn't have a lot of experience breaking up with women, and the thought of hurting Paige in the process made her feel like an asshole.

The lights went off and Paige stepped out then locked the door behind her. She smiled when she turned around and saw Shawn.

"Hey, you. You're a sight for sore eyes." She stepped forward and kissed Shawn quickly on the lips. "You want to take a walk?"

"Sure." Shawn offered her arm and Paige wrapped her hand around Shawn's biceps. No muscle twitching like she'd had with Morgan just a few hours earlier. They walked down to the lake, the pathway lit by gas lamps, a million twinkling stars, and the full moon.

"How was your day?"

"Not bad. Worked then kayaked. How about you?"

"Pretty slow today. I wish I could've gone out on the lake with you today."

Shawn never even considered inviting Paige, and that spoke volumes about her feelings for her. All she'd been thinking about lately was the stunning woman who was staying up the street from her.

"So, what did you want to talk about?"

Shawn took a deep breath and let it out before facing Paige and looking into her eyes. At that moment, that might have been the bravest thing Shawn had ever done. "I think we should stop seeing each other."

Paige's mouth dropped open, shock overcoming her face. She took a step back and looked away. Shawn had remained quiet, letting Paige process her words. Paige turned back to Shawn with tears in her eyes.

"That was not what I was expecting. I thought we liked each other, maybe more than liked. I know for myself, I could've fallen in love with you."

That statement didn't surprise Shawn, but she felt a lump in her throat that was hard to swallow around when Paige actually said those words out loud. Shawn had discovered over their time together that Paige was an excitable woman, and Shawn had witnessed that intensity when they were having sex, but that certainly wasn't enough to keep them together as a couple. And even though Shawn liked Paige, there was something about her she just couldn't put her finger on. Something that didn't sit right in Shawn's sixth sense.

"I'm sorry, Paige. I like you and we have fun together, but I just don't feel like we have a love connection."

"I see." Paige covered her face with her hands, then wiped away her tears. She moved closer and reached for Shawn's hands. "Are you sure about this?"

Shawn frowned. "I am. If you're up for it, I'm hoping we can stay friends. Like I said, I really like you."

"Just not enough to love me though, right?"

Shawn squeezed Paige's hands and slightly shook her head.

Paige kissed Shawn on her cheek and backed away. "Take care, Shawn. I hope you find what you're looking for."

Shawn stood and watched Paige walk away. While the conversation wasn't easy, she'd expected maybe a little drama, but that didn't happen, and Shawn felt the heavy weight lifted off her shoulders. Paige had been fairly calm. Maybe a little too calm for her normal behavior that made Shawn wonder if there would be a future explosion. She hoped that one day they could be friends. Shawn turned and watched the moonlight reflect off the water, and when she looked to the sky, a shooting star flew above her. She closed her eyes and quickly made a wish, just as her grandad taught her.

Shawny, whenever you see a shooting star, make a wish. But don't tell anyone or it won't come true.

All Shawn wished for was to find a woman she could connect with, one who would produce the fireworks in her soul that were as spectacular as the ones that lit the sky on the Fourth of July. Someone she wanted to spend the rest of her life with. Shawn was ready for her true love.

Chapter Eight

M organ took her cup of coffee and phone out to the deck and enjoyed the crisp morning air. There were clouds in the sky today, unlike yesterday where there was a clear blue sky while kayaking with Shawn. Morgan felt a little apprehensive when she first sat in the kayak, but with Shawn's instruction, she quickly got the hang of it. Time had passed all too quickly while listening to Shawn's stories of Lake Tahoe and the history of it. Morgan was fascinated that Shawn knew so much of this charming place, but then again, according to Shawn, she had a wonderful teacher in her grandfather. The strain of slicing the paddle through the water for two hours caused soreness in her muscles. She winced as she brought the cup to her mouth.

Morgan had thought of Shawn often last night while she started the fire, thanks to Shawn teaching her, and just sitting on the couch listening to the cracks and pops of the burning logs. She was glad she was getting to know Shawn better, and they were becoming what Morgan considered to be friends. Not only was she attractive, but she had taken Morgan under her wing. Knowing that Shawn was just down the street made Morgan feel less lonely and safer.

She took this quiet time to reflect on her relationship with Jess, as she'd done the past couple of mornings. She wasn't sure if it was the fresh air, the activities she'd done with Shawn, or just being alone, but she'd been fairly successful in quieting her mind and figuring things out for herself.

Morgan had been in love with Jess, and she never thought in a million years that she would cheat on her. She'd like to think that she'd known that they wouldn't work out in the end because it might make the betrayal a little less hurtful. Not much, but less. The night Morgan had walked in on Jess and the other woman was supposed to be a night of reconnecting with her, to get their intimacy back. Now that she'd had some time to reflect, she and Jess were never meant to be a forever couple. Still, why hadn't Morgan seen this coming at the time? Morgan and Jess had started out fast and hot, but then they had fallen into a monotonous routine with occasional sparks of excitement and adventure. Relationships that were worth having were a lot of work to keep the fire burning and looking back, Morgan knew she was putting in most of the work. Frankly, it became exhausting. She kept waiting for Jess to make more of an effort. Why wasn't Morgan worth the effort to Jess?

She understood that sometimes relationships played themselves out sooner than later. Hell, she'd been in some of those relationships. But her other exes had never cheated on her. If Jess had wanted out, she should've discussed it with Morgan like adults. They might have been able to come out of this relationship on friendly terms. But no. Morgan had not only been heartbroken, but she had been humiliated as well, and that was not something she could forgive. The humiliation and pain were what drove her to break down, redecorate her house, and to be short-tempered with her friends and colleagues. Morgan had been tempted by a pretty face that ultimately ended up burning her.

She was attracted to Shawn, there was no doubt about it. When Shawn had pulled her out of the kayak and Morgan ended up in her arms, her body had flashed heat like she'd been scorched by the sun. Her mouth went dry and her heart raced as if she'd run around the lake. Morgan had learned her lesson. She would not fall for another pretty, or in Shawn's case, handsome face and lose her ever-loving mind. She'd decided last night that Shawn was going to remain in the friend zone. Morgan wouldn't allow Shawn's charm and rugged good looks to pull her into Shawn's bed.

Morgan had waited for the blue jay to fly away from the porch railing before she went back inside to refill her coffee and make herself some breakfast. Preparing the food reminded her of Ray's Diner...

and Shawn. God, why couldn't Morgan get her out of her mind? She smiled to herself, knowing exactly the reason. She wasn't afraid to admit she'd thought more than once of Shawn's well-developed arms and shoulders, her large, strong hands, what they might feel like caressing Morgan's body, entering her, taking her like Shawn owned her.

Well, shit. She burned her eggs. She placed the pan in the sink and filled it with water, then she opened the cabinet and pulled out her trusty protein bar. She ripped open the wrapper and took a huge bite to where she couldn't chew with her mouth closed. She might as well get dressed in case she wanted to go anywhere.

The ringtone to her cell stopped Morgan in her tracks, and she retreated to the kitchen where her phone was sitting on the counter. She smiled when Jane's face appeared. Morgan hadn't talked to her since the day she arrived to let them know she was safely at the cabin.

"Hey, sweetie. How are you?"

"Better now that I know you're still alive. I was starting to get worried."

"I'm sorry, but was I supposed to call you more often? I've only been here for five days."

"Exactly! Five days where anything could've happened. You could've been kidnapped or mauled by a bear or something."

Jane's harried voice made Morgan laugh because Jane was normally a calm woman.

"You're silly, Janey. I'm having a great time actually. I spend my mornings working on myself, and I spend my afternoons playing." Morgan wondered if she should tell Jane about Shawn, knowing Jane would remember her from the diner and Morgan's ridiculous response to meeting her. Jane would be relentless with teasing at first then goading Morgan into going and having a little more fun with Shawn. Wink, wink. Nod, nod. Morgan could handle it though, and it would probably ease Jane's worry of her.

"Remember the cute butch from the diner we went to in September? Her name is Shawn, and she's my neighbor."

"Really? Small world."

"And an even smaller town." Morgan loved hearing Jane's laughter over the phone.

"I'm glad you made a friend, or is she more than that?"

Morgan nearly strained her eyes rolling them. She *knew* Jane would say something like that.

"Just friends, I promise. She helped me out of a couple of jams when I first got to town, but since then we've gone on a hike and kayaked on the lake."

"Sounds like you're having fun then. Just beware of the bears when you hike."

"Oh, my gosh. I have to tell you that we saw a bear and her cubs when we hiked a couple of days ago. I have video thanks to Shawn. Hang on." Morgan put the call on speaker and quickly texted Jane the video. "Put me on speaker and take a look." Jane's excitement was almost palpable as she commented on the video of the cubs wrestling with each other. "Jane, it was the most amazing thing I've ever seen." The adrenaline rushed through Morgan like river rapids as she recounted the story to Jane. Morgan went on to tell her about their kayaking excursion and how Jameson the dog went with them.

"Are you guys doing something today?"

"I'm not sure." Morgan interrupted her pacing to look at the clock then out the window as if Shawn would magically appear. "She said she'd call me, but she didn't say when."

"Listen, honey, I have to get back to work, but I want to hear all about your soul-searching. Call me tonight and tell me what you've learned so far."

"You got it. Have a great rest of your day, and give my love to Annie."

Morgan returned to her task of showering and dressing to get ready for her day. What that day entailed was anyone's guess.

Shawn had turned up her street and spotted Morgan walking in the opposite direction toward the lake. Shawn slowed and lowered the driver's side window.

"Hey there. Whatcha up to?"

Morgan crossed the street and leaned down with her elbows resting on the door of Shawn's car. Shawn could smell the mixture of sunscreen and perfume, and somehow the two mixed well together on Morgan.

"I was just taking a walk down to the lake. Would you like to join me?"

Shawn knew she should say no. She should make an excuse so she could distance herself from Morgan. When she'd gotten home after breaking up with Paige, she'd slid into bed and thought about their relationship and the dates they'd had. She felt it was the right thing to do, to give respect to the time they'd spent together. But just before she'd drifted off to sleep, Morgan flashed through her mind, and Shawn had sweet dreams of the two of them together. This was real life though, and if she didn't watch herself, she could fall hard for the gorgeous woman with the sexy smile. She should absolutely decline Morgan's invite.

"I'd like that. Mind if I bring the doggo to get him some exercise?"

"Of course not. Want me to wait here for you?"

"Yeah, I'll just be a minute." Shawn drove toward her house, slightly swerving to the right while watching Morgan in the side mirror. Christ, Shawn was useless when it came to Morgan. Why couldn't she just be strong and decline her invitation? She could use the excuse that she wasn't looking to start anything new, especially with a visitor. But the truth was she found Morgan funny and sweet, and she liked hanging out with her. If Shawn could just forget about the fact that Morgan was probably one of the most alluring women she'd ever met, then she'd be okay. Hell, she wasn't blind.

Shawn ran into the house and leashed up Jameson who was more than ready to go. When he spotted Morgan, he whined and pulled to get to her quicker than Shawn was moving. She let go of his leash, knowing he was safe on the barely used road, and he sprinted the rest of the way to his new best friend. Morgan put her hands out to stop him, and he wiggled his butt as he danced around her. Shawn laughed as she approached the pair.

"I guess I know how you rate with him." She picked up his leash, and they began their walk. "How was your day?"

"It was good. I talked to my best friend this morning and I told her about seeing the bears and kayaking. She nearly flipped when I sent her the video of the bears."

"Yeah, that was pretty special that you got to see them close up."

"True, but if I never see them that close again, that will be fine by me. How was your day?"

"Fine. Not too busy but steady."

They walked in silence, Shawn content to just listen to the birds singing as if they were leading them to the lake. Once they reached Shawn's dock, she unlocked the gate, and they sat on the end with their feet dangling. The water level had dropped a little since last winter due to a lower than normal snowfall so their feet weren't in danger from the ice-cold water. Jameson lay behind them soaking up the sun.

Morgan nudged Shawn's shoulder. "Tell me more about your family."

"Well, the short version is I'm an only child. My parents moved to Houston when my dad got transferred for his job. My mom works at a nursery which is perfect for her because she loves plants and flowers."

"Did you get her green thumb?"

Shawn snorted. "Hardly. I don't mind digging in the dirt, but I can never keep anything alive. I just rely on the sturdy trees to decorate my property."

"I don't garden because I work such long hours, I don't have the time to tend to anything. My weekends are spent cleaning the house, doing laundry, and grocery shopping. Tell me more about your grandparents. Your grandfather sounded like a hoot."

"Oh, he was that all right. I told you I grew up in Sacramento, and I'd spend every summer here. I'd help Grandad in the diner once I was old enough. He put me to work bussing tables and cleaning up. As I got older, he'd let me serve. I made pretty good tips, especially from his buddies that came in. There are still a few left in the area that continue to come in. I've kind of become their surrogate granddaughter. Those old codgers are fun to be around."

"And your grandma?"

Shawn looked down and smiled, recalling her grandmother's kindness and intelligence. "She was something else. They were high school sweethearts, and Grandma acted like Grandad hung the moon. Except for when Grandad would act up, then Grandma took out her trusty cast iron skillet and threatened to knock him upside the head. We all knew she was kidding because she'd never hurt a flea. Grandma taught me how to cook and bake. She'd pack us picnic lunches, and the three of us would go sit on the beach or get in the rowboat to fish. Summers up here with them were magical. Now that they're gone, I'm glad I had all that time to spend with them."

"That is special. My grandparents, both sets, lived on the East Coast, so we didn't see them often. I lost them all during my twenties and early thirties. We lived in the Midwest while I was growing up."

"What about your parents? Do they still live in the Midwest?"

"No, they're divorced. My mother lives in Florida with her new husband, and my father lives in New York with his new husband."

Wait. Did Shawn hear her right? "Your dad is gay?" Shawn could feel that her jaw dropped, and Morgan placed her fingers under Shawn's chin to help close her mouth.

"Yes, which may be the reason he took it so well when I came out. My mother on the other hand...let's just say it doesn't bother her that we live on opposite coasts. We talk only a few times a year. My dad and his husband are fantastic. They're just a couple of old queens that spend their free time seeing plays and musicals. I always have a great time when I'm with them. When they come out here, they insist I take them to Napa for wine tasting. We've been to more than a few."

The lilt in Morgan's laugh did funny things to Shawn's insides. So, Morgan was into women. Didn't that just make things more interesting? Shawn had an inkling, but she didn't want to jump to conclusions. She'd lived her life so that she didn't assume anything about anyone, and didn't know anything for certain unless she heard it from the person's mouth. And what a beautiful, kissable mouth Morgan had. A vision of Shawn's mouth on Morgan's, kissing her, teasing her, flashed before her, and she shuddered. The wind started to pick up and the billowy clouds quickly floated over the mountains, darkening the sky, and warning them of the incoming snowstorm that was to arrive later that night. The small waves on the lake started to grow.

"We should get back. The way those clouds are rolling in, it's going to get dark here pretty soon." Shawn stood and offered her hand to Morgan to help her up. Morgan held on for a few moments, and

Shawn's hand grew warm. A gentle squeeze, then Morgan released her hand.

"Thanks for coming with me and telling me about your family."

"I appreciate the invite. I had fun with you today."

The trek back uphill to Shawn's cabin left them breathing a little heavier. At least that's what Shawn was telling herself, that it wasn't the nearness to Morgan that was causing it. They reached Shawn's cabin and they stood silently looking at each other. Shawn hooked her thumb backward over her shoulder.

"That's me."

Morgan smiled and Shawn swore that her eyes actually twinkled. Morgan stepped closer and wrapped her arms around Shawn's shoulders. It took her a moment to realize that she should hug Morgan back, and she wrapped her arms around her waist. God, she felt so good in Shawn's arms. All too quickly, Morgan released her, and Shawn immediately missed the contact.

"I'll see you later."

Shawn couldn't find her voice. She just raised her hand in an attempt of a weak good-bye. Morgan got about ten yards away before Shawn could finally speak.

"Hey, Morgan?"

Morgan turned to Shawn and raised her eyebrows while Shawn walked closer.

"Would you like to come over for dinner tonight? I'm just making some beef stew and French bread if you want to join me."

"That would be lovely. What time would you like me?"

That question produced all kinds of responses in Shawn's mind, none of which were appropriate since she was supposed to keep Morgan in the "friend" territory. She looked at her watch. "How about six?"

"Perfect. See you then."

Morgan turned to go, and Shawn stood there watching her, studying her, enjoying the way Morgan's hips swayed when she walked. Morgan's sense of humor and the easy way they were able to converse were things that were catching Shawn's attention, maybe even more than the sway of Morgan's hips. Shawn felt like she could be herself and completely open up to her, something she hadn't wanted to do in the past. Shawn's ogling was caught when Morgan turned around. Shawn waved again then went inside. *Jesus. What just happened?*

Morgan changed into jeans and a sweater after taking a shower to warm up. On her walk back to the cabin, the temperature dropped dramatically, so much so that she could actually see her breath. She'd really enjoyed her time with Shawn that afternoon, and she was really looking forward to dinner with her. She'd blow-dried her hair, applied just a touch of makeup, and dabbed a little perfume in the hollow of her neck. There was nothing wrong with looking and smelling nice for a woman who invited her to dinner.

Morgan shot off a text to Jane that she'd call her the next night because she was having dinner with Shawn. Jane, always the hopeless romantic, replied with smiley emojis with hearts for eyes. She donned her coat, grabbed a bottle of wine, and got in her car for the short ride to Shawn's. The sky was ink black dotted by light snowflakes. The storm had really moved in quickly, and Morgan's breathing sped up. She didn't have much experience driving in snow, and although the streets were clear now, they might not be in a few hours. Her car was not equipped to handle snow or icy roads.

Her breathing slowed when she pulled into Shawn's driveway. She took a moment to calm herself and glance through her windshield at the snow falling. The flakes were small that melted the moment they hit the ground. Morgan opened the door and the near silence was almost deafening with the exception of the ticking of her engine. The smell of the wet pavement combined with the pine, vanilla, and crisp night air was intoxicating.

Shawn opened the door as Morgan climbed the steps to the front porch.

"Welcome. Right on time."

"You wouldn't believe the traffic I had to endure to get here. It's a good thing I left early." Jameson greeted her with a high-pitched whine and a wiggle butt.

Shawn's laugh was loud and joyful, playing sweet music to Morgan's ears.

"Yeah, there's usually always a jam in that half mile from your cabin to mine."

Shawn helped Morgan out of her coat and hung it on a hook near the front door. Morgan handed the wine to Shawn.

"This is one of the many bottles I get from Napa when I go with my dads. I hope you like it."

Shawn studied the label then looked at Morgan. "I'm not much of a wine drinker, but I love Pinot Noir, and this will go perfectly with the stew. Thank you for this."

Morgan stepped past Shawn into the living room just to the right of the front door. The couch and love seat looked comforting, and the fire burning cast a warm glow over the area. "It smells great in here. What kind of wood are you burning?"

"Cherry. I love the lasting smell it gives. Just let me put the wine in the kitchen, and I'll give you a tour. Would you like a glass now? Or can I get you something else to drink?"

"I'll take a glass of wine after you give me a tour."

Shawn nodded then ducked into the kitchen. Morgan heard the pop of the cork being released from the bottle as she continued to look around the fairly spacious living room. Shawn returned to find Morgan looking at family photographs in the built-in bookshelf next to the fireplace. Morgan held up a black-and-white photo of a couple standing in front of an old Chevy truck with large pine trees behind them.

"Are these your grandparents?"

Shawn stepped closer, and Morgan could smell the woodsy musk scent that she now associated with Shawn. It nearly made Morgan want to lean closer and smell her skin, but that would be weird.

"Yep, there they are. Weren't they cute? This was taken in the early fifties when Grandma was pregnant with Dad. They didn't move up here until 1972 when they were empty nesters."

"The cutest. Speaking of, is this you?" Morgan held up another picture. She'd recognized Shawn, maybe five or six years old, wearing cut-offs, a T-shirt with Luke and Darth Vader from Star Wars on the front, and Keds tennis shoes without socks. A baseball cap sat low on her forehead, but the smile was all Shawn. She stood holding a fish on a fishing line, and her grandfather stood next to her with his arm around her. If she could have, Morgan would have melted into a puddle in that very spot.

The blush that engulfed Shawn's face warmed Morgan even more. She lightly patted Shawn's cheek and laughed. "Don't be embarrassed. You're adorable."

"Thanks," Shawn mumbled. "Let me give you the tour."

Shawn pointed to the stairs. "That leads to the loft. It's mostly bookshelves filled with books and stuff I typically don't use." She led Morgan down the hallway to the left of the living room, and she showed her the two guest bedrooms and a bathroom. At the end of the hall was Shawn's bedroom. It wasn't a huge bedroom, but big enough to hold a queen-sized bed, a dresser, and two nightstands. Jameson's dog bed was in the corner and looked well-worn. A small flat-screen television sat in the middle of the dresser. Morgan felt a sense of intimacy when she stepped into Shawn's room, but also a little like she was invading her privacy even though she'd been invited. Despite that, she felt like she'd come home, which was crazy since they barely knew each other. What impressed Morgan the most was the en suite. A two-sink vanity, a walk-in shower, and large soaker tub were against the far two walls, and the room was colored in light blue and gray.

"This is amazing!" The bathroom didn't seem to match the rest of the house. The house felt like it hadn't been updated in the past ten years, but it was still nice and homey. But the master bath, that was something Morgan would have sweet dreams of. If she'd thought of her ideal bathroom, that'd be it. She could come home every night, take a bubble bath, and drink a glass of wine, and release the stress of her day. She had a sudden image of her in the tub with Shawn sitting on the side of the tub washing Morgan's back. Morgan shivered at the vision, but thankfully, Shawn didn't seem to notice.

"My grandparents updated the house before Grandma died, but they'd never done anything to their bathroom. This was one of the first things I'd had done when I moved in. In order to get a little more room, I took out the closet in the guest room behind my bathroom which is how I was able to get the soaker tub to fit. I also had new counter tops and appliances put in the kitchen a couple of years ago. What was their dream home is now mine."

"The whole place is lovely, Shawn. It suits you."

"Thank you. How about that wine?"

"Yes, please. I thought you'd never offer." Morgan playfully shoved Shawn from behind to get her to move faster, but she also took the time to look at how cute and firm Shawn's ass looked in her Levi's. Morgan began to feel a little stirring of lust deep in her belly. When she was younger, in high school, Morgan loved it when guys wore Levi's 501s. For some reason, it made their butts look better, and Shawn's didn't disappoint. Shawn's broad shoulders, tapered waist, long, muscular legs, tight ass—everything Morgan fantasized about. If Morgan had met Shawn in Sacramento, or rather if Shawn *lived* in Sacramento, Morgan would definitely be interested in dating her. Having flings had never been Morgan's thing. She needed to have some sort of emotional connection to her bed partner. If that hadn't been the case, Morgan felt like Shawn would be the perfect anecdote to getting over the betrayal she felt from Jess. Shawn's looks were just the cherry on top of the hot fudge brownie sundae loaded with whipped cream and nuts. As she got to know Shawn better, the more attracted Morgan was. Shawn was kind, funny, independent, generous with her time, and laid-back. What wasn't to like? It was just too bad they lived two hours away from each other. Doable but not ideal. When Morgan felt ready to date again, she wanted to be with a woman who lived close enough where they could see each other often, sometimes sleep over. The best she'd be able to hope from Shawn was a weekend here and there, depending on their schedules. But she was getting way ahead of herself.

They stepped into the kitchen for Shawn to pour the wine, and the smell of the stew made Morgan's mouth water. She ran her fingers over the butcher block countertop as she perused the area with stainless steel appliances and grayish blue cabinets.

"Shawn, my goodness. This kitchen is amazing. I love everything about it, especially the color of the cabinets. It ties in so well with the rest of the house."

Shawn laughed as she handed the glass to Morgan. "You sound like you could host one of those home improvement shows or be a Realtor."

Morgan moved her hands and arms like she was a game show assistant presenting the grand prize. "Over here, we have the updated kitchen with butcher block countertops, stainless steel appliances, and…" Morgan whispered to Shawn, "What wood is the cabinets?"

Shawn put her hand to the side of her mouth and whispered back, "Maple."

"…and Maple cabinets painted this gorgeous blue-gray color. Back to you, George."

Shawn laughed heartily with her hand on her stomach, and it made Morgan smile. "I think you definitely missed your calling, Morgan."

Morgan placed her index finger under her chin and looked up. "Hmm. Maybe. I wonder how I could get into showbiz."

"Are you kidding? With your looks, your body, your personality? You'd be a shoo-in."

The mortified widening of Shawn's eyes and the bright redness painting her cheeks made Morgan feel like she was ten feet tall, and that Shawn probably didn't mean for that comment to come out of her mouth.

"Well, uh, let me put the French bread in the oven, then we can eat."

Morgan grinned as she took a sip of wine. It appeared the attraction was mutual. That was really good to know…just in case. She leaned her elbow on the counter as she watched Shawn doctor the bread with real butter, not the spray stuff Morgan used at home.

"Do you want garlic on the bread?"

"Yes, that sounds great."

Rather than sprinkle garlic powder, like Morgan would've done, Shawn peeled and crushed the garlic cloves, spreading them generously on the bread. She wrapped it in foil and placed it in the oven. Shawn set the timer, picked up her glass of wine, and clinked it to Morgan's.

"Here's to new friends and good food."

Morgan clinked her glass and took a sip. *And maybe more than friendship. Whoa! Let's not get ahead of ourselves.*

After dinner, which was delicious, Morgan and Shawn took their glasses of wine into the living room and sat at either ends of the couch in front of the fireplace. They turned to face each other and continued their conversation from dinner.

"That was great, Shawn. Thank you so much for the invite."

Morgan took a sip of wine and stared contemplatively into the fire. "You know, I was lost when I came up here, but I'm finding my footing again."

Shawn looked up at Morgan. They hadn't discussed anything too deep at this point, except touching a little on their families. Shawn had felt that Morgan, since spending time with her, had been a little lonely and a lot lost. Shawn wanted to ask more, but she also had an inner suspicion that Morgan would open up to her when she felt ready.

"I'm glad to hear that. I'm really glad we met, and I'm really happy that you're finding your way. I've always thought this, and I may be biased, but I feel Tahoe offers up to people what they're looking for, whatever that may be. Whether it's adventure, peace, or insight, one can find it up here as long as they're willing to open up."

There was silence except for the fire crackling in the fireplace and Jameson snoring on his bed in the corner.

"I returned home from my weekend up here a couple of months ago to find my girlfriend in bed with another woman. In my own damn house. In my own damn bed."

Damn. That was some fucked up shit. Shawn sympathized with Morgan. She felt her blood boil and the urge to find said ex-girlfriend, maybe kick her ass for doing that to Morgan. If Morgan was her girlfriend, Shawn would never have the desire to look at another woman, let alone sleep with one. Shawn had so much to say, but she bit her tongue and stayed silent, allowing Morgan to continue talking.

"I lost myself. I thought maybe it was my fault that Jess strayed. I work long hours; we became complacent and took each other for granted. I was trying to do better. In fact, she was supposed to come up with my friends and me a couple of months ago, but she said she had to work. I believed her. I guess she found someone to work, all right."

Shawn saw the sadness in her eyes, but there was something else. Possibly resiliency. Morgan definitely seemed happier, more at peace than the first time they met earlier in the week. Maybe talking about her ex made Morgan sad, but she seemed determined to get over it and get on with her life.

"Anyways, I'm beginning to realize that what we had wasn't true love. Don't get me wrong, I did love her and she really hurt me, but I think what I was most upset about was that she embarrassed and humiliated me by bringing another woman into our bed. If she had loved me, she wouldn't have cheated, right?"

Shawn nodded, thinking that very same thing. "Is there anything I can do to help? Offer a shoulder? Go find your ex and slash her tires?"

Morgan laughed and placed her hand on Shawn's arm. Shawn felt the heat through her sleeve as though her skin would be forever imprinted with Morgan's hand.

"I appreciate you wanting to go all gangster on her, but you've already helped me, and I don't know how I'll ever thank you."

Shawn placed her hand over Morgan's that still remained on her arm.

"I'm glad I've helped, but there's no need for thanks. I like that we're becoming friends, and I want you to know that I'm here for you."

Morgan held Shawn's gaze, and Shawn felt it all the way to her soul. Morgan looked as if she was searching for something in Shawn's eyes. The truth? A promise? Shawn inched closer, looking down to Morgan's lips, wanting to know how they'd feel on her own. Shawn was just about to lean a little closer to what could be her sweetest destination, but Morgan cleared her throat and looked down. Shawn sat back and wiped her hand over her face.

"Shit, Morgan. I'm sorry. I shouldn't…"

Morgan placed her hand on Shawn's cheek and cupped it with such gentleness, it made Shawn lean into it.

"Shawn, I really like you, but it's not fair to you to start something when I'm going to be leaving in a little over a week. Besides, I'm not ready for anything right now. If I was in a different headspace, I'd let you kiss me until I couldn't see straight."

Shawn closed her eyes and groaned, picturing herself doing just that.

Morgan chuckled as she placed her hand in her lap. "Can we still be friends?"

Shawn squeezed Morgan's hand. "Of course we can."

Morgan stood and Shawn followed suit. "It's getting late. I should get going."

Shawn walked Morgan to the door and helped her on with her coat. "Yeah, I hope there's not too much traffic for you."

Morgan laughed before turning around and hugging Shawn, making her want to hold Morgan closer to her body. Morgan kissed her cheek and Shawn finally got to feel how soft Morgan's lips were.

"Thank you again for a great evening. Great food and even better company. Call me tomorrow?"

"Absolutely." Shawn opened the door to find about eight inches of snow in her driveway, and it was still falling.

"Holy cow! It really dumped tonight." Shawn looked at her watch and realized it'd been four and a half hours since Morgan had arrived.

"I'm not going to be able to drive my car in that." Morgan turned to Shawn and threw her hands in the air.

"Well, we have two choices. I could drive you home or you could spend the night."

Morgan squinted and Shawn felt herself blush.

"I meant you could sleep in the guest room. The snow is supposed to stop by midnight, so in the morning, I could drive you and your car back to the cabin and I can walk home from there."

"I don't know, Shawn. You think you can keep your hands to yourself?" Shawn knew Morgan was kidding by the wink Morgan threw her way, but it didn't keep Shawn's stomach from doing backflips. She held up three fingers together. "I promise."

Morgan laughed. "What? Are you a Boy Scout now?"

Shawn smiled and shook her head. "No, ma'am. But I promise to be a perfect gentleman."

"Okay, but I'll stay only on one condition."

"What's that?"

"You'll let me fix you breakfast in the morning."

"Well, I'm supposed to work, but I doubt I'll be able to get out of here without the help of a snowplow." Shawn looked upward and pursed her lips like she had to actually think about the deal. "Okay. You're on. Let me shut the house down then I'll show you to your room."

Once all the lights were off, Shawn led Morgan to her room for the night. "Let me get you a T-shirt and boxers to wear. You can find a new toothbrush and toothpaste in the guest bath."

Shawn got ready for bed, and when she came back to check on Morgan, Shawn found her under the covers—and Jameson on the bed next to Morgan, looking at Shawn expectantly.

"Come on, Jameson. Off the bed."

Jameson groaned and played dead, letting his head fall onto Morgan's stomach. Lucky dog. Morgan laughed and gave his head a scratch.

"He can stay in here if it's okay with you. It'll be nice to have a warm body next to me, even if it is a dog."

"Fine." Shawn walked in and scratched Jameson on the belly. "You mind your manners and don't snore too loud."

"I'm sure he'll be fine."

"I was talking to you."

Morgan's gasp was followed by Shawn's laughter as she started to leave. She turned back around before flicking off the light.

"Good night, Morgan. Let me know if you need anything."

"Thanks, I will. Sweet dreams, Shawn."

Shawn walked down the hall mumbling to herself about her dog being a traitor and dreams that would probably be anything but sweet.

CHAPTER NINE

The room was pitch-dark, and Morgan was snuggled up with the covers up to her chin. The creak of the door slowly opening startled Morgan awake, and she turned her head to see the shape of an imposing figure in the doorway. The figure tentatively stepped closer to the bed, standing at the side, looking down on Morgan. Morgan extended her hand, inviting her into her bed, although she still couldn't see the face. The person slipped under the covers and over Morgan before she lowered her face and slowly, thoroughly kissed Morgan. Morgan wrapped her arms around the broad shoulders and opened her mouth, allowing the woman's tongue to enter and mingle with hers.

Morgan spread her legs, and the woman had nestled her sex into Morgan's and started moving against her. Her hot breath against Morgan's neck sped up, and Morgan could feel the impending orgasm deep in her belly.

"Make me come." Morgan grabbed the woman's ass to pull her in harder, deeper. Sweat from both bodies intermingled and allowed their gyrations to speed up.

"Come for me, Morgan. I'm going to come with you."

"Yes, now. I'm coming." Morgan felt the explosion throughout her body as the woman grunted, lightly biting Morgan's neck as she too came.

Morgan ran her fingers through the short dark hair and lifted the head to stare deep into Shawn's brown eyes. Morgan lifted her head to kiss Shawn's soft lips, giving her heart time to slow down. She rested her head on her pillow and turned on her side as Shawn spooned her from behind. Thoroughly sated, Morgan grabbed Shawn's hand and held it between her breasts as she fell back to sleep.

Morgan woke a few hours later from the sun shining through the blinds of her bedroom window. She reached behind for Shawn, but the bed was empty and the sheets were cold. Did last night really happen, or was it just a dream? It must've been a dream, but judging by the wetness in her underwear, it felt completely real. God, what a night. If Real Shawn was just half as good as Dream Shawn in bed, any woman who could be with her would be in for quite a good time.

Morgan got out of bed and looked out the window to see the crystalline snow on the trees and ground. What a gorgeous sight. The sky was deep blue and the sun was shining as if Mother Nature herself said, "Just kidding." She grabbed the sweater she wore last night and pulled it over Shawn's T-shirt she wore to bed. She couldn't very well face Shawn this morning with her still-hardened nipples pointing at Shawn through the thin cotton barrier. She slipped across the hall to the guest bathroom, brushed her teeth, ran her fingers through her hair to relieve her bed head, and used the toilet, wiping away the remnants from her wet dream of Shawn. After she washed her hands, she opened the door to find Shawn coming down the hall from her bedroom.

"Good morning. How'd you sleep?"

Morgan felt the heat rise in her face, recalling the dream and seeing Shawn now in a gray hoodie sweatshirt and green and blue plaid flannel jammie pants. Her hair was sticking out in all directions, but she looked so sexy to Morgan.

"Wonderful. I woke up very relaxed." Shawn didn't need to know the real reason she felt relaxed. At least not yet. "Have the roads been plowed yet? I'm sure you have to get to work soon, so I'll get out of your hair."

Shawn grabbed Morgan's arm and slid her hand down until they held hands. Morgan's arm and hand felt warm and tingly that quickly spread throughout her body.

"Not so fast, lady. You promised you'd make me breakfast this morning. I'm holding you to that. Besides, I called one of my chefs earlier this morning and told him I'd be in later. I can't imagine it'll be too busy after the snowfall last night."

"Are you sure? I don't want you getting in trouble with the boss." Morgan winked, letting Shawn know she was joking.

Shawn smiled and had a devious glint in her eyes. "It's good to be the king."

"Indeed. In that case, I'm going to rummage through your fridge and pantry to see what I can come up with."

"Sounds good. While you do that, I'll make the coffee."

Morgan opened the refrigerator door and scanned the contents. She pulled out eggs, milk, bell pepper, mushrooms, and tomatoes. "How do omelets sound?"

"Amazing. I have some bacon in the drawer if you want to cook that."

Who didn't love bacon? Morgan opened the package and laid the slices in a frying pan. She made herself at home in Shawn's kitchen, and she had to admit to herself how comfortable she felt. Not only in Shawn's home but with Shawn herself. They'd only known each other six days, but they had a familiarity to them that made Morgan feel like she'd known Shawn for much longer.

As she chopped the vegetables, Shawn let Jameson out in the backyard to go to the bathroom. Morgan looked out the window to find Shawn and her dog chasing each other, slipping, and falling in the snow. Jameson jumped over Shawn, taunting Shawn into getting up to resume the chase. Morgan hurried to the linen closet and brought back two towels as the snow-covered human and her dog clomped up the stairs to the back deck. Morgan opened the door and handed the towels to Shawn. She closed the door on them to prevent letting out the heat. According to her father, she, in fact, had not been raised in a barn, as he'd always told her when she left the front door open.

Morgan returned to the kitchen and resumed cutting the veggies, but looked up and smiled at Shawn when she came through the door.

"Thanks for the towels. Jameson loves playing in the snow, and since you're taking care of breakfast, I thought I'd play a little too."

"You two looked like you were having fun. I was expecting you both to lie down and start making snow angels."

"I thought about it, but Jameson insisted on making snow doggies instead. It smells great in here."

Morgan finished cutting the vegetables and turned over the bacon. "Of course, it does. I mean, bacon. Am I right?"

"Spot-on. I think I could put it on anything and love it."

Morgan whipped up the eggs and poured them into another frying pan, then grated the sharp cheddar. "Shawn, would you mind making us some toast?"

"Geez, offer to cook me breakfast and you end up putting me to work."

Morgan lifted her spatula and threatened Shawn who held up her hands and surrendered.

"Yes, Queen."

Morgan laughed then gave a little swat to Shawn's butt with the spatula.

"Watch it, stud. Don't make me put you over my knee."

Shawn turned to face Morgan and waggled her eyebrows. "Promise?"

"Oh, my." The banter between Morgan and Shawn had been humorous and easy, but the thoughts that just ran through Morgan's mind made her lick her lips. She was almost painfully aware of the thudding in her chest, and she couldn't for the life of her break away from Shawn's gaze. Jameson saved the day by coming into the kitchen and nudging Morgan's hand with his nose.

"Hi, cutie-pie. Did you have fun playing in the snow with your mommy?"

He wagged his tail and Shawn cleared her throat. "No bacon for you, Jameson. Your breakfast is in your dish."

Morgan chopped the bacon and threw it, the veggies, and the cheese into the eggs, and finished the omelet. She put half on Shawn's plate and half on her own, while Shawn placed the buttered toast on the plates.

"What do you take in your coffee?"

Morgan brought the plates to the table and set them on the blue-and-white checkered placemats. "Black."

"Wow, that's impressive. I thought only old guys drank black coffee."

Morgan smacked Shawn in the stomach when she set the mugs on the table, causing Shawn to let out an "oof."

"Watch it, or I'll take your omelet and eat it myself."

Shawn chuckled as she took a seat. "I have a feeling I'm going to surrender to you a lot."

Morgan's body came to attention as she thought of all the ways Shawn could surrender to her. Morgan was versatile in bed. She could be passive or aggressive. Top or bottom. Slow or fast. Soft or rough. Well, not too rough. Morgan was quickly realizing, probably thanks to her wet dream last night, that she could see all of that with Shawn. Maybe the reflection she'd been doing was working, or maybe the fresh mountain air was helping clear her mind. She hadn't thought of Jess hardly at all for the past couple of days, other than telling Shawn about her last night, and she'd been thinking of Shawn more and more. Not that she was ready to start anything new with anyone just now, but when she was ready, she'd hoped to find someone like Shawn.

While they enjoyed their breakfast, the loud rumbling and scraping noise of the snowplow made its way up the street, clearing away last night's snowfall. Morgan looked over at Shawn. She saw the light in Shawn's eyes dim, and she imagined hers had the same effect. Their morning together was coming to an end now that the roads had been cleared. Shawn would have to get to work soon and run her business, and Morgan would go back to her cabin. Most likely, she'd think of Shawn.

"Well, I guess I should start getting ready." Shawn stood and took their empty plates to the kitchen, rinsed them off, then left them in the sink to wash later. "Listen, it might take a few hours for the remaining snow to melt off the street, so feel free to hang out, watch TV, whatever. I'll be home by three thirty, maybe earlier if we're not busy. I don't know if you have plans for later, but if not, maybe we can do something?"

Morgan noticed the red hue to Shawn's cheeks, the slight stutter in her speech. She was nervous. It was growing more obvious that Shawn was attracted to Morgan, so at least it was mutual. God, why did things have to be so complicated? They could probably hook up, have great sex for the remainder of Morgan's time at the lake, but she already liked Shawn too much to have just a fling. Besides, that wasn't really Morgan's thing.

"Thanks. I might take you up on that. Now, go get ready, and I'll take care of the dishes."

"You don't have to do that. You cooked breakfast. I'll clean them when I get home."

"Shawn." Morgan moved closer to Shawn and took her hand. "Remember that whole 'surrender' thing we talked about before breakfast?"

Shawn chuckled and squeezed Morgan's hand. "I remember." Shawn leaned down and gave Morgan a sweet, chaste kiss on her cheek. "Thank you again for breakfast. Make yourself at home."

As Shawn walked to her room, Morgan touched her cheek where Shawn had just kissed her, as if she could hold the feeling of her soft lips against her skin. It seemed that Morgan was starting to lose her self-imposed war of keeping Shawn in the friend zone. She had to try harder to keep her attraction and growing feelings in check. She shook her head and turned on the faucet, intent on washing the dishes and trying to dispel images of Shawn in her dream last night.

Morgan had just finished drying the dishes when Shawn came into the kitchen to say good-bye. She'd dressed as she normally did, with jeans and a T-shirt under her flannel, but today, she also had a black knit hat on her head. The true look of a mountain woman that again had Morgan swooning.

"Well, I'm off to work. Do you need anything before I go?"

Morgan thought that she wouldn't mind Shawn taking her quick and hard there in the kitchen before leaving for work. The way Morgan had been feeling all morning—aroused, wet, and hard—it wouldn't take long for her to come, but she couldn't voice that out loud.

"No, I'm just going to hang here with Jameson for a bit. Have a great day at work."

Shawn didn't turn to leave. In fact, she looked as if she was trying to make a decision. Morgan didn't know what Shawn was trying to decide, but she'd made one of her own. She stepped closer and opened her arms. Shawn visibly relaxed, her shoulders lowered, and she stepped into Morgan's hug. Morgan felt Shawn's arms wrap around her waist as Morgan put hers around Shawn's neck. Morgan took a deep breath in and smelled the mixture of laundry detergent and a woodsy scent, and the fragrance did something to Morgan's insides. Her body heated, and she felt her nipples harden. Jesus, the effect that Shawn had on her was nothing she'd ever experienced before. Morgan just might combust before her two weeks were up if she couldn't keep her distance from Shawn. She broke away from Shawn's body before she lost complete control. She gave a playful shove to Shawn's shoulder.

"Get out of here and go to work. We'll talk soon."

Shawn left without saying another word, and when she was safely ensconced in her vehicle, she let out the breath she'd felt she'd been holding since stepping into Morgan's arms. Even the crisp, cold air hadn't been enough to cool her overheated body. Hell, rolling around in the snow probably wouldn't do the job.

Shawn had a great night with Morgan, and an even better morning. They'd just met, but Shawn felt like she'd known Morgan for a lifetime. It was easy, too easy, to imagine a lifetime of nights and mornings with her, but Shawn knew that wouldn't be possible unless Morgan decided to move to Lake Tahoe. Shawn didn't know much about Morgan's work, but she couldn't imagine there'd be any need for an outside sales rep for medical devices in the Tahoe area. There was a decent sized hospital on the South Shore, but only a small community hospital on the North Shore, which was closer to Shawn. Damn, Shawn finally met a woman she really liked, could picture a relationship with, and she had to live and work over two hours away. Sure, people had long-distance relationships, but that wasn't what she wanted. She wanted a woman that would live with her, fall asleep together after making love, and wake up with in the morning in each other's arms.

Shawn arrived at the diner and found a nearly empty parking lot. She hadn't been wrong. It seemed the snowfall had kept most people inside today, even though it was clear blue sky and the sun was shining now. She walked through the back door to find Shorty and Melvin sitting at a small table in the back of the kitchen playing cards.

"Hey, guys. We're really hopping this morning, huh?"

"Yeah, we've had a whole three tables to serve for breakfast, but we figure once the snow melts down, people will be in for lunch."

"Not the first time this has happened, and it certainly won't be the last. I'm going to go into the office and work on the order. Anything special we need?"

Melvin made a list and gave it to Shawn. She grabbed a cup of coffee, said hello to Kerrie, the only server on staff that morning since it was so slow, and headed to her office. She'd managed to keep Morgan from her thoughts long enough to concentrate on her orders and other paperwork that needed her attention. Shawn thought about skipping out early and going back home, but the responsible business owner in her made her stay just in case things picked up a little later.

Once the diner closed, Shawn walked out to her car humming a little tune. The sky was bright blue, the sun was making its way toward the western mountains to set, and it had warmed up just enough to melt some of the snow. She had about two hours of daylight left. Not a lot of time but enough to take Jameson for a walk. Maybe Morgan was still at her house and she could go with them. Shawn felt her heart sink when she approached her house and Morgan's car wasn't there. What did she expect though? To have Morgan stay at her house all day, welcome her home after a day at work, maybe have dinner cooking? They were just friends, not lovers, not girlfriends. Morgan needed this time to work on herself, not keep Shawn company. *Get a grip, Evans.*

She opened the door to her empty cabin and noticed something was off. Where was Jameson? She called out to him, checked the rooms, then went out back. No dog. She called his name over and over until the panic took over. She felt her chest tighten, and she bent over with her hands on her knees. Her dog was gone. How'd he get out? Did he get hit by a car? Hurt by an animal? Shawn jumped in her car, lowered her windows, and started driving around the neighborhood, calling and whistling for Jameson.

Shawn saw Morgan's car in the driveway of her rental so she stopped and ran to the front door, banging on it in a rush. Morgan opened the door, eyes wide.

"Shawn, what's wrong?"

"Jameson is gone. I can't find him."

Morgan opened the door wider and Jameson came running. Shawn got on her knees, and she felt the tears sting her eyes as she opened her arms and Jameson ran into them.

"Oh, God. Are you okay? I was worried, boy."

"I decided to bring him here so we could keep each other company. I even took him for a walk."

"Jesus, Morgan! You can't just take my dog without telling me. I thought he was dead somewhere!"

The dog backed away from Shawn, sat against Morgan's leg, and whined.

"I left you a note, Shawn. It's on the kitchen counter."

"Well, obviously I didn't see it." Now that Shawn knew Jameson was safe, her adrenaline was crashing, and her anger bubbled over. "You should have called or texted me." All the while Shawn was yelling at Morgan, Morgan petted Jameson's head as if she was trying to calm him.

"You're right. I'm sorry I scared you."

Shawn turned to go without saying anything more to Morgan. "Come on, Jameson. We're going home." Shawn was at her car, but Jameson was still by Morgan's side, which pissed off Shawn even more. "Jameson, come!"

"Shawn. Please come in so we can talk. Please. I was making dinner for us."

"No, I just want to go home. Jameson, come." She opened the door, and Jameson walked down the steps. He usually ran when she opened the car door, but it appeared he didn't want to leave Morgan. He was already attached to her. Who was she kidding? So was Shawn. She needed distance from Morgan who was quickly making her way into Shawn's heart. She closed the door once Jameson was in the back seat, and she quickly got in her car and drove away before she could change her mind.

❖

Morgan watched Shawn drive away, and she had the urge to run after her, apologize until Shawn forgave her. How did this wonderful day turn into a shit show? Once Shawn had left for work, Morgan had spent some quiet time on the couch with Jameson curled up next to her. She took the dog for a long walk, enjoying the beauty of the sun shining on the freshly fallen snow. Once the snow had fully melted on the road, Morgan decided to take Jameson with her to her cabin so he wouldn't be alone for the rest of the day. She'd started dinner, read on the couch with Jameson cuddled up to next to her once again, and waited for Shawn to arrive.

It never occurred to her to call or text Shawn to let her know she had Jameson. She didn't want to bother her at work so she'd written a note and left it in plain sight on the kitchen counter. In hindsight, in Shawn's shoes, Morgan probably wouldn't have seen the note either if she was panicking. She had to find some way to make it up to her. She dialed Jane's number and smiled when she picked up.

"Hey, Morgan. Are you okay?"

Morgan looked at her watch and winced. She hadn't realized it had gotten so late, but it was almost nine p.m. "I'm so sorry to call so late. The time just got away from me."

"It's okay, sweetie. We were just watching a movie, but we've seen it before so we can talk."

"Are you sure? I don't want to be a bother."

"Honey, when have you ever been a bother? Now, what's going on?"

Morgan went into detail of the past couple of days, and how things ended that afternoon.

"I feel so bad for freaking her out."

"I'm sure you do, but I also feel she overreacted a tad much. I mean, you did leave a note. Should you have texted her? Sure. But it wasn't like you were careless with her dog. Besides, since when do you like dogs?"

"I love dogs actually, but it wouldn't be fair to have one with the number of hours I work."

"I can't believe in all the years I've known you, I didn't know you were a dog lover."

"Well, now you know. Can you please help me out? I don't know what to do about Shawn."

"What does it really matter, Morgan? I mean, you'll be coming home in a week. You might not ever see her again."

Just the very thought of never seeing Shawn again added more queasiness to her already turning stomach. She and Shawn were becoming friends, even though it was apparent she had a huge crush on her. Plus, all the nice things she had done for Morgan, the thought that Shawn was upset with her didn't sit right, and she felt her world had slipped slightly off its axis.

"But I want to see her again. We've become friends. She's a great person, and I want to keep in touch with her, maybe visit her once in a while."

The silence on the other line was deafening. Morgan pulled the phone away to make sure they were still connected. Then she heard it.

"Oh, no."

"What?"

"You've fallen for her."

"What? No, I haven't." Had she? There was the dream, sure. And there might have been a wee bit of flirtation. "Listen, I'm not looking to date anyone right now."

"Honey, love seems to find us when we aren't even looking. I'm not saying you're in love...yet. But you can't deny there's an attraction there. If there is, and it's something you might want to pursue in the future, just apologize to her again. If she's half as nice as you say she is, she'll forgive you."

"Whoa! Just...whoa! There's no love. Not any kind of love going on up here. Don't say that word again."

Jane laughed over the phone, but it didn't ease Morgan's stress at all. "Okay, no love, but at least attraction. Can I say attraction, or are you going to blow another gasket?"

Morgan chewed on Jane's advice for a moment. She was right. There was an attraction between them brewing, and even though Morgan wasn't ready to act on it, she still wanted Shawn to forgive her. Even if they were nothing but friends, Morgan wanted Shawn in her life.

"Okay. I'll go down to the diner tomorrow morning, have breakfast, and apologize again. I just hope she'll forgive me. Thanks, Janey, for everything."

"Anytime, sweetie. Anything else you want to talk about?"

Morgan thought about telling her about the hot dream she had about Shawn last night but quickly squashed that idea. "No, I'm good. Actually, a lot better now that I've talked to you. I miss you guys."

"We miss you too, Morgan. Let's have dinner when you get back to town. Now, get some sleep, and in the morning, go get her, tiger."

Morgan laughed, and God, it felt so good. "Night, Jane. Give Annie a kiss for me."

Morgan slid between the sheets, ready for sleep. The sooner she could fall into slumber, the sooner she'd wake up, the sooner she'd see Shawn.

CHAPTER TEN

Morgan didn't get much sleep. She kept seeing the desperate look on Shawn's face when she thought she'd lost her dog. That desperation turned to anger, and Morgan kept dreaming that Shawn cut her out of her life and said she never wanted to see her again. Morgan hoped that that was just a nightmare and not a reality. She took extra care getting dressed and putting on makeup, hoping to entice Shawn into forgiving her. Morgan pulled into the parking lot a little after eight a.m., and she checked her makeup and hair once more in the visor mirror before exiting the car.

The butterflies were fluttering in her stomach, and she wiped her sweaty palms down the front of her jeans. She took a slow deep breath in and let it out before opening the front door. The jangle of the bells on the upper part of the door announced her arrival. Shawn wasn't at the counter. Morgan quickly looked around and wondered if Shawn took the day off since her car wasn't in the driveway when Morgan drove by. Her disappointment quickly turned to excitement and her heart raced when Shawn came through the swinging door that presumedly led to the kitchen area, or maybe her office. When Shawn saw Morgan, she slowed her stride. Shawn's frown was not what Morgan wanted to see, but at least she was still moving toward Morgan instead of going back through the door.

"Hey." Shawn's greeting definitely wasn't a "hey, great to see you," but more of a "hey, I guess you're here to let me have it."

"Shawn, I am so sorry for not calling or texting you to let you know I had Jameson. I can't imagine the fear you went through when you couldn't find him. I promise that I'll never do that again.

But please say you'll forgive me. I don't want to lose you. Or our friendship."

Shawn smiled a little. That could be promising. "I'll forgive you on one condition."

"Anything. Just name it."

"That you'll forgive me for being such a dick to you yesterday. I was going to come by your place when I got off work to apologize. I was way out of line talking to you the way I did. I'm sorry, Morgan. I don't want to lose our friendship either."

Morgan felt the dreaded weight lift from her shoulders. "I wish I could give you a big hug right now."

Shawn's smile could've brightened the darkest room, and she stepped closer with her arms open. "Come here."

Morgan stepped in and just like that, all was right in the world again. She could feel Shawn's back muscles tighten as she wrapped her arms around Morgan. Now was not the time to think of Shawn hovering over her, body slick with sweat, muscles flexed as she drove herself into Morgan. She cleared her throat as she remembered they were in Shawn's diner. She released her hold, her body heated and her panties wet. That was going to be uncomfortable.

"Hey, Shawny. Who's your friend?" An older gentleman at a table with three other men laughed when Shawn blushed.

Shawn ducked her head and spoke softly into Morgan's ear. "I have to introduce you to those guys. They were good friends of my grandfather's, but don't pay them no mind. They're nosy old codgers."

Morgan looked up into Shawn's eyes. "I'd love to meet them."

Shawn grabbed Morgan's hand and led her to the table. "Guys, this is my friend Morgan Campbell. Morgan, that's Ernie, Dave, Bill, and this ugly mug is Jack."

Morgan smiled and shook their hands. "It's a pleasure to meet you, gentlemen."

"Are you here to have breakfast, young lady, or are you just going to make googly eyes at our Shawny?"

Morgan barked out a hearty laugh as Shawn turned the deepest shade of red she'd ever seen on a person. That Jack guy was a hoot and a troublemaker, Morgan could tell. This could be fun. "Can't I do both, Jack?"

The men laughed and Morgan winked at Shawn. She could handle these guys, and it was just a little bonus to see Shawn a bit off kilter.

Ernie jumped up and grabbed another chair, whacked Dave on the arm and told him to scoot over. "Why don't you join us, honey? You can sit next to me."

Normally, a man other than her dads calling her honey would've given Morgan an opportunity to use a few choice words, but she knew deep inside these guys were harmless and not condescending.

"I'd love to. Thank you." Ernie held the chair for Morgan and when she sat, he helped scoot her in.

"What can I get you, Morgan? I recommend the banana nut pancakes."

"That sounds perfect, Shawn. Could I also get some coffee?"

"Sure." Shawn pointed at each of the men. "Y'all behave and don't go telling stories."

Once Shawn left, the four men all looked at Morgan. It somehow felt like she was about to be interrogated, and she was tempted to look around for a bright light for them to shine in her eyes.

"How do you know our Shawny, honey?" Jack looked over the rim of his mug as he took a sip of coffee.

He had a head full of thick gray hair and a twinkle in his bright blue eyes. Morgan could tell he was the leader of this group, like a big brother.

"Well, I actually just met her a week ago. I've rented a cabin up the street from hers and she's been nice enough to help me with some things."

The guys looked at each other, Bill rolling his lips in to keep from laughing probably now that Morgan reran that sentence back in her head.

"Get your mind out of the gutter, Bill." Morgan calling him on that got the other guys to burst out laughing. Bill was a skinny man, also gray-haired, as well as a gray goatee. Morgan pegged him as the joker and troublemaker of the group.

Shawn came back with Morgan's coffee and refilled the other mugs on the table. "What's so funny?"

"I was just telling them how we met. Anyways, gentlemen, and I use that term loosely," Morgan winked at Bill, "Shawn has been nice enough to take me hiking and kayaking since I'm here by myself."

Dave nodded. "Our Shawny is as nice as they come. We all love her like she was our own granddaughter. Her granddaddy was one of our best friends." Dave was a bulk of a man, his protruding belly preventing him from getting too close to the table. He had a face full of hair, including a long beard that reminded her of Santa Claus. Ernie looked to be the youngest of the group with salt-and-pepper hair and a decent physique for a man his age. He was the quiet one of the group.

Touched, Morgan looked at Shawn and grinned. She'd only known Shawn for a week, and she already knew that she was special.

"You guys are just buttering me up so I'll comp your meal." Shawn clapped her hand on Jack's shoulder before she left to help a customer.

"Where are you from, Morgan?"

"Sacramento."

"And what do you do?"

"How long will you be here?"

"Where's your family?"

They shot off question after question, from all different directions, and Morgan felt like her head was spinning. She could take it though because they were just looking out for Shawn, and she appreciated that.

"All right, guys. Leave her alone and let her eat."

Morgan's eyes widened when she saw the pancakes Shawn set in front of her. There were three large pancakes topped with sliced banana, walnuts, and whipped cream. There were smaller dishes with butter and syrup, but she doubted she'd need that. She slowly and methodically cut the cakes into tiny squares then looked up to see five sets of eyes on her. She stabbed a banana then a square of the pancakes and held it in front of her mouth. The anticipation seemed to be killing the spectators, so she opened wide and closed her lips over the fork and let the warm sweetness envelop her taste buds. She moaned her pleasure and held her thumb up. She loved seeing Shawn pleased, and she knew inexplicably that she wanted to continue doing so.

The guys had finished their breakfasts before Morgan even sat down, so she encouraged them to tell tales of Shawn and her grandparents while she ate. She was only able to eat three-quarters of her breakfast before she felt like she'd burst, and she pushed her plate away. Since the breakfast crowd had dwindled, Shawn pulled up a chair after taking Morgan's plate away, and she joined them with her own cup of coffee. Shawn sat next to Jack, and it warmed Morgan's heart to see his affection for her. He placed his arm behind Shawn's chair and started rubbing her neck, causing Shawn's head to fall forward. Morgan wished it was her that was rubbing Shawn's neck muscles, soothing her into submission. Again, with the dirty thoughts. Morgan could be in some real trouble if she didn't rein in her lust.

They spent another thirty minutes together before Jack stood, followed by Ernie, Dave, and Bill.

"Well, ladies, us old guys better get going so we can get on with our day." Jack took Morgan's hand and helped her stand before wrapping her in a gentle grandfatherly hug. While they embraced, Jack spoke softly. "I like you, honey. I like you for Shawny. But if I hear you hurt her, I'll send my wife after you with a wooden spoon."

Morgan looked into Jack's eyes, knowing he was just looking out for Shawn's welfare, and seeing the love he had for his surrogate granddaughter.

"I would never do anything to intentionally hurt Shawn, sir. You have my word."

"Good. I hope to see you again real soon. Join us anytime for breakfast. Shawny knows the days we come in."

Morgan hugged the other three, then they all hugged Shawn after paying for their meal. Shawn came back over to the table and sat with Morgan.

"How did you like the pancakes?"

"I think it's my new favorite breakfast, but I'm in a total food coma. I might just pass out when I get back to the cabin."

"Oh, that's too bad because I was going to ask if you wanted to watch the sunset from Sand Harbor. It's across the lake from here and the Tahoe sunsets are gorgeous."

The thought of watching a sunset with Shawn perked up Morgan. "Well, I can take a little nap until you get off work. I'll be well rested."

The smile that lit up Shawn's face made Morgan want to do anything she asked.

"Great! I'll pick you up at four. I gotta get back to work, but I'll see you soon."

"I can't wait. I just need my check."

"There isn't one. Jack insisted on buying your meal even though I told him I wasn't going to charge you."

"Can I just tell you how much I already love those guys? They're a riot, and they sure do love you. Thank you for introducing them to me."

"They're pretty far gone on you, too."

"I'll fix us something to eat while we watch the sunset."

"You don't have to do that. I can fix something."

"Nonsense. You're working and I have the time. I'll see you soon, right?"

"You will. And, Morgan? I'm really glad you came in today."

Morgan quickly hugged Shawn, not wanting to linger and get worked up again. "I am, too."

Shawn raced home after work, grabbed Jameson, a warm blanket, and a jacket before heading to Morgan's. She was just exiting the car to knock on Morgan's door when she stepped out onto the porch holding a bag in one hand and her jacket under her other arm. Shawn went to her and grabbed the bag from her so Morgan could lock the door.

"Still not willing to leave your door unlocked?"

"Old habits die hard. Besides, you never know when a random dog might come along, open the door that's unlocked, and jump up on the couch with me."

"Happens to you a lot, does it?"

They both got in the car and closed the doors.

"You have no idea. It's a total thing. Hi, Jameson. Ready to see the sunset?" Jameson licked Morgan's face and Shawn laughed.

"I hope you don't mind dog slobber."

"Not from this handsome guy."

Shawn turned her SUV left on Highway 89 and followed the road along the North Shore. Morgan had filled Shawn in on the stories Jack, Bill, Dave, and Ernie told about Shawn.

"Those guys are great, but they can sure embarrass a person. They're also very nosy, especially about my love life." Shawn gripped the steering wheel and she glanced over at Morgan. "Uh, I mean, not that I have a love life to talk about or anything." Geez, she kept putting her foot in her mouth when it came to Morgan.

"So, you're a virgin?"

"No!"

Morgan laughed and placed her hand on Shawn's arm that was still gripping the wheel.

"I'm just kidding. Not that being a virgin at, what? Thirty-five? Is a bad thing."

"I'm thirty-eight, I'll have you know, and I lost my virginity in college, thank you very much."

"Tell me about her. I mean it's still a while before we get there, right?"

"Seriously? You really want to know?"

"I'll share mine if you share yours."

Oh, man. Morgan had no idea what she did to Shawn with her suggestive words and her constant touching. All of it was driving Shawn mad. How was Morgan able to keep her in a constant state of arousal without even knowing it? Or did she? No, Morgan wouldn't do that. Besides, she'd brushed off Shawn when she went to kiss her the other night. She said she wasn't ready for anything, and Shawn would abide by Morgan's wishes. But still. Shawn was only human.

"All right, but it's not that interesting. It's kind of crappy actually. I was a freshman playing on the college's softball team. One of the seniors on the team had a friend a few years older than her. I was at a team party one night, and my teammate's friend started hitting me up. We ended up in a vacant bedroom, and she started kissing me. I was a little on edge because I'd never kissed a girl, or woman before. But she was telling me how cute she thought I was, what a good player I was, how she couldn't believe I was single. She said she really wanted to kiss me, and I thought I was going to lose it. I was so flattered that I allowed her to take my hand, and she led me to the room. Anyways, she took her time in the beginning, kissing me. Then she placed her hand on my leg, and it startled me. God, I was such a dork."

Shawn glanced over to see Morgan's eyes and attention on her so she felt compelled to continue.

"We kept kissing and touching each other, and before I knew it, she was undressing me, and she put her hand inside my underwear. She had me so worked up, I popped off like a sixteen-year-old boy. My breathing hadn't even returned to normal when she kissed me, told me to get dressed, and she left the room, leaving me there with just my sports bra and underwear on. Well, I got dressed and went to look for her so we could talk and hang out, maybe exchange numbers, but she'd left."

The car was quiet except for the hum of the engine and the radio playing softly. Shawn looked over to Morgan who looked incredulous. Her eyes and mouth were equally wide open.

"Pretty shitty, huh?" Shawn looked back at Morgan who was shaking her head.

"That's one of the worst stories I'd ever heard. I can't believe she just did that to you."

"Yeah. I felt so ashamed, especially after my teammate said that was her friend's MO. It took me a while before I wanted another woman touching me."

"God, Shawn. I'm so sorry that your first time wasn't with someone caring. I mean, come on! She just left you there."

"Well, she didn't know it was my first time."

"That doesn't matter." Morgan threw her hands in the air, and Shawn thought she might hit something. "Any decent person would stick around, maybe talk a little. But she just left you."

"Morgan, it's okay. I got over it. My follow-up was a much better experience, and that first woman actually taught me what *not* to do. I learned to always treat my lovers with respect and make sure we're on the same page."

They pulled into the parking lot of the beach, and Shawn backed into the space so they could sit in the back to watch the sunset. She released the rear lift gate, put down the third-row seat so Jameson could join them, and sat in the back. Morgan started pulling foodstuffs out of the bag and opening the containers that had salami, cheese, gourmet olives, and crackers. She handed a bottle of wine and a corkscrew to Shawn to handle that task. Everything looked delicious, including the Pinot Grigio.

Morgan beamed. "It's a charcuterie board without the board. I also cooked a chicken breast for Jameson." She looked so proud of herself that Shawn had to consciously keep her hands from grabbing Morgan's face and kissing her senseless. Instead, she used her hands and mouth to nosh on the food Morgan had prepared, letting her know that everything tasted great. They still had about thirty minutes before the sun set, plenty of time to eat and talk some more.

"Your turn."

"My turn? For what?"

"I told you mine. Time for you to tell me about your first time."

Morgan handed Jameson a piece of chicken and he gently took it from her fingers. "After hearing your story, I don't think I want to tell you now."

"That bad?"

"No, it was much better than yours. I don't want you to be jealous."

Morgan laughed when Shawn started tickling her and Jameson barked at their antics.

"Okay, okay. I'll tell you. Geez. So, here it is. My high school girlfriend and I had sex in my car after the movies one night. That's it."

Shawn shook her head. "That's all I get?"

"What more do you want?" Morgan covered her mouth since she'd just taken a bite.

"Don't make me tickle you again. How old were you? How long had you been together? What happened to her? What movie did you see?" Shawn asked innocently, batting her eyes and giving Morgan her sweetest smile.

"We were both eighteen. We'd been together for a year. She went away to college. And I don't remember the movie. I think Julia Roberts was in it."

"Morgan! I swear, it's like pulling teeth with you."

"Okay, fine. Her name was Gemma. Probably still is. She and her family moved into our neighborhood the year prior, we had some classes together, and we became friends. I had an immediate crush on her."

"What was it about her that attracted you?"

"I'm not sure exactly. She was cute in a girl-next-door type of way. She was super smart and so funny. There were many times I cried from laughing so hard with her. I wasn't out in high school. In fact, I was still trying to figure out why I was more attracted to girls than boys. Anyways, the summer before our senior year, we spent our days at the community pool, and our nights having dinner at each other's houses. One night, we hugged good-bye, but it was different. It felt different, than our normal hugs. When we broke apart, she kissed me on the mouth, but she looked shocked and ran into her house. I was a mess because it finally clicked for me that I was a lesbian. We didn't speak for a week and it nearly killed me. I missed her so much and I kept replaying that hug and kiss in my mind over and over again. Finally, I couldn't take not seeing her so I drove to her house, picked her up, and we went for a drive. Sorry this is so long. Are you bored yet?"

Bored? No. Riveted? Yes. Shawn was enjoying listening to Morgan, even if it was about her having sex for the first time. "No, go on."

"We confessed our feelings for each other and then we kissed. It was awkward at first. Teeth banging into each other, you know? But we practiced. A lot. But we were both too scared to do anything more. We spent the entire school year just holding hands and kissing, a little over the clothes action." Morgan wiggled her eyebrows, making Shawn laugh. "Over the next summer, we couldn't spend enough time with each other. We were both going away to college on separate coasts. One night, we went parking after the movie, and we got braver, probably because we knew our time together was coming to an end. We fumbled around, fondling each other in the back seat of my tiny Honda Civic." Morgan laughed recalling the memory and it made Shawn smile.

"We finally unbuttoned and unzipped our shorts, and we stuck our hands in each other's underwear. It took longer than it should have to orgasm, but we didn't know what the hell we were doing. We finally came, almost at the same time, and we spent the rest of our night holding each other until we had to go home because of curfew."

"That was such a sweet story. And now I *am* jealous that your first time was special."

"Yeah, it really was."

"Morgan, look." Shawn pointed across the lake where the sun was starting to set. The sky was a magnificent mixture of orange, pink, and purple breaking through the few clouds in the sky.

Morgan's mouth opened, which she quickly covered with her hand. When she turned to face Shawn, her eyes were wet with unshed tears. "That's the most beautiful thing I've ever seen."

Shawn kept her eyes on Morgan and said quietly, "Sure is."

It took a moment for Morgan to realize Shawn was talking about her. The glow of the fading sun put this ethereal light on to Morgan's face, and Shawn thought she looked like an angel. Morgan placed her hand on Shawn's cheek, and Shawn looked into Morgan's eyes, down to her mouth, and back up into her eyes. Shawn's breathing quickened, as did her heartbeat. When Morgan leaned closer, Shawn's eyes closed, and she felt the softness of Morgan's lips. The kiss didn't last long, way too short in Shawn's opinion, but it was probably the sweetest kiss she'd ever had. The fact that it was with Morgan at sunset in her most favorite place made it all the more special.

They turned their attention back to the sunset, but Shawn couldn't think of anything else except for Morgan's lips on hers. She wasn't sure what she was supposed to do. Morgan had made it clear that she hadn't been interested in a fling. Shawn thought their kiss must've been a "being in the moment" thing for Morgan. Shawn wouldn't make the first move out of respect for Morgan's wishes, but if Morgan decided to change her mind and want to get together with Shawn, she certainly wouldn't turn her away, even though she wanted more. The more time she spent with Morgan, the more she wanted of her. It would be impossible not to fall for her, which, inevitably, would lead to a broken heart that Shawn wasn't sure would heal. The sky had darkened, the sun had disappeared completely behind the mountain, and the temperature was dropping.

"You ready to head back?"

Morgan shrugged. "I guess so. I wish that could've lasted longer."

The sunset or the kiss? Shawn wondered because she definitely wished the kiss lasted longer. They packed up the food, folded up the flannel blanket they'd used to cover their legs, and headed out of the parking lot. They spent the first few minutes talking about the sunset and the view from that side of the lake. Shawn told Morgan that Sand Harbor was a popular place for people to photograph because of the blues, greens, and turquoise of the water, not to mention the clarity. There were also large boulders that stuck out of the water that made it fun to kayak around.

"Whatever happened to Gemma?"

"Excuse me?" Morgan looked at Shawn like she didn't know who or what she was talking about.

"Gemma. Your first? Whatever happened to her?"

Morgan sighed and looked out of the window. So many thoughts and emotions ran through Morgan that day. She was lost in thought as she glanced at the lights and buildings in the small towns they passed by as they drove back home. That was an interesting word to describe Morgan's vacation cabin. The longer she was there, the more it felt like home to her. Shawn could also have a little to do with it, but she didn't want to think about that while Shawn was asking about Gemma.

"We both left for college at the end of the summer. We tried to do the long-distance thing, but there were too many miles between us. We haven't kept in touch. Life just got in the way, I guess. Last I heard, she was living in Washington."

"Have you tried to find her on social media?"

"I'm not on any sites. I have no use or need for it. The people I'm interested in keeping in contact with, I call or text."

"Wow! I guess you're one of the few that don't use it."

"Am I missing out?"

Shawn laughed. "Probably only on rage or indignation on social justice and politics. Oh, but there are some pretty cute puppy and kitten videos."

"Hmm. I don't think cute videos are good enough reason for me to join them."

They were almost back to the cabin, and their night would be coming to an end. Maybe that was a good thing for Morgan. She'd kissed Shawn. She'd told Shawn a few days ago that she wanted to be friends, but Morgan now found herself wanting more, which was confusing her. She knew Shawn would be interested just by the way she looked at her. Shawn's eyes were telling if one was paying attention, and Morgan definitely was. They should probably talk about the kiss but not tonight. Morgan needed some time alone to think about what she wanted.

They pulled into Morgan's driveway and Shawn put the gear in neutral. Morgan was torn between reaching over the center console to hug Shawn and fleeing from the car.

"Thanks for tonight. I had a great time."

"Same here. Listen, I have a ton of things to do after work tomorrow, but I'm off the following day. How about we take a drive around the lake? I can take you to some beautiful spots if you want to take some pictures. We can take a hike, grab some lunch. Interested?"

Morgan was definitely interested. Plus, not seeing Shawn tomorrow would give Morgan time to get her thoughts and feelings under control.

"That sounds fun."

"Great. I'll pick you up at five thirty a.m."

"What? Why so early?"

"You'll see. Dress in layers."

Now Morgan's curiosity was piqued. "Okay, I'll be ready." Morgan reached into the back seat to pet Jameson on the head. "I'll see you later, cutie-pie." Then she reached over and petted Shawn on the head, making Shawn laugh. "I'll see you later."

"What? I'm not a cutie-pie?"

Morgan looked at her and raised her left eyebrow. "Oh, you're something all right. Good night, Shawn."

"Night, Morgan."

Once Morgan opened the door then closed it behind her, she heard Shawn's car back out of her driveway. Shit. What was she going to do about her growing feelings for Shawn?

CHAPTER ELEVEN

O kay. Let's recap this past week, shall we?" Morgan spoke to herself out loud as she paced the hardwood floor of her rental cabin. She hadn't planned on going anywhere that day, which was a good thing, because quite frankly, her head was spinning with all of the feelings she'd been having. She'd found Shawn attractive when she'd been in Tahoe a couple of months ago even though she had a girlfriend at the time. However, getting to know Shawn, Morgan realized the attraction went beyond Shawn's rugged good looks. As the days passed and they hung out more, Morgan felt herself slipping away from being lonely. There seemed to be a powerful chemistry between them, one that she'd been trying to hold at bay. When Morgan was with Shawn, she never thought about Jess. It was almost as if she'd been completely voided from her mind.

Morgan was losing the fight. She'd opened up to Shawn about Jess, a little about her family, and last night, she talked about Gemma. She found Shawn extremely easy to talk to, and she also had this need to touch her, no matter how innocent or not. Shawn was sharing her town and all of the things she loved about it with Morgan, like Shawn wanted her to see all the best parts. In turn, Morgan wanted Shawn to see the very best in her. She wasn't a mountain girl, but the Sierras were already calling to her. She could see the allure of living there, and the thought may have crossed her mind one or five times.

And Morgan kissed Shawn. She couldn't help herself. She was powerless to the powerful kiss. It wasn't long. Hell, there wasn't even tongue involved, but Morgan felt the intensity all the way to her toes.

It felt like a fire burned hot and bright in her the moment her lips touched Shawn's, but Morgan pulled away. She had to. She had no explanation for Shawn as to why she'd kissed her even though Shawn didn't ask. On the drive home, Shawn didn't even bring it up, instead asking more about Gemma. Maybe it was because Morgan shot her down that night she got snowed in at Shawn's. Shawn had moved in to kiss Morgan, and she stopped her, saying she just wanted to be friends. Shawn had abided by Morgan's wishes, but now Morgan seemed to be changing her mind.

"Here's the thing though," Morgan continued wearing a path in the floor with her back-and-forth movements. She often did this when she was practicing a presentation, pacing and speaking out loud in an empty room with no audience. "Shawn is someone I feel totally comfortable talking to about this. I just have to work it all out in my head so I have my thoughts organized."

Maybe, just maybe, Shawn would be up for testing the waters with her. Maybe they could try dating, even though it was long-distance, it was only a two-hour drive. They could see each other every other weekend, taking turns going up and down the mountain. Shawn was fairly busy with the diner, but she was the boss, so she could probably manage to take a weekend off here and there. She would talk to Shawn about it tomorrow. If Shawn agreed, they could take things slow, enjoy Morgan's last week there, and make a plan to see each other again.

Morgan nodded her head, agreeing with everything she planned out because Morgan was a planner. She needed that to feel centered and organized. She took a deep breath in as she closed her eyes, counted to five, then let the breath out slowly. She was almost back to feeling her normal self.

"Good talk, Morgan."

Shawn had endured a restless sleep, replaying the conversation she'd had with Morgan, watching the sunset with her sitting by Shawn's side, feeling the softness of Morgan's lips as they met hers. That one little kiss had Shawn so worked up, she thought talking more about Gemma on the way home would douse her arousal. It had somewhat, but by the time she'd gotten into bed, she'd replayed that kiss at least a hundred times in her head, and her arousal spiked back up. She'd tried to take care of herself, but it was a futile effort because she'd wanted Morgan's hands and mouth to make her come. Shawn wasn't sure that would ever happen though. She wanted to kiss Morgan, touch her, make love to her. But she wanted more. She wanted Morgan to be her girlfriend, maybe have a life together, which was crazy since they'd only known each other for a week. Thinking about all of that had Shawn tossing and turning all night.

Shawn thankfully had been busy at work, which kept her from collapsing from exhaustion. That and the five cups of coffee she'd drank during what felt like a forty-five-hour shift. She'd been burning the candle at both ends the past four days or so, keeping Morgan company and doing things with her. Prior to Morgan coming into town, Shawn typically was active after work but quieted down by six thirty or seven p.m. and in bed by eight thirty since she woke up at an ungodly hour. Even though she'd been lacking her normal sleep routine, the time she'd spent with Morgan, she wouldn't trade for the world. Even if nothing romantic happened between them, they'd still be friends, and Morgan would still be in her life. But damn it, she wanted more.

After work, Shawn had gone to the grocery store where she ran into Paige. They were both in the produce section, and while Paige was checking out eggplant, which made Shawn shudder, she considered turning in the other direction. Had it only been three or four days since breaking up with her? Spending time with Morgan had both sped up and slowed down time. She only had another week before Morgan would be heading home, and the very thought of it wanted to make Shawn cry. And she wasn't a crier.

She'd made up her mind to turn in the other direction when Paige looked up and saw her. Shit.

"Shawn! Hey." Paige waved in Shawn's direction, so Shawn pushed her cart toward her.

"Hi, Paige. How are you?"

"You mean since you broke up with me?"

Shawn winced. The tone in Paige's voice indicated she wasn't kidding around with Shawn, and that she was hurt. She didn't think she'd broken up with Paige badly, as if there was a good way to break up with someone, but she didn't think she'd been an asshole about it.

"I'm sorry, Paige. I didn't mean to hurt you."

Paige waved her hand as if she were shooing a pesky bug away. "Please, I'm fine. We're still friends, right?"

"I'd like to be." That was the truth. This town was way too small to not be friends with an ex. It was a guaranteed way to continue running into them time and again.

"In that case, how about you come over for dinner tomorrow night? I'm making eggplant parmigiana."

Shawn loved Italian food, however the *mere* mention of eggplant made her want to puke. She loved most vegetables, but eggplant and Brussels sprouts never made the list. "Sorry, I can't. I have plans tomorrow night." She was hoping after spending the day together with Morgan that she'd allow Shawn to take her for dinner.

"Oh, do you have a new girlfriend already?" The smile that Paige had on her face didn't reach her eyes, and Shawn heard the hostility in her words. This was more of what she'd been expecting the night they broke up

"No, I'm just spending the day with a friend that's leaving town in a week." That was the absolute truth. Morgan was her friend, although Shawn wanted more, and she was leaving in a week. Shawn also wanted longer. Paige looked like she was about to breathe fire. "Look, I have to finish shopping so I can get home to Jameson. I'll see you around."

Shawn didn't give Paige a chance to say anything more as she turned her cart around and headed to the opposite side of the store. Paige's cart had looked full enough that Shawn had hoped she was nearly finished with her shopping, and Shawn wouldn't have to see her again. At least not that day.

She'd managed to get her groceries and get out of the store without seeing Paige again. She wondered if she and Paige actually could be friends, yet after their exchange earlier, Shawn wasn't so sure. Paige had seemed more than a little bitter when Shawn mentioned Morgan. To assume Shawn had a new girlfriend already was an insult to Shawn, although truthfully, Shawn's attraction to Morgan was quickly getting to be off the charts. It was getting increasingly difficult to keep her feelings in check. There weren't many times throughout the day now that Morgan hadn't crossed her mind, and she was now regretting telling Morgan she wouldn't be able to see her today. Shawn would just have to find something to keep her occupied.

Once she got home and put away her groceries, she took Jameson out back. Her house was on a half-acre of land, but she'd had a fence put up in the backyard so Jameson could go in and out of the doggie door during the day. The fence wouldn't stop a bear from getting in the back, but at least Jameson could scare it away. With days like today, when she'd get home too late to take Jameson out for proper exercise, she'd throw a ball for him to fetch until he tired out.

After about thirty minutes of fetch, Shawn brought her exhausted dog inside, and she started on dinner. It was pitch-dark, and when she looked out her kitchen window, she could see a light in the distance through the trees. That was where Morgan was. What was she doing? Was she cooking dinner as well? Reading a book? Talking on the phone? She was so close, yet Shawn stayed home. She'd thought about inviting Morgan to dinner. How pathetic was she? Shawn didn't even know Morgan a week ago, and now she couldn't go a day without seeing her? Come on, Shawn. Stop being ridiculous. She'd see her tomorrow and they'd spend the whole day together. She decided to send off a reminder text to Morgan after she'd put dinner in the oven and fed her dog.

Hey, you. Just making sure we're still on for tomorrow.

Absolutely! But why so early? Morgan sent a crying emoji and a sleeping emoji.

It's a surprise, but if you really want to sleep in, we can skip it.

No, I'm just being a baby. I'm excited for our adventure.

You'll love it!

Promise? Winky emoji.

Shawn felt the thud in her chest that seemed to arrive anytime Morgan said anything flirty or suggestive. Shawn could play that game too.

With all my heart. Winky kiss emoji.

Shawn saw the dots indicating that Morgan was texting then they'd disappear. When the next message came through, Shawn smiled.

I'll hold you to that. Good night, Shawn.

Sweet dreams, Morgan.

Shawn placed her phone on the coffee table when she sat on the couch with a freshly opened bottle of beer. She was so excited to play tourism director for Morgan tomorrow. There were so many things Shawn loved about Tahoe, and she was so happy to show them to Morgan. Thankfully, she was already exhausted, and hopefully, she wouldn't have trouble falling asleep tonight. As long as she didn't think about kissing Morgan.

CHAPTER TWELVE

Morgan's alarm on her phone went off at four forty-five a.m., and she had half a mind to throw it across the room. Who in their right mind got up this early while on vacation? Shawn better have a very good reason for getting her up this early. Morgan had washed her hair the night before so all she had to do was take a quick rinse in the shower and pull her hair into a ponytail. She'd checked the weather last night and knew the temperature would be mild. She wore a sweatshirt over a T-shirt, jeans, and her hiking boots. She'd packed a small tote with a baseball cap, sunscreen, and her sunglasses, as well as a couple of bottles of water and small bags of mixed nuts for a snack. Shawn had been fairly secretive about this excursion, but she was fairly certain they'd be stopping for breakfast at least.

At five thirty on the dot, Shawn knocked on Morgan's door. Just the sight of Shawn made Morgan's heart race. She'd decided that she would talk to Shawn about her attraction, however she wasn't against it happening organically. That was good because Morgan wasn't sure if she'd be able to keep her hands, or lips, off of Shawn.

"Are you ready for your adventure, Ms. Campbell?"

"All set, Ms. Evans. Show me your Lake Tahoe."

Shawn opened the passenger door for Morgan, closing it once she was safely inside. *My, my. Shawn definitely knows how to act like a gentlewoman.* Morgan had a feeling Shawn was talented in many areas.

Shawn started the car and looked over at Morgan. She looked like a kid headed to Disneyland. Even in the dark, Shawn's smile was bright, and Morgan felt blessed to see this side of her. When they turned right on Highway 89 from their street, Morgan was a little disoriented. Although she'd been there for a week, she hadn't ventured south of her cabin. Shawn had her bright headlights on as there were no other crazy people on the road at this time on a Sunday morning. Neither of them was really saying much. Morgan knew her silence was due to not having a proper cup of coffee yet. Morgan felt Shawn's silence might be due to her excitement. If Morgan had lived here, she was sure she'd be excited to show someone the sights as well.

A short time later, they pulled into the parking lot of Emerald Bay State Park. The sky was starting to turn from pitch-dark to a dark purple. The ridge of mountains east of the lake were rimmed in an orange-yellow hue that promised a spectacular daybreak.

"This is the best place to watch the sunrise. It's not too busy now, but in about fifteen minutes, the parking lot will be packed so we'd better hurry."

"Where are we going?"

"You'll see." Shawn grabbed a blanket and thermos of coffee and led the way for the best view. Shawn navigated climbing the large boulders with ease. Morgan? Not so much.

"Hey, a little help here?"

Shawn turned around and sheepishly smiled. "Sorry. Hang on. Let me put our stuff down and I'll come back and help."

Shawn returned and guided Morgan around the large boulder and followed a dirt path to reach their destination, the back side of the rock had nooks that could be used as steps.

"Seriously, Shawn? We couldn't have taken this way to begin with?"

Shawn shrugged. "Yeah, but this way isn't as fun as climbing rocks." Shawn looked like a child who was scolded for not cleaning up after herself.

"How did you do that with your hands full?"

Shawn spread out the blanket for them to sit on then held onto Morgan's hand as she helped her sit. "Lots of practice, I guess. I've been doing it since I was a kid. I'd go explore the woods when I came to visit my grandparents, which included climbing a lot of rocks."

"Your childhood sounds like it was a lot of fun coming up here."

"It was. Here, let me pour you a cup of coffee." Shawn pulled two paper coffee cups out of her small backpack, and she poured each of them a cup of the strong, hot liquid.

Morgan took her first sip of coffee for the morning, and she sighed once it warmed her throat. The sky continued to slowly lighten, the stars and moon faded, and Morgan shivered as a slight breeze of cold air tickled her face.

"Cold?"

"A little. Not too bad."

Shawn took Morgan's cup and placed it next to hers. "Here, sit in front of me." Shawn spread her legs, and Morgan hesitated. Sweet Jesus. Shawn was slowly killing her, yet her pulse quickened despite being at death's door. What Morgan wouldn't give to feel the sensation of being between Shawn's legs, and she was offering. She crawled closer then scooted back until her behind was nestled into Shawn's center. While she'd been repositioning herself, Shawn pulled something out of her pack and opened it.

"What's that?" Shawn placed it in front of Morgan and wrapped it around her.

"It's a safety blanket. It will keep you warm."

Morgan turned her head to look back at Shawn. "What will you use to keep yourself warm?"

Shawn smirked. "You." Shawn wrapped her arms around Morgan. "Is this okay?"

Morgan nodded, not trusting her voice. She was sure it would be high and shaky, giving away more of Shawn's effect on her. Morgan took a deep breath, the cold air nearly burning her lungs, but her insides were on fire. There she was, sitting between Shawn's legs with her arms loosely around Morgan's waist, waiting to watch the sunrise in one of the most beautiful places Morgan had ever seen. She felt like she was the lead in a rom-com film, or the protagonist in a romance novel.

"What did you do yesterday?"

Shawn's words broke her out of her trance of waiting for the sun to dawn a new day.

"Nothing much. I meditated in the morning, did some yoga. I spent most of my afternoon sitting outside reading."

"I tried meditating a few times, but it was too still for me, you know? I like to be active, and I feel like I get my peace when I'm kayaking on the lake or hiking through the wilderness. It's still quiet, and I can still think while being active."

"Meditation is new to me, and at first I had a hard time quieting my mind. But in a way, what you do is meditation. What do you think about while you're active?"

Morgan felt Shawn shrug by the slight lift of her arms that were still around her waist.

"I don't know. I guess I think about my family, how I miss my parents. I talk to my grandfather a lot, especially when I'm on the water."

"How often do you see your parents?"

"Oh, about twice a year, but it's usually them that come to see me. I'm always so busy with the diner so it's hard to get away."

"Don't you go on vacations?"

"Not really. Why would I? I mean, look where I live. I don't have a desire to go anywhere else. I prefer the mountains to the beach. Where was your last vacation?"

Morgan chuckled and leaned her head back on Shawn's broad shoulder. "Here, actually. The first time I met you. Although the trip was cut short because there was a work emergency. That's when I discovered Jess was cheating on me."

Morgan felt Shawn's arms tighten around her and she placed a kiss to Morgan's temple.

"I can't believe she did that. If you were my girlfriend, I'd never look at another woman."

Morgan stayed quiet as she took to heart what Shawn said. For some reason, Morgan wanted to believe her. But as much as she felt like she'd been healing, the thought of Jess cheating on her still tore at her heart. She was still cautious of her well-being and her still fragile heart. She wasn't interested in being with someone who was a player or couldn't keep it in their pants when a pretty face came along. She wanted to love and be loved by a woman who would be faithful to her. She needed to try and trust again.

"I'm a believer in things happen for a reason. If I hadn't gone down the rabbit hole after the breakup, I wouldn't be here with you at this very moment. And this is exactly where I want to be right now. I really like that we've become friends."

"I wouldn't want to be anywhere else right now either. I mean, check out the sunrise."

Morgan looked straight ahead and could see the top of the sun break the peak of the mountain. She'd heard some of their fellow sunrise watchers' commentary, but honestly, no words could do it justice. Morgan watched as the sun slowly rose, bringing more yellow than orange to meet the purple sky. She wasn't sure why, but she felt this was a turning point in her life. A peaceful sensation came over her, like she could see the colors more clearly, she was able to breathe easier, and she felt like she'd come home.

The feel of Shawn's arms around her, Shawn's chin resting on Morgan's right shoulder as they watched the sunrise had Morgan feeling things she'd never felt before. She'd loved and lost a few women in her life, women who she felt could have been long-term, but she'd never felt this strongly for any woman as she felt for Shawn in that moment. She didn't know if it was a fleeting moment, one captured in the beauty and stillness of the sun rising over the mountains, but Morgan felt like she needed to explore her feelings for Shawn.

The past two months, but particularly the past week, had been life-changing for Morgan. She felt like she'd grown mentally and emotionally so much that she felt like a new woman. One who wanted to do more for herself, do more for others somehow. She wasn't sure what yet, but she was certain that would come to her when the time was right. She wanted to live life to its fullest, take chances, and embrace love. Morgan reached behind her and grabbed Shawn's head as she turned her own.

"Kiss me, Shawn."

Shawn turned a little more and slowly approached Morgan's lips with her own. She didn't question Morgan. She didn't say a word. She just did what Morgan commanded of her, and Morgan thought that was very sexy. The anticipation alone made Morgan wet, and her clit twitched. When their lips finally met, Morgan felt the explosion of the sun beyond the ridge light up behind her eyelids. She opened her mouth slightly to allow Shawn's tongue to slowly enter and touch her own tongue. Morgan sighed her pleasure, yet regretted the time and location. There were people around them, preventing Morgan from fully exploring Shawn's mouth. She slowly ended the kiss but kept her eyes closed. She felt Shawn's forehead meet her own and Shawn's ragged breath tickle her skin.

"That was some kiss."

Morgan's laugh was shaky. Despite her wanting to take it slow, Shawn's attention, her chivalry, her kiss was confusing Morgan. Right now, she wanted all of Shawn, future heartache be damned. "It sure was. And I want to do a lot more than kissing, but I'm really looking forward to you showing me more of your Tahoe."

"Let's go then."

They stood and gathered their things, and once they were off the boulder, Morgan took Shawn's hand in hers. It felt right, their fingers interlocked, fitting perfectly together. Shawn's fingers squeezed hers as she turned back to smile at Morgan. That smile set off a heatwave throughout Morgan's body, as if it was midday in the summer, and the sun was shining directly above. Some of the other spectators headed toward their cars now that the day's opening show had ended. Others made their way across the street to the trail head for Eagle Falls. When they reached the car, Shawn opened the door for Morgan, and once she was inside, Shawn closed the door for her. Morgan kept her eyes on Shawn through the side mirror as she walked to the back of the car, opened the rear door, and deposited their belongings.

Shawn climbed into the driver's side, started the car, and pulled out of the parking lot, then headed south again on Highway 89 toward the South Shore. Once they were on the road, Morgan boldly grabbed Shawn's hand and held it in her lap. When Shawn looked at her, Morgan could see the question on Shawn's face. Morgan smiled and winked before pulling Shawn's hand up to her lips and kissed it.

"That sunrise was...I don't have the words to describe it. Beautiful and amazing just aren't strong enough adjectives."

"I see the sunrise almost every morning from the diner's windows, but I don't think they've ever been as gorgeous as the one today."

"Maybe it was the company."

Shawn laughed and squeezed Morgan's hand. "I have no doubt about it."

They were quiet for a few minutes while Shawn maneuvered the hairpin turns leaving Emerald Bay. Once they'd reached flat road, Shawn brought Morgan's hand to her mouth and kissed it as Morgan had done earlier.

"So, can we talk about the kisses?"

Morgan could hear the quiver in Shawn's voice. Nerves? Arousal? Both? Morgan owed it to her how she'd been feeling of late, especially since she'd told her early on that she just wanted to be friends.

"Yes, of course."

Moments of silence passed as did the pine and aspen trees out the passenger window.

"I've discovered some things about myself this week, which had a little to do with you. I'm forty-one years old, and I've worked hard my entire life. I have a few great friends and many acquaintants, but I don't do a lot of things for myself. It seems I'm always going and going and never stopping long enough to enjoy life. I've always looked for the next client, the next sale, the next bonus check. This past week, I've realized there's more to life than work. I've learned to discover the beauty in things, to be adventurous, and that's because of you, Shawn. I want to be present, to live in the moment, and not let special things or people pass me by. That includes you." Morgan took a deep breath, trying to slow her hammering heart. "I'm attracted to you, Shawn. I like the way you live your life. I like the way you love your family. I like how you love your dog."

Shawn laughed, and the deep timbre in Shawn's voice caused Morgan to smile.

"I know I'm only here for a little while longer, but we live only two hours apart. I'm hoping you'd be interested in dating me, to see if there's something more between us, because I think there is." Once Morgan had her say, she quieted to let Shawn voice her thoughts. Shawn's silence was deafening to Morgan's ears, and she feared she said too much too soon.

"I'm attracted to you too, Morgan. I've enjoyed my time with you."

Morgan could feel a "but" coming on that would lead to Shawn's denial.

"I do have concerns though. I want to eventually settle down with a woman I can fall asleep and wake up with in my arms. To fall in love with a woman I can share my life with. That's my end goal."

Morgan started to speak, but Shawn held up her hand, indicating she wasn't finished.

"With that being said, I would like to see where things with us could go. The one thing I need from you though is complete honesty. If it's not working out, then we let the other know. I'll be honest with you, as well."

Morgan felt like she could breathe again, and her body thrummed with excitement and possibility. "I agree to those terms, Ms. Evans. Shall we shake on it?"

Unplanned, yet simultaneously, they both started shaking and wiggling in their respective seats, causing them to burst out into nearly uncontrollable laughter. Shawn wiped the tears from her eyes.

"I have a better idea."

Shawn pulled over into a turnout, placed the car in park, and leaned over the center console to fully envelop Morgan's lips with her own. Morgan grabbed the sleeve over Shawn's shoulder and pulled her closer. The feel of Shawn's tongue gliding with her own made Morgan want all of Shawn, wanted her weight on Morgan's body, wanted her sex filled with Shawn's fingers, or perhaps a toy. Morgan wanted to grab Shawn's naked ass, grip her fingers in the muscled flesh, and pull her closer, deeper into her.

"God, Shawn." Morgan breathed heavily. "We need to stop, or I'll demand you take me back to your cabin and fuck me for the rest of the time I'm here." Morgan's panties were soaked. That, and her rock-hard clit, would make for a lot of discomfort today.

"That sounds like a great idea. I'll turn us around." Shawn looked over her left shoulder to check for cars, and Morgan reached out to stop her.

"No, you promised me a drive around the lake, but first, I need you to feed me."

Shawn looked at Morgan and had one eyebrow raised.

"Breakfast, Shawn. Feed me breakfast. Get your mind out of the gutter, dirty girl."

"Trust me when I say you'll like me dirty, baby."

Morgan let out a whoosh of air. "Jesus."

Shawn chuckled as she pulled back out on the roadway. On the drive to what Shawn called "the second-best breakfast place in Lake Tahoe," Morgan studied Shawn's hand in hers They were strong and sure, a little calloused, most likely from kayaking and mountain biking. Morgan noticed a few faint linear scars, prominent veins, and freckles under her tanned skin. Her nails were blunt and clean, her fingers thick. A lesbian's wet dream come true. Morgan had to put a lot of effort into *not* imagining how they'd feel inside her, stroking slow and easy at first, morphing into fast and powerful to bring her to orgasm. Nope. Nuh-uh. Not going to think about that at all. She lowered her window to allow the crisp air to cool her down.

All during breakfast, Morgan and Shawn mostly spoke with their eyes. Shawn's gaze was hungry, and not for food, Morgan assumed. She was fairly certain she was giving Shawn the same look. Morgan had never felt more conflicted in her life. She wanted both to enjoy the day and scenery with Shawn driving around the lake, yet she wanted to hurry back to Shawn's cabin and have sex with her all day and night. She could be patient, but holy mother, if Shawn kept looking at her the way she was, she would just crawl into the back of the SUV and let Shawn have her.

After breakfast, Shawn suggested they go gamble for about an hour to let their food digest before going for a hike. Morgan wasn't much of a gambler, that was always Jessica's thing when they came up to South Lake Tahoe, but she didn't mind playing a little video poker. Not more than five minutes after sliding a twenty-dollar bill in a video poker machine, her machine drew a royal flush on one hand. The bells whistling from the machine and the light flashing overhead had Morgan and Shawn going crazy, jumping up and down. A smattering of people gathered around despite the casino being nearly empty on an early Sunday morning. Morgan had won a progressive jackpot worth over a thousand dollars. Shawn hit the Cash Out button and took the ticket that was dispensed, placed it in her wallet, and slid another twenty into the machine.

"Hey! That's my ticket, you slot machine jackpot thief."

Shawn laughed and spoke into Morgan's ear. "I'm just keeping it safe until we leave. Then you can take it to the cashier and get your money. Now hush and keep playing."

They spent the next forty-five minutes playing, and Morgan had won around another two hundred dollars while Shawn broke even. As they walked to the ticket kiosk to cash out her winning tickets, Morgan wrapped her arm around Shawn's waist and pulled her closer.

"I think I can become a professional gambler. This is easy!"

Shawn nodded. "I think you're right. I'm all for anything that will keep you here."

Morgan pulled Shawn to a stop and faced her before giving Shawn a chaste kiss since they were in public. Shawn's firm and slightly chapped lips felt wonderful against Morgan's, and she wanted to kiss Shawn as much as she could. Once they got back to Shawn's car, she and Shawn kissed again, this time with more heat. Morgan felt like a sixteen-year-old girl making out with the hottest girl in the school. Shawn gripped her waist and squeezed it like a cat pawing a soft blanket. Her clit throbbing synced up with Shawn's gentle movements. Morgan moved her hand and found the inside of Shawn's right thigh inching slowly toward her center. Shawn let go of Morgan and stopped her hand from progressing farther.

"God, you have no idea what you're doing to me, Morgan. I'm about to come in my jeans."

Morgan could feel her eyes widen and her breathing quicken. "Yes, let's try for that." She started moving her hand again and Shawn stopped it. Again.

"Nuh-uh. The first time we have sex, we'll be completely naked in a soft bed so I can take my time with you."

"Shawn, you're killing me here."

Shawn picked up Morgan's wandering hand and brought it to her lips, sucking her index finger into her mouth, making Morgan's stomach flip. She felt her eyelids grow heavy with lust, and desperately needed Shawn to relieve her of her aching need.

"What a way to go though, right? I promise, I won't leave you unsated when the time comes."

"I'm holding you to that, Evans. Fine. Start the damn car and let's continue on." Morgan smiled to let Shawn know she understood, but inside, she was a complete mess. If Shawn's kisses completely undid her this way, Morgan thought she might *actually* die when they finally had sex.

The rest of the drive was incredible. They stopped at a few vista points so Morgan could take pictures. The sun was shining high above, the cloudless sky a deep blue that matched the lake water. They pulled into Sand Harbor parking lot where they watched the sunset two nights ago, and they went for a walk along a newly built pedestrian trail that rimmed three miles of the eastern shore. To see the sights, the white boulders in the water and the colors of the water in the daylight left Morgan in awe. Greens morphed into turquoise, which morphed into a deep blue, and Shawn explained the change in colors had to do with the depth.

They strolled hand in hand, enjoying the light breeze that ruffled Shawn's thick hair. Morgan took a deep breath, smelling the mixture of pine and vanilla that Morgan now associated with the clean air and trees of Tahoe. They watched a few sailboats and motorboats dash across the water, leaving crystal wakes behind them.

By the time they got back to Shawn's car, Morgan was starving, her breakfast long worked off by all the hiking and walking they'd done. Shawn promised her the best lunch in the best diner in all of Lake Tahoe. They pulled into the parking lot of Ray's Diner, and Morgan looked to Shawn.

"So, how do you want to do things. Are we walking in as friends or potential lovers?"

Shawn's eyes grew dark, and Morgan had an idea of what her answer would be.

"There's no 'potential' about it. It's just a matter of time."

Morgan fanned her face. "Oh, my."

Shawn chuckled as she exited the car, walked to the other side, and opened the door for Morgan. Shawn grabbed her hand and led her through the door to the diner that smelled of cheeseburgers and French fries, the evidence of breakfast long gone. They waved at the servers and to Melvin and Shorty through the pass window. Shawn led them to a corner table in the back of the restaurant that was in front of a window where they could continue their day with a lakeside view.

"How's it going, boss? You couldn't find a classier place to take this gorgeous woman to?"

Morgan felt herself blush in front of the server she knew by face but not by name. Shawn ignored the comment.

"Morgan, this soon-to-be-fired lady is Kerrie. Kerrie, this is Morgan."

"It's so nice to finally know your name, Kerrie. And don't worry...Shawn knows better than to fire her best employee."

Melvin and Shorty stepped out from behind the kitchen door, and one of them cleared his throat.

"The name's Melvin, ma'am, and I believe *I'm* the best employee here." Melvin's white T-shirt was stained with grease from running the grill. The other gentleman stood well over six feet tall and built like a brick house shoved Melvin out of the way an extended his hand. "I'm Shorty, ma'am, and I think *I'm* the best employee here."

Morgan laughed while Shawn shook her head. "It's nice to meet all of you. If I may offer an opinion, the food I've had here has been nothing short of spectacular." Morgan looked at Kerrie. "And the service is exemplary. Shawn is lucky to have the three of you working with her."

The smiles on each of their faces told Morgan they loved her opinion.

"In that case, what can we get you? It's on the house."

Shawn's eyebrows raised into her forehead. "Hey! We don't give away free food."

Kerrie stepped closer to Morgan and slid her arm around her shoulders. "Well, boss, we're giving you the check to pay, so technically it's on the house since you own the joint."

"If anybody pays, it should be Morgan. She took twelve hundred dollars of Harrah's money on video poker this morning."

"Great job, Morgan." Kerrie's hand squeezed Morgan's shoulder, and she got nods from Melvin and Shorty. Morgan and Shawn were the only two customers in the diner since they only had an hour to closing. Once Shawn suggested the club sandwich to Morgan, Melvin and Shorty went back to the kitchen to get started on their late lunches while Kerrie filled two glasses of iced tea for them.

"You know…" Shawn leaned closer to Morgan and placed her hand on her knee. "I wanted to take you out for a nice dinner tonight, but I'm not sure we're going to have any room left in our stomachs after we eat the monster sandwiches."

Morgan placed her hand over Shawn's and guided it up her leg, closer to where she needed, wanted to be touched. "I have an appetite for something other than food tonight."

"Christ." Morgan's heat made Shawn want to keep her hand where it was, but when Kerrie brought their plates to the table, Shawn withdrew her hand and sat up tall in the chair.

Morgan took a piping hot fry off her plate, blew on it to cool it off, then dipped it in ranch dressing. She slowly brought it up to her mouth and licked off a drip of the dressing. Just the sight of the tip of Morgan's tongue had Shawn thinking of what that tongue could do to her.

"I say we box up this food and have it for a snack later."

Morgan took a bite of the fry and slowly shook her head. "Now why would I want to do that?" Morgan took a small slice of bacon from her sandwich and took a delicate bite, showing a bit of her teeth.

Shawn was tempted to spread a little bacon grease on her if the flavor made Morgan do that with her mouth. Lunch took longer than it should have due to Morgan's teasing, but Shawn didn't mind the show. As it got near closing time, Morgan used some of her earlier winnings to buy their lunch and leave a very generous tip. They bid their good-byes to Kerrie, Melvin, and Shorty.

"Do you want to come over for a while or go back to your cabin?" Shawn stole a glance while trying to keep her eyes on the road.

"I think I'll go back to the cabin." Morgan's answer disappointed Shawn. They'd had a great time together, and Shawn wasn't ready for it to end.

"I want to get cleaned up then I'll come back over to your place, if that's okay."

Now we're talking. "Yes, I'd love that. I'll take doggo for a walk and wear off some of his energy." Shawn pulled into Morgan's driveway and turned off the ignition. She hurried over to open the door for Morgan and held her hand as they walked to the door.

"I'll see you soon, right?"

"How about two hours? You can go for a walk and get cleaned up."

"Yes." Shawn grabbed Morgan's hips and pulled her closer. "I can't wait." She kissed Morgan. Gentle. Soft. Until Morgan wrapped her arms around Shawn's neck and deepened the kiss. They went at it for minutes, maybe hours. Who knew? Time spent with Morgan had a way of being distorted especially when she was kissing and teasing Shawn. They finally broke free, both gasping for breath, and Shawn felt her legs might give out.

"Um, yeah, so I'll see you in a couple of hours." Shawn nearly tripped as she walked backward toward her car, unable to pry her eyes from the stunning woman standing on the front porch. Shawn fumbled her keys as she tried to put them in the ignition. She would definitely need to get a grip on her emotions before Morgan came over later, but would that even be possible? At that point, Shawn realized she really didn't care.

CHAPTER THIRTEEN

Morgan showered and got ready for her night with Shawn. They both knew they were going to have sex after the way they'd behaved all day. They'd been flirting and teasing each other relentlessly. An entire day of foreplay had left Morgan hot and horny. She'd almost taken care of herself, but she wanted Shawn to do that for her. It had been months since another woman touched her. Hell, the last time Jess had touched Morgan was a good three to four months before they broke up. Even then, it was hurried, as Jess seemed like she had better things to do. In all the time they'd been together, Morgan had never been as worked up as Shawn had her today. Luckily, Morgan had packed a few bra and panty sets, sexy silk and lace numbers in black, red, and turquoise. Tonight, she wore the turquoise as they reminded her of the water they saw on the East Shore.

She took extra care in doing her hair, light makeup, and dabbing a few spots on her neck and between her breasts with her favorite perfume. Unfortunately, she didn't have a sexy dress to wear over her sexy lingerie. She only had jeans, short-sleeved and long-sleeve button-down shirts. Her stomach flip-flopped as she got ready, the anticipation of having sex with Shawn nearly killed her. She took one more glance in the mirror, satisfied with how she looked, and more than satisfied with her lingerie selection. She hoped Shawn would be satisfied. Morgan chuckled to herself. Morgan would never leave Shawn dissatisfied.

She knocked on Shawn's front door and heard Jameson's thundering gallop. When Shawn opened it, Morgan's mouth went dry. Shawn was dressed in black jeans and a tight black T-shirt that did nothing to hide her muscular arms and shoulders, small firm breasts, and her trim waist. Her short dark hair was slicked back, and she looked positively dangerous and delicious. And now nerves hit Morgan hard like a punch to her gut, and she wondered what the hell she'd been thinking. Starting something with Shawn a week before she left town? Wait a minute. This was Shawn. They were friends with the potential for more. They were fine. She was fine. Shawn kissed Morgan's cheek when she stepped inside. Shawn took her jacket and hung it on the coat tree near the front door.

"Are you okay? You look nervous."

Shawn walked past Morgan to the kitchen where she'd poured them both a glass of wine and handed it to Morgan.

"I guess I am a little. I'd been thinking about this, us, for a few days, and I guess I got a little worked up."

"Come here." Shawn took Morgan's hand and led her to the couch where they sat next to each other. "Nothing has to happen. We can stay friends if that's what you want. I'm not the type of person who would pressure someone into having sex with me."

Morgan smiled as she relaxed. "I think I know that about you."

"Good. Now, we can watch a movie. I can make some popcorn, although I don't think it will pair well with this wine."

"That's where you're wrong. Popcorn goes very nicely with this Malbec."

"Ha! Good to know. But if you want something else, I have cheese, salami, and crackers if you get hungry."

"Thank you, Shawn." Morgan squeezed her hand. "I think a movie would be great."

If Morgan expected to see disappointment on Shawn's face, she didn't get it. She was a little surprised since they'd been working each other into a wild frenzy all day long, but Shawn was the poster child of cool. No sweat droplets over her upper lip or forehead. No sweaty or clammy hands. No heavy breathing. Just cool Shawn taking a sip of wine and scrolling through the guide on her television to pick out a movie for them. She stopped at a title.

"Have you seen this?"

Morgan had in fact seen the lesbian movie Shawn stopped at. In fact, Morgan had gotten herself off while watching it by herself one night. She certainly wouldn't mind watching it again.

"No, I haven't. Is it good?" A little fib to get them in the mood. Morgan knew it was an okay movie as far as the acting was concerned, but who didn't have a crush on the lead actress. Besides, the sex scenes were off the charts smoking hot.

"I haven't either. Let's try it."

And so began their movie-watching date. About halfway through the movie, during a particularly racy scene, Morgan noticed Shawn squirming a little. Morgan felt her body heat up. The lead character reminded Morgan a little of Shawn. Not in looks, but by her confidence when it came to seducing her love interest.

"I'll be right back." Shawn stood. "Need anything while I'm up?"

"No." The word squeaked out of Morgan's mouth as if she'd just sucked in some helium. She cleared her throat. "No, I'm good."

Once Shawn left the room to go to the guest bathroom, Morgan turned off the TV and left their empty glasses of wine on the coffee table. She stood outside the bathroom door waiting for Shawn to emerge. The door finally opened, and Shawn stood before Morgan who had her back pressed against the wall. Morgan was more than worked up from watching the sex scenes in the movie, and she desperately needed Shawn to take care of it and take her now.

There was only slight hesitation before Shawn took two long strides to reach Morgan. Shawn grabbed Morgan's face with her strong hands and kissed her senseless. Morgan dropped her hands to undo the buttons on Shawn's jeans. She pushed them and Shawn's white cotton boxers down to her ankles while Shawn unbuttoned Morgan's shirt. Shawn lowered her head over Morgan's sexy bra, and she bit and sucked on her nipple before turning her attention to the other one. Morgan grabbed the back of Shawn's head to pull her in closer, wanting and needing Shawn's mouth to bring her nipples to rigid points.

"Fuck." Morgan released her grasp of Shawn's head, unbuttoned her jeans and slid them down, leaving her soaked panties in place.

Shawn released her grip on Morgan's nipples and took notice of Morgan's lingerie.

"You are so gorgeous." Shawn's breathing was hard and Morgan's chest was heaving.

"Fuck me right here, Shawn. I need your fingers in me."

Shawn slid her hand inside the silk that covered Morgan's sex and immediately thrust two fingers in her, quickly adding a third easily, Morgan was that hot and wet for her. Morgan's legs were stuck with her shoes still on and her jeans around her ankles. She wanted Shawn to pick her up so Morgan could wrap her legs around Shawn's waist while she fucked her hard, but it seemed like Shawn had no problem with gaining purchase with her fingers thrusting inside Morgan's sex. Morgan reached down and glided her fingers over Shawn's full, plump clit. Shawn bucked forward into Morgan's hand as they rode each other into oblivion. It didn't take long for either one to cry out as they came, which wasn't a surprise due to their teasing all day and the movie's sex scenes.

They breathed heavily, still pressed against each other as they came down from their explosion.

"Jesus. That was so much better than I imagined."

Morgan ran her fingers through Shawn's damp hair. "Oh, yeah? You imagined this, did you?"

"To be honest, from the first time you came into my diner with your friends."

Wow. Morgan hadn't expected that comment, even though she immediately crushed on Shawn the first time she saw her despite still being with Jessica. "Take me to your bedroom, Shawn. Show me all the things you imagined doing to me."

Shawn kicked off her shoes, then her jeans and boxers, picked up Morgan in her arms and carried her to her bed. Shawn was giving her swoon-worthy material. Once Morgan was seated on the bed, Shawn knelt down and took off Morgan's boots, then slowly slid off her jeans and underwear. Morgan reached behind and unhooked her own bra and tossed it to the pile of her discarded clothes. Shawn still had her shirt on so Morgan grabbed the hem and pulled it over Shawn's head along with her sports bra. They were both now naked, finally, although you'd never hear Morgan complain about the hallway.

Shawn spread Morgan's legs wide and barely touched Morgan's still sensitive clit with the tip of her tongue. Morgan could feel the walls of her sex clench, urging Shawn to refill her with her fingers. Shawn didn't obey. She seemed content to slow things down, and it made Morgan want to grab the back of Shawn's head to encourage her to go faster.

"Shawn, God, I need to come again."

"You will, baby. When I'm ready for you to. You taste so good, I want to take my time."

Shawn dipped her tongue into Morgan's opening and thrust in and out a few times before she withdrew and resumed flicking Morgan's clit up and down, side to side before Shawn sucked her in and stroked her slowly. Morgan could feel herself swell against Shawn's tongue and lips. Shawn must've been ready to let Morgan come because she started sucking harder, faster, pulling Morgan's clit farther into her mouth until she exploded, coming all over Shawn's face.

Morgan's breathing was heavy and her heart racing, feeling like she'd just sprinted a marathon. Morgan was dead. She was sure of it. Otherwise, she'd be able to move, but she couldn't with her jelly arms and legs. Shawn dropped soft kisses up and down Morgan's inner thighs, kissed her mound, then slid on top of Morgan and kissed her mouth. The taste of her on Shawn's lips was intoxicating, and it made Morgan want more of Shawn's mouth. Just not on her clit. Her clit was dead. Nobody had ever killed her clit before. Not even close.

"Just give me a minute to recover. I seem to have lost all control of my limbs."

Shawn chuckled before kissing a tender spot just below her ear. "That good, huh?"

"Nuh-uh. Awful. Worst sex I've ever had."

Shawn looked at her and raised an eyebrow. "Is that so? Maybe I should try again." Shawn started to move down when Morgan reached for her.

"No. Don't you dare go back down there just yet."

"Do you have the energy to scoot all the way on the bed?" Morgan's legs were still dangling off the side.

Morgan scooted her body like she was a sea lion which caused Shawn to laugh. "It's sexy, right? My wiggling is turning you on. Don't deny it."

"Honestly, seeing you naked has me turned on. You're so beautiful, Morgan."

The softness in Shawn's eyes did something magical to Morgan's insides, and she miraculously raised her arms to bring Shawn closer. Morgan spread her legs so Shawn could nestle between them. She laid on top of Morgan with her arms on either side of Morgan's head. Shawn started rocking her pelvis into Morgan's while holding eye contact.

"You feel so good."

Morgan reached up with her hands and fondled Shawn's small breasts, squeezing the flesh then pinching her nipples into hard stones. "I think that's my line."

Shawn reached down with one hand and spread hers and Morgan's lips apart, exposing their clits before Shawn started rocking again.

"Does that feel good, baby?"

Morgan nodded while she bit her bottom lip. She mimicked the dream she had and grabbed Shawn's ass, digging in her fingers and wrapping her legs behind Shawn's.

"You feel so good fucking me, Shawn. I want you to keep going until you come all over me."

Shawn must have liked Morgan talking to her because she began thrusting harder, faster. Morgan imagined Shawn wearing a strap-on while doing this, and it took her to the brink of her third orgasm of the night.

"Shawn, fuck. I'm going to come again. Are you close?"

"Yes." Shawn grunted, her hips bucking wild until she slammed into Morgan one last time, causing both to shout out their climax. Sweat pooled in the small of Shawn's back, and Morgan wiped it away as she rubbed her hands up Shawn's back, along her neck, and into her hair. Shawn had collapsed onto Morgan, taking Shawn's entire weight, and she thought nothing felt better than this other than the brain-shattering orgasms. Shawn breathed hard into Morgan's ear, causing chills throughout her body. After a few minutes, Shawn rolled off Morgan, and she felt the absence of Shawn's body on hers intensely.

Shawn lay on her stomach next to her, and Morgan rolled toward her, kissing her cheek, ear, neck, letting her lips linger in each spot.

"Are you okay?"

Shawn nodded with her eyes closed, a grin spreading across her face. "Never better. You?"

"I feel fantastic."

"Good." Shawn kept her eyes closed while Morgan ran her fingers through Shawn's hair slow and gentle. The grin remained on Shawn's face as her breathing slowed into slumber. Morgan reminisced about the day they'd spent together, and she quickly decided this was probably the best day of her life. Morgan pulled the blanket off the footboard of Shawn's bed and covered them. She kissed Shawn on her forehead and wrapped her arm around her, holding her close through the night.

Chapter Fourteen

Shawn's alarm woke her way too early, but Morgan didn't even stir. Shawn wanted nothing more than to spend the day in bed with Morgan and to continue where they left off last night. Shawn's clit was still throbbing, especially with Morgan's arm wrapped around her. Seeing her blond hair sprawled across the pillow, Shawn had never seen a more beautiful sight. The light from the moon slivering through the slats on her blinds made Morgan look celestial. But being the owner of a diner beckoned, and she had to answer the call. She managed to slide out from Morgan's arm without waking her, and she headed to the guest bath to get ready so she wouldn't disturb her.

Thirty minutes later, she sat next to Morgan and placed a kiss on her cheek.

"Baby." Shawn spoke softly.

"Hmm."

"I have to go to work."

"No. Come back to bed." Morgan's voice was raspy and soft from still being mostly asleep.

"I wish I could but feel free to stay as long as you want. Text me later."

"Mm. Okay. Bye, baby."

And just like that, Morgan was back to sleep.

Shawn closed the door to her bedroom and met Jameson by the back door to let him out. When he came back in, Shawn placed his bowl of food on the floor.

"Morgan's still asleep, pal. Let her rest, and I'll be back soon. Be a good boy."

A little while later, Shawn felt her phone buzz in the pocket of her jeans as she was ringing up a customer. Once they'd left, Shawn pulled her phone out to see she had a text from Morgan.

Your bed and dog miss you.

Shawn smiled as she texted back.

Just my bed and dog? Nobody else?

The door to the diner opened, and Jack and crew came in. "Hey, guys. Your usual table is open and ready for you."

Nope. None that I can think of.

Huh. That's too bad. I might cry. I can feel the tears forming. Shawn sent off the crying emoji.

Aw, I don't want to make you cry. Okay, I miss you too.

Good. Come have breakfast. My grandfathers just arrived.

Be there in 20. Kiss emoji.

Whew, the feeling swirling in Shawn's tummy had her a little dizzy and a lot excited. She came from behind the counter and headed to the guys' table.

"Good morning, friends. I just got a text from Morgan and she's on her way if you want her to join you."

"Are you kidding? She's the perfect start to our day." The twinkle in Jack's eyes told Shawn he was a little smitten with Morgan. Hell, why wouldn't he be? Shawn was a lot smitten with her, and she felt her body hum with excitement at the thought of seeing Morgan soon.

Kerrie brought over four cups of coffee and placed them in front of Jack, Bill, Dave, and Ernie.

"Morgan's on her way, Kerrie, so can you bring her a cup when she gets here?"

"Sure thing, Dave. Did Shawn tell you that she and Morgan spent the day together yesterday?"

Shawn shot Kerrie a look that clearly conveyed she should keep her mouth shut.

Bill's face lit up. "Whoa! Shawny, way to go!"

Jack raised his eyebrows to Shawn. "The real question is, did the date last through the night, Shawny?"

"Shush, old man. You know I don't kiss and tell."

Ernie's head tilted the way Jameson's did when he heard "go" or "walk."

"So, there was kissing, eh, Shawny? Atta kid."

"Listen, don't say anything to Morgan. I really like this woman, and I don't want her thinking I'm spreading her business all over town."

Shawn's comment caused a hurt look on all their faces.

"You know us better than that, Shawn Evans."

Shawn bowed her head. She hadn't been taken to task like that since her grandfather was alive, and she had the gall to talk back to him once. Only once. "I'm sorry. You're right. I just haven't felt this way in a long time, maybe ever, and I don't want to do anything to screw it up."

"We understand, kid. We'll behave ourselves. Well, speak of the devil."

"And the devil shall appear." Morgan walked toward them while shedding her coat. She was glowing, her smile was bright, and she looked happy. Really happy. Shawn hoped she'd been a part in that.

Morgan went around the table kissing all the guys on the cheek and giving Kerrie a hug. She'd waved to Shorty and Melvin on her way to the table. Shawn clearly saw that Morgan felt quite at home here.

"Hi." Shawn pulled out a chair for Morgan.

"Hi, yourself." Morgan kissed Shawn on the mouth before she sat down. Shawn felt the heat rise in her cheeks, and the older men were silenced as their mouths hung open. Morgan looked at each one and shrugged her shoulders.

"What?"

Jack pointed his index finger at Morgan. "You just kissed our Shawny."

Morgan looked at Shawn and winked. "I think she might be my Shawny now too."

The table was silent as the four men looked at each other then erupted in celebration. Kerrie stood next to Jack with a huge smile on her face. The ruckus caused Morgan and Shawn to smile themselves, and Morgan grabbed her hand.

"How did this happen?" Jack asked.

"When did this happen?" Dave asked.

"If you gentlemen don't mind, I'll tell you all about it during breakfast."

"Don't tell them everything, honey. Even if they're being relentless."

"Don't worry, baby. I'll keep it PG-13."

The four men moaned their displeasure, and Morgan and Shawn laughed.

"I'll leave you to it then." Shawn gave Morgan one more kiss before heading back behind the counter. She couldn't help but smile as she kept stealing glances at Morgan, assuming she was telling the grandfathers about their day together. She had the guys hooked as they paid rapt attention to her words. Occasionally, they'd all turn and look at Shawn, who would just give them a wave. Other times, the guys would laugh and give Shawn a thumbs-up. It made Shawn's heart swell with affection to see how easily Morgan fit in with the guys. She wished she could join them and get Morgan's take on yesterday, but since Shawn had given her three orgasms, she'd say it went pretty well. She mentally buffed her nails on her shirt.

The guys and Morgan stayed for a couple of hours, and Shawn would occasionally stop by to see if they needed anything. When they finally got up to leave, Shawn gave the guys hugs and kissed Morgan.

"You want to get together later?"

"Absolutely. Call me when you get home and we can take Jameson for a nice long walk."

Shawn watched her walk out and she stood on the sidewalk talking to the guys for another fifteen minutes. She hugged them good-bye before driving away. Jack immediately came back in with a huge smile on his face.

"What do you want, old man?" Shawn knew her smile matched Jack's.

"Nice job, Shawny. From Morgan's tell of it, you planned a romantic day yesterday."

"I did, indeed, Jack. I had to pull out all stops so I could impress the girl."

"That you did, Shawny. We love her already. Your granddad would love her too." He pointed his finger at Shawn for the second time that day. "Don't screw it up."

"No, sir."

Jack took Shawn's hand and kissed it over the barrier of the counter. "Love you, kid."

"I love you too, Jack. Now get out of here, and let me get back to work."

Jack gave another wave as he exited the diner. Shawn swallowed down the lump in her throat. Jack and the fellas were excellent surrogate grandfathers, and they always watched out for her. She couldn't love them more if they were related by blood.

A long four hours later, Shawn called Morgan as soon as she got in the car. She didn't want to wait until she got home.

"Hey, handsome."

Shawn laughed and blushed at the same time. She looked in the rearview mirror to see her cheeks redden.

"Hi, yourself, gorgeous. I'm just leaving the diner. Meet me at my house in twenty?"

"I'm already here, and I already took Jameson for his walk. Dinner's on the stove, and we're just waiting for you."

"How'd you get in?"

"I left it unlocked, silly. You told me you never lock the door. Besides, how else was I going to get back in to surprise you with dinner?"

Shawn shook her head as she pressed down on the gas pedal, daring to go as fast as it was safe to on the mountain roads.

"You're something else, you know that?"

"I do know that, and you can show your gratitude later in the bedroom."

Shawn's stomach flipped just at the thought of them in the bedroom.

"Gladly. See you soon."

When Shawn arrived home, she opened the door. "Honey, I'm home."

Morgan came out of the kitchen wearing an apron and nothing else.

"Holy…" Shawn blindly reached down and pet her dog on his head as Morgan walked toward her.

"Are you ready for an appetizer?" Morgan stood with her hand on her hip and a look of come hither on her gorgeous face.

How in the holy fuck could someone sound so sexy? Oh, right. This was Morgan we were talking about.

"I think I could use a little nibble." Shawn picked up Morgan, and she wrapped her legs around Shawn. She carried Morgan into the kitchen and sat her on the counter before leaning in and owning Morgan's lips with her own. The kiss was hot and fierce, as Shawn had been thinking of kissing Morgan, and doing other delectable things to her, all day long. Shawn reached behind her and untied the apron strings and lifted it over Morgan's head. Morgan's chest was flushed and her nipples hard and dark. Shawn went to work feasting on Morgan's breasts, first one then the other, sucking and gently biting her nipples until Morgan moaned her pleasure. After getting her fill, Shawn moved down, kissing and licking the space between Morgan's breasts, down to her stomach, dipping her tongue in her navel.

Shawn could smell Morgan's arousal, and it made her mouth water. She knelt in front of Morgan, spread her legs farther apart, and took her into her mouth. Morgan was ready for her, hot, wet, and swollen, and Shawn wanted to stay in that position all night. The taste of Morgan and the smell coming from dinner heightened Shawn's senses, and she had to swallow her own saliva along with Morgan's juices.

Morgan reclined on her elbows, and Shawn reached up to play with her breasts. Morgan lifted her legs and rested her feet on Shawn's shoulders, allowing Shawn even better access. Shawn continued to suck Morgan's clit deep in her mouth and work Morgan's nipples between her thumb and index finger. Morgan's moans got louder, and Shawn knew she was close. She inserted two fingers into Morgan's opening and quickly thrust them in and out.

"Fuck, Shawn. I'm coming. Don't stop." Morgan sucked in a deep gasp and screamed her pleasure as Shawn continued to stroke Morgan's hardened clit between her lips. When she felt Morgan soften, Shawn licked the juices that drenched Morgan's sex. She stood and leaned over Morgan, now on her back with her eyes closed. Shawn kissed her way up her stomach, kissed each breast, and laid her head down on Morgan's chest.

"You made me see stars." Morgan chuckled and ran her fingers through Shawn's hair.

"It's your fault, greeting me in nothing but an apron."

"If this is what the reward will be, then I'll do it every day." Shawn slipped her hands under Morgan's shoulders to help her sit up, then she wrapped her arms around her, holding Morgan close to her. Shawn was quickly falling for Morgan like a meteor shooting out of the sky. She just hoped she wouldn't crash into a ball of flames.

They'd spent the rest of the afternoon in Shawn's bed taking turns pleasing each other before growling tummies got them out of bed to eat dinner and pay some attention to Jameson, who'd been a very good boy sleeping in his bed in the living room while his human and his new friend made all kinds of weird noises.

They spent the next couple of hours on the couch with Jameson between them, watching a movie. They held hands that rested on Jameson's side, and it appeared to Shawn that both Morgan and her dog were happy and content. Shawn looked over at Morgan who seemed enthralled with the movie.

"When's your last day here again?"

"You trying to get rid of me already?" Morgan winked to let her know she was kidding, but Shawn had already heard it in her voice.

"Well, yeah. I have to think about the other women I sleep with so they don't get jealous."

A dark cloud came across them as Morgan snatched her hand away from Shawn. She sat for a moment staring straight ahead then she leaped to her feet. She headed toward the door when Shawn hurried to catch her.

"Seriously, Shawn? What the fuck?"

"I'm sorry, Morgan. I was only kidding."

"You know my story. Why I'm here in the first place. I'm not interested in being a side piece with a player, you understand?"

"I'm sorry." Shawn pleaded, her voice strained and her body chilled. "It was an insensitive thing to say."

"You're right, it was. Listen, I'm going back to my cabin. I need a little time to cool off. We'll talk later."

"Morgan, please."

"Not now, Shawn. I have to go."

Shawn stared at the pine door that closed behind Morgan. How stupid could she be? Shawn knew that Morgan had been cheated on, but honestly, she was just joking. She didn't think before those idiotic words came flying out of her mouth. It was kind of true that she'd been a little bit of a player, but that was the old Shawn. She'd have her flings with tourists and when they'd leave, she'd be on to the next one. But she was different now. She was older, she thought smarter, but after her comment to Morgan, that didn't seem to be the case. She was done with sleeping around. She wanted that special woman she could settle down with, spend the rest of their lives together.

She plopped down on the couch and folded her hands between her knees. Now what? She'd have to find a way to make it up to her. It was too early to declare her feelings for Morgan, although Shawn was having *all* the feelings. But she needed to do something to convince Morgan she was done playing around. Jameson placed his paw on Shawn's arm and whined. He really was an empath, and Shawn enlisted his help to get Morgan back.

CHAPTER FIFTEEN

Morgan was exhausted. After she'd left Shawn's house the night before, she spent the evening drinking wine and listening to ballads on Pandora. She'd thought about calling Jane, but she needed to think first. She'd had such a delightful day yesterday, having breakfast with Shawn's surrogate grandfathers, then greeting Shawn when she came home only to have sex all afternoon.

Morgan's feelings were growing for Shawn, and she knew that they were always joking with each other. But what Shawn had said struck like a knife to her heart. Shawn really hadn't discussed her past sex life, and honestly, Morgan hadn't wanted to know. But did she now? She could see Shawn as a player when they first met, before she knew the real Shawn. But spending time with her, it was difficult to see that now. It's possible Morgan overreacted, but she still needed time to process what it all meant.

Morgan cared deeply for Shawn, and spending all that time with her, Morgan dared to imagine settling down with her. She'd been trying to keep her growing feelings tamped down before they gained momentum like a snowball rolling downhill, gaining speed and force, that would eventually smash apart once it hit a wall or some other immoveable object. Maybe Shawn entering her life now was happening for a reason. Maybe it was showing Morgan that not all people were shitty like Jessica. Shawn's compliments and actions certainly made Morgan feel like she was special, that she mattered. And maybe the off-the-charts sex was just an added bonus. Maybe

Morgan could try to keep her feelings locked up and just enjoy the rest of her time here with Shawn. Maybe she still had lessons to learn from this trip.

All of her thinking and wondering left Morgan drained and craving a nap. She wanted Shawn there with her to use her own special way of putting Morgan to sleep, then spooning behind her with her arm wrapped around Morgan's body.

A while later, she had no idea of the time, she heard scratching at the door. She must've fallen asleep on the couch. What was that sound? Was it a bear? Some other wild animal? She looked out the window and was both relieved and curious. Morgan opened the door to find Jameson sitting on her doorstep with an envelope in his mouth.

"How did you get here, Jameson?" Morgan took the envelope from his mouth and he barked once. She unfolded the piece of paper and couldn't help but laugh.

Dear Morgan,

Please forgive my hooman. I talked to her last night. Told her she's dumb sometimes. But I love her. Now I love you too. I miss you. My hooman said she wants to make it up to you. Maybe she give you cookie like she give me.

Love,

Jameson

Morgan knelt and threw her arms around the dog's neck as he bathed her in kisses.

"Lucky dog."

Morgan looked up to see Shawn peeking around the corner of her cabin.

"No, you're lucky that your dog wrote me this note. Now, where's my cookie?"

Morgan laughed when Shawn pulled a giant cookie wrapped in saran wrap from behind her back. Shawn seemed apprehensive to move closer to Morgan, but she soldiered on. She handed the cookie over to Morgan who took a couple of seconds to look it over.

"Chocolate chip?"

"Of course."

"What would you say if I told you I hated chocolate chip?"

Shawn's jaw dropped. "First, I'd question your sanity because who doesn't like chocolate chip? Then I'd ask you what your favorite cookie was, and I'd go back to the bakery to get it while eating the chocolate chip cookie I got for you."

Morgan stared at Shawn, remaining silent. She felt bad when Shawn started to shift her weight from foot to foot.

"Good thing chocolate chip is my favorite."

Shawn visibly relaxed, her shoulders lowering from her ears. "I really am truly sorry, Morgan. I obviously didn't think about what I was saying, but I want you to know that I'd never intentionally hurt you."

Morgan reached for Shawn's hand and they sat on the front porch. "I know. Let's just forget it ever happened, okay? I overreacted rather than stayed to listen. And I should've stayed. I know you're a kind person."

Shawn lifted Morgan's hand to her lips and kissed it.

"Can I take you to dinner tonight? There's a great restaurant nearby that serves steak and seafood."

"I'd love to, but I don't have anything fancy to wear. Just jeans."

"No worries. It's a pretty casual place. How about I pick you up in an hour? The place opens at five for dinner, we can eat early, then I can spend the rest of the night making it up to you."

"And just how do you plan on doing that?"

"By doing whatever you want." Shawn's confidence appeared to be coming back with her quirked eyebrow and cocky smile. Morgan loved that about Shawn, and oddly enough, it made her feel wanted.

"I have a whole list of things you can do to and for me, so you're going to need lots of food to give you energy. Lots of protein. Now get out of here so I can get ready." Morgan scratched Jameson's chest, who was sitting on her left. "Thanks for talking sense into your human, cutie-pie. You did good."

Shawn stood. Jameson licked Morgan's cheek then joined Shawn. "See you soon." Shawn and her dog cut through the woods to get back to the street, and Morgan jumped up. She needed to get ready for tonight.

❖

Shawn and Morgan had a nice dinner, both ordering filet and lobster tail, but only Shawn finished the entire meal, including the baked potato and steamed veggies. Shawn's gut had been twisted up all day in anticipation of apologizing to Morgan and hoping she forgave her, and she hadn't been able to eat anything. Now that Morgan had forgiven her, Shawn was famished. She nearly asked Morgan if she could finish what was left on Morgan's plate, but she didn't want to appear to be a glutton. Besides, she had a feeling Morgan was going to make Shawn work her ass off later, and it was a very welcome feeling.

"Do you want to stay over?" Shawn asked on the drive home.

Morgan's smile was Shawn's answer and her heart rate ramped up.

They were greeted at the door by Jameson and his wiggle butt. It was always nice to be welcomed home with such enthusiasm. Morgan and Shawn spent a few minutes giving him some love and belly scratches, then Shawn headed to the kitchen, calling out behind her. "You want something to drink?"

"Just water."

Shawn was pouring a glass of water from tap since Tahoe water was much better tasting than bottled. Shawn felt arms snake around her waist and hands untuck her shirt. Those clever hands stroked Shawn's stomach, and she felt the rippling through her skin and muscles.

Shawn turned off the faucet and looked over her shoulder. "Need something?"

Morgan didn't say anything, just kept moving her hands north until they covered Shawn's breasts. Shawn felt herself grow wet and her clit throbbing matched her heartbeat.

"You're driving me crazy."

"Mmm. Good." Morgan bit Shawn's shoulder and she reached her arms back to grab Morgan's hips, pulling her pelvis into Shawn's ass.

"Remember when you said earlier that you'd do anything I wanted?"

Morgan pinching and pulling Shawn's nipples had her gasping for breath. "Yes. Anything."

"Do you have a strap-on?"

Shawn tried to turn around, but given Morgan's smaller stature, she sure was strong. "I do."

"I really want you to fuck me with it. I was imagining how that would feel the other night when you were on top of me, bringing me to my third orgasm. I imagined your cock filling me up and making me come until I see stars."

Shawn unbuckled her belt, unbuttoned and unzipped her jeans, and took Morgan's hand and placed it inside her boxers. "See how wet you just made me?"

"Impressive but not half as wet as I am. I think I'm going to have you start with your mouth on me, and when you make me come, I want you on your back so I can ride you as you fill me up."

Shawn's legs nearly gave out and her body felt like it was on fire. "Let's go." Shawn grabbed Morgan's hand and nearly ran to her room. She rummaged through her nightstand and pulled out her boxer brief harness and dildo. She started to walk toward the bathroom to get ready, but Morgan stopped her.

"I want to see you put it on."

Shawn had always put it on in private, but hey, at this point, she'd do anything Morgan asked or told her to do. She removed her shirt and bra, kicked off her boots, and slid her jeans and boxers off. Morgan didn't take her eyes off Shawn's hands as she placed the dildo through the cock ring then stepped into the harness. The base of the dildo pressed against her hardened clit, and Shawn knew it wouldn't take much to make her come. But tonight was about Morgan and Shawn's repentance for being a dick the night before.

"Sit on the bed and watch me, Shawn."

Shawn sat, and Morgan started her slow striptease. She methodically undid each button while never taking her eyes off Shawn. Morgan opened her blouse to expose her black lace bra, and she reached up and played with her breasts. Shawn slowly stroked her dildo as Morgan put on her little show.

"Hands off, Shawn. No starting without me." Morgan pushed her jeans off her legs, again slowly and exposed her matching black thong. "You like this?" Morgan was squeezing her breasts again, pinching her nipples through the lace.

"I love it."

"You're really going to love this." Morgan knelt in front of her, licking the tip of Shawn's dildo with her tongue. She then took it into her mouth, and Shawn thought she would come right there. Shawn loved being a woman, and her womanly parts, but at that moment, she wished her cock was real so she could feel Morgan's mouth on it. Morgan placed her hand at the base of Shawn's cock and started moving it in time with her mouth sucking it in and out. Watching Morgan take her made Shawn dizzy, and she felt the beginning of her orgasm build with frenzy.

"Fuck. I'm going to come, baby."

"Yes, Shawn. I want you to come in my mouth." Morgan went back to sucking and stroking her, and Shawn felt her eyes roll back. She placed her hand on the back of Morgan's head but didn't apply any pressure. She didn't need to. Morgan was doing a fantastic job all on her own. Shawn felt the orgasm deep in her belly and she buckled forward as she came while calling Morgan's name. Shawn fell back on her bed, her breathing harder than she could ever remember.

While Shawn was semi-unconscious, Morgan must've stripped out of her lingerie because she climbed on top of Shawn until her pussy was hovering over Shawn's face, and she didn't think she'd ever seen a more beautiful sight.

"I can't wait, Shawn. I need your mouth on me."

Shawn got her second wind as Morgan lowered herself to Shawn's face. She could smell Morgan's arousal, and her mouth watered. Shawn held onto Morgan's hips as she drank her in, alternating between sucking Morgan's clit and thrusting her tongue into her opening. Morgan rode Shawn's face like she owned it. Morgan reached back and grabbed Shawn's breasts, holding on for dear life as she started trembling.

"Fuck, Shawn. Your tongue is incredible. Suck my clit, baby, and I'll come all over your face."

Morgan's dirty talk made Shawn's clit swell again, and she had to really concentrate on bringing Morgan to climax.

"Baby, please. I need to come now."

Shawn sucked her hard, keeping Morgan's clit in her mouth. She didn't dare deviate now when Morgan was so close. Morgan bucked her hips, cried out, and fell forward. Shawn turned over and kissed Morgan's back, waiting for her to come down off her high. Some licks, kisses, nibbles along her ass, her back, her neck. Morgan's skin tasted so sweet on Shawn's tongue, a mixture of citrus and sweat. Shawn didn't think she could ever get enough.

Morgan raised her hips higher in the air while she rested her forearms on the bed. "Keep going, baby." Shawn had never admitted this to anyone, but this was her favorite position of all time while wearing her strap. She used her finger to gather the wetness Morgan still had on her sex, and Shawn lubricated the dildo before gliding it in. She moved slow, allowing Morgan to adjust to the girth.

"You okay?"

"Oh, yeah. Never better. Now get to work, stud."

Shawn chuckled as she slowly withdrew to the tip then went back in. She did this over and over, but when Morgan's hips started moving back into her, the base of the dildo slammed into Shawn's clit. *Shit. Just hold on until Morgan comes.* Her pace increased with the timing of Morgan's movements.

"I'm coming again, Shawn. Oh, God."

"I'm going to come inside you, baby. Let me know when you're close."

"Now! I'm so fucking close now." Morgan started screaming Shawn's name and she slammed into her one more time before she climaxed. Morgan collapsed on the bed with Shawn closely behind. Shawn was still buried deep inside her, and she didn't dare move until Morgan told her to. Shawn could almost feel Morgan's sex walls spasming, squeezing her cock. Morgan reached behind her and grabbed Shawn's hair, pulling her closer.

"That was incredible, lover."

"Mmm, you ready for me to pull out?"

Morgan shook her head. "I wish you could stay in me forever. But, yes, you can pull out now."

The thought of forever with Morgan had been making its way into Shawn's mind since late last week. Shawn stood, pulled her harness off, and tossed it on the floor.

"I'm going to let Jameson out. Get under the covers, and I'll be right back."

After Jameson was taken care of and the house was shut down, Shawn returned to her bedroom to find Morgan under the covers, fast asleep with her golden hair sprawled across her pillow. Shawn stood there, watching Morgan's slow breathing, her skin still glowing from the sex they'd just had. That was the moment Shawn realized she was falling in love with Morgan Campbell.

Chapter Sixteen

Morgan woke to an empty bed, Shawn up obviously long ago given the coolness of the sheets. The sun was shining through the slats of the window. It looked to be another glorious day in Lake Tahoe. Morgan stretched the soreness of her body and limbs, evidence of her workout with Shawn the night before. Morgan had had some great sex with other women, but with Shawn, it was out of the stratosphere hot, hot, hot. Shawn knew her way around Morgan's body. Morgan hadn't had so many orgasms in so little time as she'd had with Shawn. She smiled and became wet while thinking how Shawn had fucked her hard the previous night. She slipped her fingers into her sex, tempted to make herself come when her clit twitched, but she wanted to savor the feeling for the rest of the day until Shawn could take care of the problem herself. And, oh, what a problem to have. Morgan felt like she'd been rebirthed.

In the week and a half that she'd been in Lake Tahoe, Morgan felt like she'd become a new woman, like she had shed the skin of her former self. Almost. She still had feelings of insecurity that kept some of the walls up around her heart. She'd love to admit that she fully trusted Shawn, but if she was being honest with herself, Jess had done such a number on her, she sometimes didn't trust her own judgement. She was trying though. It was part of her self-discovery. She'd learned to quiet her mind, to slow down, to pause long enough to enjoy the true beauty, both of nature and people. Morgan had a sense of home here with her new friends, and she felt the sting in her eyes when she thought about returning to Sacramento in a few days.

She'd miss her walks down to the lake, the smell of the clean air, her new friends at the diner, and especially Shawn.

She shook her head to escape the negative feelings that crept into her mind. She wasn't leaving forever. Morgan and Shawn were dating now. She'd be back. Morgan realized that she wouldn't mind to be the one always doing the traveling because that would mean she'd get to see her new friends more often.

It wasn't like she was unhappy in Sacramento. Her best friends were there. Her job that she loved was there. However, she'd been feeling stagnant, like sitting water that was attracting pesky mosquitos. Even when she was living with Jess, her life was vanilla, plain. No time for fun. Morgan had needed a shake-up in her life. She'd needed to for quite some time. And she got it in Tahoe. Her life would be better now that she'd come here.

Morgan got out of bed and dug a T-shirt and sweatpants out of Shawn's dresser. She had her own sweats to wear that she'd left there, but having Shawn's clothes on made her feel closer to her lover. Morgan wasn't sure if "lover" was the right word to use now. She was a great friend, and they were now officially dating. But it was more. Morgan's feelings and affection were growing. Dare she say she may be falling hard for her kind, gentle mountain woman? Yes. Morgan was teetering on the edge, and she hoped Shawn was strong enough to catch her when she fell and wouldn't break her heart.

Morgan heard Jameson barking and it sounded like it was coming from the backyard. She made her way to the back door where she saw the dog going ballistic at a juvenile black bear that was standing on Shawn's fence. His hackles were raised, and he held an aggressive stance toward the bear. Shit! What was she supposed to do? The only thing she could think of was to get the dog out of the dangerous situation. She opened the back door, her heart pounding, her entire body shaking, and her voice quavering as she yelled at the bear to leave. She screamed and yelled over and over until the bear finally jumped down on the other side.

Danger aborted, she came down from her adrenaline rush, her legs gave out from under her. She plopped down on her behind, body shaking violently now, and tears spilled over and down her cheeks.

She wrapped her arms around Jameson when he ran to her and sat by her side, licking her tears away.

"You crazy dog. Don't scare me like that again. I don't know what I'd do if anything bad happened to you."

It was then that Morgan realized she did love everything about Shawn, including her incredibly brave dog. After plenty of kisses from Jameson, Morgan's heart rate slowed and she felt the strength in her legs return. They went back inside so Morgan could call Shawn and tell her what happened. When Shawn answered, Morgan started crying again just from the relief she felt in hearing her voice.

"Baby? What's wrong?"

"A bear." Morgan tried to squeak out the words in between sobs. "Jameson."

"Are you okay? Is Jameson?"

Morgan took a deep breath and tried to calm down because there were in fact okay.

"Yes, we're both fine. It just scared the shit out of me."

"I'll be right there."

The fact that Shawn was about to drop everything to come home for her and the dog made Morgan fall a little harder and a lot deeper for Shawn.

"No, sweetheart. We're okay, really. I was just so scared, but the bear left. Really, don't come home."

"Are you sure? The crew could manage without me."

"I'm sure. But the fact that you're willing to come home to be with us means so much."

"Morgan, I care about you. Of course, I'd want to help."

"I care about you too, honey. Stay at work, but if it's okay, I'll just stay here with Jameson until you get home. I don't want him to have another encounter."

"If you have other things to do, don't feel you need to stay. Jameson stays home alone all day all the time."

"I'm not doing anything, so it's no problem."

"Okay. Listen, I'll be home in a little while, but if you need anything, don't hesitate to call."

Morgan hung up and went over to sit on the couch with the dog. Jameson laid his head in Morgan's lap, and she ran her fingers over his head. She recalled how scared she was to find him and the bear that morning.

"For being a sleepy little town, there is some excitement around here, huh, doggo." She smiled when Jameson beat his tail on the couch cushion.

Now that her adrenaline crashed, she was exhausted and she was tempted to take a nap. She instead grabbed the remote and turned on the television. She was halfway through an episode of a game show when the front door opened. Morgan turned around to see Shawn come through the door. Although Morgan had told her she didn't have to come home, now that she was there, Morgan's relief almost felt palpable.

"What are you doing here?" Jameson left her lap to greet her, and Morgan followed.

"I live here." Shawn laughed and opened her arms, inviting Morgan in.

"Smart-ass." Morgan slapped Shawn's stomach before Shawn could wrap her arms around her.

"We weren't that busy, honestly, and it was either I leave or I send a server home. I hate to take away potential tip money from any of my workers, so I opted out. Besides I only have four more days before you go home, and I want to spend every second I can with you."

Morgan stood on her tip toes and kissed Shawn like she hadn't seen her in months. "You are just the absolute sweetest person I've ever met."

A blush crept across Shawn's cheeks, and she ducked her head. "Aw, shucks."

"Now that you're home, what do you want to do for the rest of the day?"

Shawn waggled her eyebrows, which made Morgan laugh. "I was gonna say let's go take a nap, but for the activity I wanted before the nap, I think we should have lunch first to give us energy."

Morgan squeezed Shawn and took in a deep breath to smell Shawn's scent.

"I'm craving pizza. Anywhere near that's good?"

"I know just the place. Then we can walk around town and just make a day of it. What do you think?"

"Sounds perfect."

Once Morgan got dressed, Shawn drove them to Tahoe City and parked in the parking lot beside the small pizza place that looked like a log cabin. They stepped inside and were greeted immediately by the woman behind the counter.

"Well, well. If it isn't Shawn Evans. What brings you here?"

Shawn guided Morgan up to the counter with her hand on the small of her back. The place smelled like tomato sauce, spices, dough, garlic, and pepperoni. Morgan was in heaven, and she already liked the motherly figure behind the counter with her silver-streaked hair in a bun and flour on her red-and-white checked apron that matched the plastic tablecloths throughout the place.

"The best-looking woman who owns the best tasting pizza place. How's it going, Ronnie?"

"Better now that you're here, sweetheart. Who's this woman that's too good-looking to be seen with the likes of you?"

Morgan smiled at Shawn. "No truer words, Ronnie. This is Morgan Campbell. Morgan, Veronica Sellars, Ronnie to her friends."

Morgan and Ronnie shook hands over the counter. "It's so nice to meet you. Shawn assures me this is the place to satisfy my pizza craving. Please tell me she's telling the truth."

"She is honestly telling the truth. We're the locals' favorite, or so says the banner out front."

"See? I told you." Shawn wrapped her arm around Morgan's waist and pulled her closer.

"Ronnie, it all looks and smells so good. What do you recommend?"

"The combo. Everything on it." Without hesitation, Morgan went with Ronnie's recommendation, and ordered the combo.

"Coming right up. It might be a little chilly to sit out on the back deck, but go show it to her anyway, Shawn."

Shawn led Morgan through a side door that opened to a walkway that connected to the back patio overlooking the Truckee River flowing below them. Each side of the river was decked with tall pine trees and other greenery. The river was lazily flowing, but Shawn assured Morgan that in late spring and summer, the river would be raging from the snow melt.

"It's beautiful out here, but Ronnie is right. It is a little chilly. Let's eat inside if it's all right with you."

"Of course. Let's go back in and get our drinks."

They'd spent the better part of an hour eating pizza, drinking iced tea, and talking to Ronnie and her husband, who'd been busy making the pizzas. Once they'd finished off the pie, they hugged Ronnie and her husband good-bye, Morgan promising she'd be back. Shawn had been right. That pizza had been one of the best Morgan had ever had, and now she was stuffed to the gills.

Shawn took Morgan's hand as they strolled through town, going into different shops. Morgan was interested in buying something from a local artist, either a piece of artwork or jewelry. In the third store they went into, a woman came up to Shawn, threw her arms around her, *and* kissed her on the mouth. Morgan may have growled, and her claws may have come out. Who the hell was that woman kissing on her girlfriend? Um, okay. Morgan could use that term. Maybe. Kind of.

"Morgan, this is my best friend, Marcy."

Marcy hugged Morgan so hard that she nearly lost her balance. Morgan's claws retracted knowing that she was Shawn's best friend.

"I've heard so much about you. I'm so happy to finally meet you."

Morgan tried to recall if she'd heard about Marcy, and she didn't remember Shawn mentioning her. Weird since they're best friends. Morgan didn't want to say she'd never heard of her before because… well…rude.

"Likewise. Is this your store?"

"It is." The pride in Marcy's smile was evident.

"It's fantastic. I can't wait to look around."

"Anything you want. I'll give you the Friends and Family discount."

"Thank you. That's very kind. I'm going to take a look."

Shawn kissed Morgan on the cheek. "I'll catch up to you. I want to talk to Marcy."

Shawn watched Morgan walk away and she could feel her smile grow wider as she kept her eyes on Morgan's ass that filled out her jeans in such a good way. The punch to her shoulder took her attention away, and she rubbed the sore spot.

• 178 •

"What's the big idea? That hurt."

"Stop being a baby. I barely touched you. So, that's the woman you told me about? The tourist?"

Shawn felt her cheeks warm, as well as the rest of her body, as it did anytime she thought of Morgan. She took off her jacket and tucked it under her arm.

"It is. What do you think?"

"She's gorgeous. Is she why I haven't talked to you lately?"

Shawn ducked her head, embarrassed she hadn't made the effort to call her friend that she normally spoke to at least every other day.

"Guilty. I'm sorry. She's only here until Saturday and I wanted to spend as much time with her as possible."

"It's okay, buddy. I understand. How're things going with her?"

"Jesus, Marce. Morgan's amazing. We're having such a great time together." Shawn told Marcy all of the adventures she and Morgan had.

"Is she good in bed? She looks like she'd be good in bed." Marcy whispered low enough that Morgan wouldn't hear her.

Shawn didn't say anything but fanned her face instead.

"You dog! Snagged another one without even trying."

Shawn chuckled and held her finger up against her lips, telling Marcy to keep it down. "Believe me, I've been getting A's for my effort, but she's worth it. I'm hoping I'm done snagging women because Morgan has become very special to me."

"You've fallen in love with her."

Shawn didn't know what to say. Marcy was her best friend, and she usually told her everything, but she didn't want to do anything to jinx her relationship with Morgan. Besides, it was too early to be in love.

"I don't know if it's that far yet, but it could be heading that way."

Marcy hugged her again because that was the type of person Marcy was. A hugger. Very tactile. At first, it made Shawn a little uncomfortable, but she was now used to it, and she'd become a hugger herself.

"Have I given you enough time to catch up?" Morgan walked up and kissed Shawn on the cheek, and Marcy laughed.

"I like her, Shawn. Did you find anything you like?"

"So many things. You have a great shop, Marcy. I'll definitely be back before I leave. I might buy one of everything in here if I can fit it all in my car."

Marcy's smile got bigger. "I like you even more now. I hope we get a chance to hang out soon."

"Likewise. I'll be back."

They said good-bye and continued on their stroll.

"Ooh, ice cream. Let's get some."

Shawn started to panic. They were coming up on Paige's shop and Shawn would not take Morgan in there. They had great ice cream, but the way Paige behaved in the grocery store a few days ago, Shawn didn't trust her to not say something or shoot daggers at Morgan. Shawn actually thought about letting go of Morgan's hand, but it felt so good, she knew she'd feel the loss. Even if it was only for ten seconds, it was too long for Shawn. Maybe Paige wouldn't see them.

"Okay, but not here. I know a better place." Shawn glanced in the window and saw Paige watching them. Shawn felt the need to dodge the imaginary dagger Paige was shooting her way. *Shit. That's going to cause some words next time I run into her.* Shawn prayed that Paige wouldn't come running out of her shop after them. They turned a corner and went into an art gallery Morgan got excited about.

The farther into the gallery they got, the more Shawn relaxed. Her phone buzzed, and she took it out of her pocket to see she'd had a text from Paige. Fucking Murphy's Law.

Who's that woman you're with?

Did Shawn ignore her or text back? If she didn't, would Paige blow up her phone with more texts? If she did answer, would Paige still blow up her phone? Shawn decided to put the phone on Do Not Disturb and put it back in her pocket. She'd deal with it later. She didn't want to think about Paige. The only person she wanted on her mind was Morgan.

They meandered their way through a few more shops before Shawn took Morgan to the only other ice cream shop in town that wasn't owned by Paige. They had both settled on single scoop cones, Shawn with pistachio and Morgan with peanut butter and chocolate, and they ate them on the way back to the car. Once they were in the car headed back home, the stress that plagued Shawn for the previous hour miraculously released from her shoulders. That is, until she read the texts she knew Paige sent. But that would be for another day, another time, when Morgan was gone. Until that time, except for work, her time would be happily filled with Morgan and only Morgan.

When they went to bed that night, there was a different air between them. Shawn could feel it. The previous nights had been filled with lust-craved sex. Tonight, they stood before each other next to the bed, slowly undressing. When they were completely naked, they stepped into each other's arms, kissing slowly, deeply. There'd been no rush. No frenzy. Each kiss, each touch was deliberate.

They got under the sheets and faced each other on their sides. Shawn caressed Morgan's cheek. Shawn wanted to kiss Morgan, but the desire to look into her eyes, to try to look in her soul while she touched her was greater. She traced Morgan's eyebrows with her fingers, ran her thumb across Morgan's bottom lip. They followed the contours of her jaw, down the slender lines of her neck, across her collar bone. Morgan's eyelids fluttered closed with the delicate touches.

"Look at me, Morgan. Keep your eyes open and look into mine."

When Morgan's blue eyes, darkened with arousal, opened and connected with Shawn's brown eyes, she continued her tactile journey over Morgan's body. She ran the palm of her hand over Morgan's exposed flesh, causing goose bumps in the wake. Down her arm, back up to her shoulder, between the valley of Morgan's breasts. Morgan's lips made an O when Shawn rimmed her nipple with her index finger, bringing it to a rigid peak and a shade darker.

Shawn moved her hand lower down Morgan's belly, over the trimmed blond hair at her center, and Morgan bent her knees to open up for Shawn. No words had been spoken during this journey, but so much had been said. Shawn's fingers slid through Morgan's folds, spreading the abundant wetness over her clit.

"Oh, Shawn."

"Keep looking at me, baby."

Morgan obeyed but Shawn saw she was heavy-lidded. With each slow stroke Shawn's fingers made over her clit, Morgan's hips moved with them. Shawn entered her with two fingers, curled them up to rub that magical spot, then withdrew to spread more wetness around Morgan's sex.

"What are you doing to me?" Morgan's voice was raspy and breathless, and Shawn knew she'd never heard anything sexier in her life.

"Making love to you."

Shawn continued the same rhythm until Morgan's hips started chasing the orgasm Shawn was waiting to give her. Shawn loved seeing Morgan this submissive to her touch, so open to what Shawn wanted to give her. And Shawn wanted to give her everything. Morgan gripped Shawn's ass and held on as Shawn gave Morgan her release. Shawn never took her eyes off Morgan as she came, and to witness such exquisite beauty nearly brought her to tears.

The rest of the night was spent slowly making love. It was a night of meticulous exploration, and long after Morgan had drifted off to sleep in Shawn's arms, she continued to caress Morgan's skin, memorizing the feel of it beneath her fingertips. It was too early to voice her words, but if she didn't expel them, she felt like she might die. She kissed Morgan on the cheek and whispered in her ear.

"I love you."

CHAPTER SEVENTEEN

Morgan woke that morning for the second time. The first, Shawn woke her before she left for work, giving her a lingering soft kiss that continued to speak of the lovemaking from the night before. Now, Morgan was flying high, taken there by Shawn's hands and mouth. She'd never felt like that, been made love to so sweetly as she'd been by Shawn. Morgan felt her walls around her heart crumbling down. In all honesty, Shawn had been chipping away at those bricks since they'd started becoming friends. When Morgan made the trek up to Lake Tahoe a week and a half ago, she didn't have any designs on meeting someone, let alone start to fall for someone. She'd come to the mountains for self-discovery, self-betterment, and self-love, and along with achieving that, she'd also met a woman she could see having a relationship with, maybe even a happily ever after. The walls around her heart were starting to crumble.

Morgan liked the woman she was becoming, and she loved the woman she was when she was with Shawn. Morgan wasn't religious, but she'd found her spiritual home in this small town with her new friends, and she knew she was a changed woman. She'd discovered there was more to life than working too-long hours and allowing toxic people into her life. That was going to change when she returned to Sacramento. Jane and Annie might not even recognize her. Morgan chuckled at the thought. Morgan missed them so much and couldn't wait to see them again, to tell them everything, especially about her and Shawn. She was already thinking about asking Shawn if Morgan could bring Jane and Annie with her one weekend so they could all meet, three of the most important people in her life.

Morgan got out of bed and got ready. She wanted to have breakfast at the diner then she had an errand to run. When they'd been in Marcy's shop the day before, Morgan had seen some pieces of jewelry and art she wanted to buy. One of the art pieces she wanted to give to Shawn to hang in her room. It was a painting of a Tahoe sunset from Sand Harbor, almost identical to the scene they'd witnessed. It was the night she realized she was falling for Shawn.

On the drive over to the diner, Morgan's body tingled with each mile in anticipation of seeing Shawn. When she pulled into the parking lot, she couldn't get out of her car fast enough. She walked through the door, the charming little bell announcing her arrival, and her first look at Shawn made every person, every noise in the diner disappear. Their eyes locked, and the smile on Shawn's face was bright enough to light the darkest night. That smile was for Morgan, and Morgan's was for Shawn.

"Hi." Only the counter separated Morgan and Shawn.

"Good morning, beautiful."

God, just the sound of Shawn's voice stirred arousal deep in Morgan.

"I missed you this morning."

"Same. I would've loved to stay in bed with you all day, but we can do that tomorrow. I'm taking the next two days off to spend with you before you go home."

The thought of leaving this magical place made Morgan want to cry. Sure, her house, job, best friends were in Sacramento, but Morgan could envision Tahoe being her home.

"Then I better get some breakfast so I can be ready for you."

Morgan decided to sit at the counter and eat so she could be closer to Shawn. She needed as much time as she could get to soak in all of her.

"What's on your agenda for today?"

"Just running a couple of errands. There were some things in Marcy's shop that I wanted to get, then I thought I'd do a little grocery shopping so I can make you a special dinner." Morgan thought of the idea on the way to the diner. She'd buy something to fix for dinner, something nice, but she hadn't decided on what yet. She wanted to have a candlelit dinner and romantic evening with her new love,

Shawn. She envisioned listening to soft music in front of a fire, maybe slow dancing, then continuing their dance in the bedroom. Since Shawn wasn't working tomorrow, there would be no need for sleep. They could make love all night long, and Morgan would find a way to show Shawn how deeply she cared for her.

"Aw, babe. You don't have to do that. I can make dinner or we can go out."

"Don't argue with me, baby. I want to do something special for you."

The blush that engulfed Shawn's cheeks warmed Morgan's entire body, and it earned Shawn a kiss. When Morgan finished eating and Shawn refused to charge her for her meal, Morgan pulled a twenty-dollar bill out of her wallet and left it on the counter for a tip. She kissed Shawn once more.

"I'll see you later, baby."

A short while later, Morgan had entered Marcy's shop, but there was a different woman behind the counter who Morgan didn't know. She knew what she wanted to buy, but she wanted to look around a little more before making her purchases. She'd been looking through prints of Lake Tahoe to take back home when she heard a woman's voice ask for Marcy, and she sounded angry. The woman at the counter informed her she was in the back. The woman strode with purpose through a doorway in what Morgan assumed was Marcy's office. *Uh-oh. This looks like drama.*

"That fucking Shawn Evans!"

Morgan's ears perked up and she couldn't help but move a little closer to eavesdrop. Normally that wasn't her style, but if this had to do with Shawn, Morgan wanted to know.

"Calm down, Paige. What's going on?"

"I saw her yesterday holding hands with some other woman."

Yeah, that was me, psycho.

"They walked right by my ice cream shop like Shawn wanted to flaunt her new fuck in front of me."

"Okay." Marcy sounded like she was trying to calm this Paige woman down.

"I can't believe how quickly she moved on. I mean, she just broke up with me last week, and she already has a new sidepiece. She was probably already fucking her before she broke up with me."

"I just met her yesterday. She's only in town for a few more days is what Shawn told me."

"Damn her. Shawn's never going to change. She'll never settle down. She'll continue to go from one tourist to another, oblivious to the hearts she's breaking."

Hold on for just a damn minute!

"Shawn's always been a player and always will be. She's not interested in any kind of relationship or commitment. That woman she was with yesterday is a damn fool if she thinks she's going to change Shawn's wandering ways. But if all Shawn wants is a fuck buddy, I can be that for her. She's fucking hot in the sack."

"Paige, please. That's my best friend you're talking about."

"Oh, shut it, Marcy. You've slept with her yourself so you know I'm right."

"Oh, you're right. She definitely knows what she's doing, but I still don't want to talk about it. It's ancient history."

"It's all that practice, going from one woman to the next."

Morgan felt the tears well in her eyes and her heart started to break. She thought Shawn was different. She thought Shawn cared about her. Shawn knew what Morgan went through with Jess, how betrayed she felt, and now she did the same damn thing to her and to other women. Morgan thought she was going to be sick. She managed to find the strength in her legs to carry her out of Marcy's shop when all she wanted to do was collapse. She'd barely heard the woman behind the counter calling out for Morgan to have a nice day. Morgan made it to her car and sat behind the wheel stunned and numb. What was she going to do? She took a few more minutes to think before she finally came to a conclusion. She started the car and drove back to her cabin, trying not to let the tears flow or the hurt consume her or the anger rage through her. She couldn't even look at Shawn's home as she passed by.

Morgan went directly to the bedroom and packed her clothes and toiletries. She didn't bother packing up her food, just threw it in the bear-proof cans along with the stupid book Shawn had given her just a few days after she arrived in Tahoe. She thought about going to Shawn's to pick up the few pieces of clothes she'd left there, but she didn't feel she had the strength to step foot in Shawn's home.

The place they'd had sex, talked, laughed. And Jameson. Oh, man, if she saw Jameson right now, she'd lose her shit. No, she'd let Shawn throw out what Morgan had left behind and get her house ready for the next woman she'd bring to her bed.

"Good-bye, Jameson. I'll miss you," Morgan whispered as she drove by Shawn's house. She turned left on Highway 89 that would normally take her to the diner, but today, now, she'd pass it by, not taking another glance, and keep driving until she got to the interstate that would take her back to the city. Away from her new friends. Away from Shawn.

Shawn had been looking forward to tonight since having seen Morgan earlier that morning. She loved that Morgan wanted to make her dinner although it was completely unnecessary. She just wanted to spend time alone with Morgan and make a plan for the next time they'd see each other. She was going to make the most of the next two days. She needed to get her fill of Morgan until the next time they'd see each other.

Shawn was disappointed that Morgan's car wasn't in her driveway. Maybe she was still out running errands or exploring. She threw the ball for Jameson in the backyard for a while after she'd texted Morgan that she was home. The sky was growing dark, and she still hadn't heard from Morgan. She texted her again, and when she didn't hear back, she called her. It went straight to voice mail.

"Hi, baby. I was just wondering when you were coming over. Should I turn on the oven for you? Anything I can do to help prep for dinner? Let me know. I can't wait to see you."

Another hour went by and no word from Morgan. Shawn was starting to freak out a little, so she hopped in her car and drove to Morgan's. The cabin was dark and Morgan's car wasn't in the driveway. She looked in all the windows, and there were no signs that she'd been there. Shawn turned on the flashlight on her phone and looked in the garbage can. On the top, she found the book she'd given Morgan.

"What the hell is going on?"

KC RICHARDSON

Shawn called her again and it went straight to voice mail.

"Morgan? Where are you, baby? I'm getting worried. I'm at your cabin and it looks like you left. Please call me."

Shawn ran her fingers through her hair and turned around in a circle as if she'd find Morgan standing behind her, playing a practical joke. But this shit wasn't funny. Where the fuck was she?

She drove home and paced the living room, not knowing who to call. Then she thought of Marcy. She dialed her number.

"Hey. Did you see Morgan today? She had planned on buying some stuff from you, then we were going to have dinner together, but she's not here, she's not answering her phone or my texts. I'm freaking out here, Marce."

"Calm down, Shawn. I haven't seen her today, but I've been holed up in my office most of the day. Have you called the hospital?"

"Jesus, no! If anything happened to her, I don't know what I'd do." It wasn't uncommon for car accidents to happen there, especially with the winding mountain roads or wild animals darting out, causing a driver to swerve. That wouldn't explain, though, why Morgan's stuff was gone from the cabin.

"Call the hospital then call me back. I'm sure she's fine, honey."

Shawn hung up without saying another word and called the local hospital. She had a friend that worked as a nurse so Shawn asked to be transferred to her department.

"Hey, Linda. I need a favor."

"Shawn? Are you okay?"

"No, I'm freaking out. I was supposed to have dinner with a friend tonight, and I can't get a hold of her. Can you check to see if she's been admitted? Maybe she had an accident. Her name is Morgan Campbell."

"Hang on." Shawn heard the clicking of the keyboard. "No, nobody here by that name and no Jane Doe in the ER. Sorry."

"Thanks, Linda. Let me know if you hear anything."

Shawn hung up and sat on the couch, feeling like her legs were going to give out. She rested her elbows on her knees and her head in her hands. Should she go out and look for her? Shawn didn't even know where to start. She hadn't seen or spoken to Morgan since ten that morning, and now it was eight p.m. Morgan could be anywhere. Jameson sat at her feet and whined, making Shawn look up.

"I don't know where she is, buddy. I can tell you that I'm really worried."

Her phone dinged, alerting her to a text message. Shawn thought she'd cry when she saw it was from Morgan.

I've left Tahoe. Don't call me. Don't text me. I never want to hear from you again, Shawn Evans.

"What the hell?"

Morgan, what's wrong? What happened? I've been so worried.

Save it, Shawn. You'll forget all about me when the next notch on your headboard arrives in town.

What the hell was she talking about? What the fuck happened to bring this one-eighty turn?

Morgan, please tell me what happened?

Fuck this. Shawn dialed the phone and it went straight to voice mail. Shawn screamed in her empty house. "Morgan!" Jameson cowered and went immediately to the corner of the living room.

Morgan! Please talk to me. What did I do? I can't fix it if you won't talk to me.

Shawn held her phone in her hands like it was her lifeline to Morgan. Hell, it was. She was gone. Shawn couldn't just show up at her house since she didn't know where she lived. Shawn stared at the screen, willing another message, a call, anything from the woman who'd made her way into Shawn's heart in such a short amount of time. But her phone remained silent. The house was quiet. Too quiet. And the silence allowed Shawn to hear the pieces of her heart shattering.

Chapter Eighteen

Morgan had been holed up in her home since arriving on Thursday afternoon. It was now Sunday morning, and she was still wearing her pajamas for the third day in a row. The only thing she'd had any energy for was brushing her teeth. Her hair looked like a rat's nest, she had dark circles under her eyes, and she was pale as a ghost. When her doorbell rang mid-morning, she was none too happy to have to answer the door. She'd thought about ignoring it, going back to bed, and crawling under the covers. The sound of the key unlocking her door demolished Morgan's plans.

In walked Jane and Annie carrying a large paper bag and three paper cups with lids. Morgan could smell the hot bagels, but she had no appetite. Morgan didn't greet her friends, just continued to sit in an oversized easy chair, pulling her legs under her.

"You look like shit. Here, eat this." Jane placed a blueberry bagel smeared with cream cheese and a cup of hot coffee on the reading table next to her chair.

"I'm not hungry. What are you guys doing here?

Annie came into the living room with their bagels and coffee, and sat on the couch next to Jane.

"If I recall, you texted us Thursday night, telling us you're home, and didn't want to talk about it. About what? We have no idea because you didn't tell us. We decided to give you a couple of days to calm down from whatever or whomever you're pissed at, but today it stops."

Annie took a bite of her bagel and nodded as Jane spoke. She wiped errant cream cheese off the corners of her mouth.

"Looking at you now, I'm guessing it has to do with Shawn."

Morgan looked up from her lap and pointed at Jane. "Do not mention her name again."

Jane and Annie looked at each other and took another bite of their respective bagels in unison.

"What did she do?"

"I told you, I don't want to talk about it. Why won't you listen to me?"

Annie took another bite so Jane continued. "Because we know you'll want to talk about it eventually, so it might as well be now so you can move on."

Morgan felt the tears sting her eyes, and she wiped them away, angry that she'd given so much power to Shawn to hurt her that way. She covered her face with her hands since the tears wouldn't stop. She felt one of them sit on the chair arm, probably Jane since Annie was uncomfortable with girl stuff such as feelings except when it came to Jane.

"Oh, honey. What happened?" Morgan felt Jane's arms wrap around her, and Morgan fell into her.

"She broke my heart," Morgan managed to get out between sobs. When she calmed down, she explained what happened, how she overheard Shawn's best friend and ex. "She had a girlfriend when we first met, and she didn't tell me."

"Was there any reason for her to tell you? I mean, you two had just met. You weren't technically even friends yet."

"She could've told me when I opened up to her about Jess. She could've told me when we kissed for the first time."

"Seriously? Come on, Morgan. 'Wow, that was a great kiss, but you should know I just broke up with someone.' Talk about a lady boner shrinker." Annie always had a way with being blunt. No holds barred. That was not what Morgan wanted right then.

Jane held her tighter as she told Annie to shush. "Tell me about your time there. Before you heard that conversation, how were you feeling?"

Morgan wiped away more tears and wiped her nose with her sleep shirt sleeve.

"Baby, can you get Morgan some tissue? That was disgusting." That comment made Morgan huff out a chuckle.

Annie handed a few tissues to Morgan, and she thanked her.

"Prior to hearing that conversation, things were going really well. She was attentive, romantic, protective. We laughed a lot. When we agreed to start dating, we both promised we'd be honest with each other. She lied to me."

"Well, not technically." Annie was playing devil's advocate. "It's not like she was sneaking around with other women while you were there with her."

Morgan threw her arms in the air and raised her voice. "She lied by omission!"

Jane rubbed Morgan's back in an effort to calm her down. It wasn't working. Well, maybe a little.

"Let me ask you something. If you hadn't gone up to Tahoe for your self-care mission, if you hadn't found Jess cheating on you, would you have told Shawn about her? Think about it. That's not the kind of thing you bring to the table on a first date, even if that first date lasted a week."

God, why couldn't Jane and Annie just let her wallow in her pity party? She just wanted to mourn the loss of what could've been. Not only had she began falling for Shawn, but she loved Jameson, Shorty, Melvin, Kerrie, Jack, Bill, Dave, and Ernie. The thought of never seeing them again almost broke her heart as much as Shawn did.

"Listen, I know you're hurting right now. But there was something special brewing between you and Shawn. Maybe if you give her the chance to explain, you might be able to work it out." Jane kissed the top of Morgan's head. "Damn, lady. How long has it been since you bathed or washed your hair? The stench is making my eyes water."

Morgan laughed, which actually felt really good. "Fuck off. I didn't invite you here to insult me."

Annie took another bite of her bagel, shrugged, and spoke around the food in her mouth. "You didn't invite us, we barged in, so I guess we deserve it. Now, eat your bagel, go take a *very* long shower, and get dressed. You don't have to go anywhere, but it's time to pick yourself up, put on your big girl panties, and raise your chin."

Morgan looked up at Jane, appalled at how Annie just spoke to her.

Jane shrugged. "She's right."

"Fine." Morgan pushed herself up and sent Jane flying onto the floor, laughing her ass off. Morgan pointed to Jane. "You deserved that." Jane laughed harder. Morgan shot Annie a dirty look as she walked by her on her way to her room.

Morgan turned on the water for her shower, took off her clothes, and looked at herself in the mirror. Three days of barely eating made her gaunt and pale. She ran her hands down her naked chest and under her breasts, lifting them up. Doing that reminded her of how Shawn loved playing with her breasts—teasing them, squeezing, nibbling, pinching, and biting. It never took long for her to grow wet when Shawn played with them. She didn't know if she'd ever feel as wonderful and sexy with another woman's touch as she did with Shawn's. At this point, she could never imagine being with another woman ever. Tears trickled down her cheeks.

Morgan stepped under the hot spray of her rain showerhead, letting the water soak her hair. She lathered the shampoo and scratched her scalp with all the soap. She squirted some Stress Relief shower gel on her loofa and took her time scrubbing the stink and bodily oils off her skin. Morgan had stayed in the shower for about twenty minutes, taking care of her body and soul, letting the tears flow, not trying to stop them. When they finally ceased, Morgan turned off the water and gently dried her skin with a soft bath sheet. She applied deodorant, face cream, and body lotion, then combed the tangles out of her hair before tying it up in a ponytail.

Morgan returned to the living room after dressing to find Jane and Annie watching a football game on the television and three Bloody Marys sitting on the coffee table in front of the couch. Jane patted the cushion next to her to invite Morgan to sit down and enjoy her nutritious breakfast drink decked with green olives, a pickle spear, and a celery stalk. Man, that hit the spot. Extra spicy too? Despite being peeved at her friends, they sure did know how to take care of her.

"So, Morgan, Annie and I are headed to Tahoe in a couple of weeks for the Thanksgiving weekend to ski. Would you like to join us? Maybe give Shawn a chance to explain?"

The question surprised Morgan in more ways than one. "Um, guys. There's no snow up there."

"Yet. They're expecting a big storm next week and Homewood and Heavenly are opening up for Thanksgiving, either with fresh snow or man-made."

Morgan was sure she wouldn't be ready for that trip, to be within driving distance of Shawn.

"Thanks, but I'll pass. You have fun though."

They spent the rest of the day watching football, drinking all the Marys, and snacking on chips, dips, and salami and cheese. It turned out to be a pretty decent day for Morgan. She had her friends, she showered and got dressed, and she only thought of Shawn a hundred times that day instead of the thousands since she'd returned home. She'd be ready to jump back in the saddle and return to work tomorrow. What she needed was to stay busy. The busier she was, the less time she'd have to think of Shawn and all she'd left in Tahoe.

Shawn had the past couple of days off from work since she'd planned on spending it with Morgan. Instead, she'd spent the days with her phone attached to her hand, hoping and praying that Morgan would contact her, but she was radio silent. There were so many times, hundreds, thousands that Shawn went to text or call Morgan, but her wishes were clear. She didn't want to talk to Shawn. She needed to figure out how she'd get Morgan back. If only Morgan would talk to her and tell her what happened. Shawn would do anything to rectify it.

Sunday morning, Shawn began her day by willing her brain to tuck Morgan away into a corner so she could make it through her workday. She didn't want to say anything to her friends because they'd ask the questions she didn't have the answers to. When she got home from work, she could unpack thoughts of Morgan and cry if she had to.

As they were setting the tables for the upcoming breakfast rush, Kerrie had been the first to ask.

"How was your time with Morgan, boss?"

"Oh, good. She's home now." Shawn continued placing the coffee mugs on the tables.

"That's it? That's all you have?"

"Um, yep. That's pretty much it." *Hold it together, Shawn. Now's not the time to break down.*

"When are you going to see her again?"

"Um, it might be a while. You know, returning to work after three weeks, I'm sure she's going to be pretty busy." Shawn kept busy herself, unwilling to look Kerrie in the eye. They'd known each other long enough that Kerrie would see Shawn was lying. "I'll be right back."

Shawn went into her office and shut the door behind her. When she sat in her chair, she felt the tears start to form, and she pressed her palms into her eyes to stop them from falling. She took a few deep breaths, rubbed her face vigorously with her hands, and applied some eyedrops to get rid of the redness she knew had colored her eyes.

When she returned, it was close enough to six a.m. that she unlocked the diner door and allowed the first customers in a few minutes early. The busier she got, the more likely she'd be able to hold her shit together. At least she knew her grandfathers wouldn't be in until tomorrow. That gave her a whole day to get her emotions in check. No problem, right? She was tough, and if Morgan didn't want her, that was Morgan's loss. Shawn was a good person. She was ready to find someone to settle down with. She thought that maybe Morgan could've been that someone. Okay, that was enough of that. She couldn't concentrate on work if she kept thinking about Morgan.

By the time Shawn got home from work, she was mentally exhausted. It was really hard work keeping Morgan out of her mind. What she needed was a good run to clear her head. She changed into her running clothes, leashed up Jameson, and off they ran. She headed toward the lake, crossed the street once it was safe, and continued on the pedestrian/bike path adjacent to the shore. The temperature was chilly, and she could see her breath. The smell of fall permeated the air. This was Shawn's favorite time of the year. The smell of smoke coming from chimneys, the earthy aroma of the fallen leaves and cold dirt, the clean smell before the first major snowfall were all wonderful, but all she could think about was Morgan.

Shawn pictured them snuggled up on the couch wrapped in a wool blanket, watching the wood burn in the fireplace. They'd drink hot chocolate with whipped cream, maybe a splash of Baileys to increase the warmth as the hot liquid made its way from their mouths to their stomachs. Shawn could picture them taking walks, hand in hand, wearing flannel-lined jeans, parkas, sweaters, and wool caps to keep their heads and ears warm. Jameson would walk with them, occasionally darting into the woods and returning with a stick for Shawn to throw him. Of course, he'd run to it, smell it, then keep walking, quickly losing interest in his recently found bounty.

They would sleep in Shawn's bed with the winter flannel sheets colored in greens and blues, a thermal blanket, and a down comforter draped over them. Morgan would sleep in Shawn's arms with her head on Shawn's shoulder. That wouldn't be happening now. Shawn would walk alone with her dog, she'd sit on the couch with her dog, and she'd go to bed alone.

Shawn was so into her head that she didn't notice Jameson step in front of her until it was too late. She twisted her ankle in trying to avoid falling on her dog and did a face-plant onto the black asphalt. Jameson whined and came back to her, licking the side of her face. She laid sprawled out for a few moments, wiggling her fingers and toes, making sure everything worked. As she tried to stand, her ankle gave out, unable to bear any weight. She rolled over and sat with her legs out in front of her, wondering how she was going to get home. She pulled her phone out of her pocket to discover her screen had cracked but thankfully still worked.

"Marcy, I need you to come get me. I hurt my ankle while on a run and I can't stand on it."

"Jesus, Shawn. Where are you?"

"I'm about two miles north of my dock. I'll be the load sitting down with her dog next to her."

"I'll be right there. Don't move."

Shawn barked out a harsh laugh. Like she could go anywhere. Ten minutes later, Marcy pulled up next to her and rushed over to Shawn. She put Jameson into the back of her car then came back to help Shawn up.

"Put your arm around me."

Shawn placed a little bit of weight on her ankle and yelped in pain.

"I'm going to need you to take me home to get my wallet then take me to the ER. I'm going to need X-rays."

"No problem, honey."

Marcy flipped a U-turn and when they arrived to Shawn's, Marcy took Jameson in the house and grabbed Shawn's wallet off the entryway table where Shawn told her it would be.

When they got back on the road, Marcy glanced at Shawn. "How did this happen?

Shawn shook her head and scrubbed her face with her scraped up hand. "I was thinking about Morgan and didn't notice Jameson in front of me. I tripped over him."

"Still haven't heard from her?"

"No, and I have a feeling I won't. I just wish I knew what happened, why she's so mad at me."

Marcy let out a deep breath. "I've been thinking, and I know it's a long shot, but Paige came to my shop Thursday morning, bitching about seeing you with another woman, whom I'm guessing was Morgan. She said things that if Morgan was in the shop around the same time, she may have overheard."

"What kind of things?" Shawn could feel her blood boil. She'd received numerous texts from Paige after she saw them in town on Wednesday, but Shawn hadn't looked at them until Friday when Morgan was gone. Paige had sounded all kinds of batshit crazy with what she'd said to Shawn. She could only imagine what she said to Marcy.

"That right after you broke up with her, you started seeing this other woman. That you were never going to change, that you only wanted to have flings with tourists. I know I shouldn't have, but I let her rant, hoping she'd run out of steam. I finally had to shut her down when she started saying if all you wanted was a fuck buddy, she could be that for you. You dodged a bullet with that one, buddy."

Shawn tried to recall what Morgan's texts said, and she scrolled through the messages. *Save it, Shawn. You'll forget all about me when the next notch on your bedpost arrives in town.*

Shawn slammed her hand on the dashboard.

"Fuck! God dammit, Marcy, she probably overhead you. Why didn't you tell me this before?"

"I didn't know, Shawn. I had no idea that Morgan was there in the shop. Paige stopped by a little after ten a.m. What time did Morgan leave the diner?"

"A little before ten. Shit! I have to talk to her, explain that she wasn't a fling with me. That I wanted a relationship with her and only her."

"Well, it's going to have to wait." Marcy pulled into the parking lot of the hospital near the ER and went to find a wheelchair. Thankfully, X-rays were negative for fracture, but the doctor told her she had a bad sprain. She had to use crutches and a walking boot for the next couple of weeks. Shawn declined pain medication, intent to control the pain and swelling with ice and anti-inflammatories.

When Marcy got Shawn home, Shawn lay on the couch with her leg elevated, and Marcy placed an ice pack over her ankle. While Marcy was in the kitchen making soup and grilled cheese sandwiches, Shawn texted Kerrie, Melvin, and Shorty to let them know of her injury and that she wouldn't be in for a couple of days. They replied that they'd come by tomorrow after work with some meals for her. She was really lucky to have such great friends, and she owed them big time with all of her absences lately.

When her phone rang a minute later, Shawn gasped when she saw Morgan's name through the cracked screen.

"Morgan?"

"Hi, Shawn." The sound of Morgan's voice made Shawn want to weep. "I think we should talk."

Shawn nodded as if Morgan could see her. "Yes, I want that so much."

At the worst possible time, Marcy came into the room.

"Here ya go, babe. Gotta get some food in you to give you some energy for later."

"Are you fucking kidding me? I've been gone for four days and you already have another woman in your home? Unfuckingbelievable."

"No, Morgan. It's not like that. I—"

"Stop. We're done. I thought I'd made a mistake by not giving you a chance to explain things. The only mistake I seemed to have made was meeting you. We're through."

The click from Morgan hanging up sounded like a loud blast in Shawn's ear.

"Morgan? Morgan? Fuck!" Shawn threw her phone into the stone hearth of the fireplace where it shattered into pieces. Shawn looked at Marcy standing still, eyes wide like a deer caught in headlights, holding the tray of food.

"I love you, Marce, but you have the worst fucking timing. That was Morgan. She heard you. Now she thinks you're the next woman I'm sleeping with."

"God, Shawn, I'm so sorry. Let me call her and explain."

Shawn laughed mirthlessly. "That would be great, but I don't know her number by heart. It was programmed into my phone." Shawn pointed to the fireplace and the broken pieces that came from her hand.

Marcy placed the tray of food on the coffee table.

"I guess we're going to have to get you a new phone."

"Thanks for taking care of me tonight, but I really need to be alone right now. Could you lock the door behind you?"

Shawn knew she sounded harsh, and the evidence was clear by the look of Marcy's fallen face and frown.

"I'll come by to see you tomorrow morning, check to see if you need anything," Marcy said before closing the door.

Once she was alone, she threw her arm over her eyes and finally allowed the tears to fall. For being one not to cry much, her tears sure had been overflowing the past few days. When the ice on her ankle started to melt and soak the couch cushion, she grabbed her crutches, threw the ice bag into the sink and hobbled her way to bed.

CHAPTER NINETEEN

The Thanksgiving holiday was in full swing in Lake Tahoe. All of the area ski resorts were open and there'd been a total of two feet fresh snow that had fallen in the previous few days. The sky was deep blue and the sun shining on the pristine powder made the snow crystals blink like a million diamonds. Ray's Diner was bustling with locals and tourists, fueling their bodies prior to hitting the slopes. All in all, it should've been the perfect day, yet Shawn was miserable.

It had been two weeks since she'd talked to Morgan. Well, not exactly talked. Morgan yelled at Shawn with the misunderstanding that Shawn had replaced her so quickly. As if that was possible. She couldn't even text or call her because while she replaced her broken phone, there had been some sort of glitch where she lost a lot of her contacts. Not all, but a lot, including Morgan's. That had effectively ended Shawn's chance of trying to explain to Morgan that she hadn't replaced her and didn't think that would ever happen. Without the remote possibility of Morgan actually coming to see Shawn, she was stuck wondering what could have been.

By the end of the first week after Morgan left, Shawn had been shuffling around the diner, struggling to put on a happy face for her customers. Her breaking point had come when Jack paid a house call one afternoon.

"Shawny, what's going on? You've been moping around like someone kidnapped your puppy. Are you missing Morgan that much?"

Her lip quivering and tears stinging her eyes, Shawn told Jack what happened and why she thought it happened.

"I don't know what to do, Jack. I don't have her number, I don't have her address. If I did, I'd drive to Sacramento and bang on her door until she talked to me."

"Google her, Shawny."

Shawn laughed as she rubbed her eyes. "I did. I couldn't find anything on her. She's not on social media. It's like she's a ghost. She's not, though, right? You saw her? You talked to her?"

"Listen to me, honey. That girl loves you. Maybe she just needs some time to figure things out."

"If she loved me, she wouldn't have left. If she thought we had something special, she would've stayed and talked to me."

Jack hugged her and rubbed her back as her own grandfather had done when she was younger going through some sort of heartache.

"Keep the faith, honey. She'll come back when she's ready. In the meantime, we all love you and we're here for you."

It had been a few days since Jack's pep talk, and it made Shawn feel a teeny bit better knowing she had such wonderful friends that would help her get through losing Morgan. But Shawn knew she'd never get *over* losing Morgan.

Her ankle had been healing, but she was still in her walking boot. The holiday weekend crowd meant she'd been on her feet all day, and her ankle was now throbbing. Toward the end of the lunch rush, she'd gone back to her office with a bag of ice, removed her boot, and elevated her leg with the ice wrapped around her ankle. After twenty minutes, she'd taken the ice off and was strapping the boot when Kerrie knocked on her door.

"Hey, boss. There are a couple of women at table three that asked to speak to you. Want me to tell them you left?" Kerrie and her other employees had been walking on eggshells around her since finding out Morgan left, doing anything to avoid her short temper.

"No, I'll be right out." Shawn hoped those women wanted to tell them how great her diner was and not to complain. She just didn't have the energy to deal with any bullshit right now. She saw the two women sitting close together, sipping on iced tea. They looked happy yet nervous.

"Good afternoon, ladies. I'm Shawn Evans. You wanted to speak to me?" Shawn plastered her best smile to her face even though she hadn't had much to be happy about lately.

"Hi, Shawn. It's so nice to meet you officially. I'm Jane and this is my wife, Annie."

Shawn thought they looked a little familiar and she somehow knew the names.

"We're Morgan's best friends."

Shawn felt her heart drop into her stomach and her heart race. Morgan's best friends. Here. In her diner.

"Would you be able to join us for a moment? We won't take much of your time."

Shawn plopped down into her chair, the strength in her leg muscles weakening as she heard Morgan's name.

"Is she...how...is she all right?"

Jane looked to Annie, and Shawn knew what the answer was by their facial expressions.

"Actually, no. She's not all right. She'd kill us if she knew we were talking to you, but we felt we needed the whole story, not just her version. You want to fill us in?"

Shawn felt the heat enflame her face and her hackles rise. "No, I don't. This is between Morgan and me. I'm having a hard enough time without being attacked by her best friends." Shawn started to stand when the larger of the two, Annie, placed her hand on Shawn's forearm.

"Attacking you is not why we're here. Our best friend is miserable, and if there's any way we can help her not be, we want to try. Please sit down and hear us out."

Shawn reluctantly sat and crossed her arms over her chest. They did seem earnest, so Shawn felt the least she could do was hear them out. And if they helped her have one last chance at winning Morgan back, then she'd owe them big time.

"Shawn, I spoke with Morgan a couple of times while she'd been here, and she seemed so happy. She sounded like a different person, in touch with herself and her feelings. She sounded lighter, almost giddy, since the two of you started hanging out, becoming friends then lovers."

Shawn felt her ears warm and her body flush at the memories of her and Morgan having sex, making love. The last night they'd been together, she'd felt a shift in her heart when they'd made love. Shawn had dared to dream of a future together.

"Then she returned home three days early, not talking to us and trying to shut us out. She told us that she overheard your best friend and your ex say how you only want to bed tourists, and you move from one to the next. Is there any truth to that?"

So, Marcy was right. Morgan did overhear them. She had the sudden urge to go find Paige and…and…she didn't know what. She wasn't a violent person, and it was Shawn's fault for getting involved with her in the first place, then letting the relationship go on as long as it did. She realized the night she broke up with Paige that she had feelings that Shawn didn't share, and she had a feeling Paige wasn't going to take the breakup well. She'd been expecting the other shoe to drop with Paige, and the hell if she hadn't just dropped the shoe but threw it at Shawn's head.

"To be honest, that's how I had lived my life since moving here. It wasn't that I wasn't interested in having a girlfriend, but there aren't many local lesbians here that I could date. But I'm not that person anymore." Shawn paused, not knowing if she could trust these women, Morgan's friends, to keep an open mind, but what the hell did she have to lose? She'd already lost Morgan. "Before Morgan came up here, I'd been dating Paige. I knew from the beginning that she wasn't the one, but a few of my friends talked me into giving it a chance. She and I were dating when Morgan arrived. We had just started becoming friends when I finally broke up with Paige."

"Did you have feelings for Morgan?" Shawn saw Annie squeeze Jane's hand when she'd asked that question.

"More than I've felt for anyone in a very long time. Even though I was attracted to Morgan, I didn't push her into anything because of what she went through with her ex. I figured, if all we could be was friends, I'd be a lucky son of a bitch to have Morgan in my life. She's an incredible woman, but I'm sure you know that."

Shawn took a deep breath and looked out the window to the lake to give her a moment to collect her thoughts. What she said next could make or break her in the eyes of Jane and Annie.

"My time spent with Morgan was nothing short of spectacular. I'm not going to go into detail about our sex life because what I feel for her has nothing to do with sex if I'm being honest. It seemed without trying, Morgan wound her way into my life, and into my heart. I was so happy every minute I got to spend with her, and I wanted to spend *every* minute with her. I loved how she interacted with my friends, how she seamlessly made her own friendships with them. She made me feel special, and all I wanted was to make her happy, to give us a chance at a possible future together."

Shawn saw Jane and Annie smile at each other, then Jane frowned at Shawn.

"She called you almost a couple of weeks ago after we convinced her to talk to you. She told us she heard another woman in the background saying some suggestive things." Annie's eyebrow raised, challenging Shawn to explain that.

Shawn pointed to the walking boot. "I was out running and I sprained my ankle. My best friend picked me up, took me to the ER, then brought me home. She'd been taking care of me, getting me dinner, when Morgan called. I'll admit that Marcy and I dated years ago, but we were better off as friends. She's been my best friend, and I don't have any romantic feelings for her at all. As a matter of fact, I couldn't imagine being with anyone except Morgan."

Jane's eyes rolled up and she shook her head. "I swear, I love Morgan with all my heart, but that one has the worst habit of jumping to conclusions. Listen, Shawn, you need to fix this with her. She's been miserable so I know she has feelings for you."

"I can't."

"Why the hell not?"

"I threw my phone that night after Morgan hung up on me. I lost her number. I don't know her address or who she works for. I was ready to drive to Sacramento to scour the town looking for her, but it's a big city. I didn't know where to start."

The smile that lit Jane's face was brighter than the sun shining over the lake.

"Well, hell, woman. Let me give you her number and address. Show up at her front door if you have to, but for God's sake, don't give up on her. If you're able to get her to see your side of things, I can promise that she'll be all you ever need in this life."

For the first time since Morgan left, Shawn felt a sliver of hope make its way into her heart.

"So, you guys believe me?"

"Is there any reason not to?"

Shawn laughed. "Hell, no. Morgan means the world to me, and if I can get her to talk to me, I'll make her sure of that." Shawn called Kerrie over and handed over a pen and order pad to Jane.

"Kerrie, this is Jane and Annie, Morgan's best friends. They're encouraging me to go after Morgan."

Kerrie wiped her brow in an exaggerated fashion. "Thank Goddess. Shawn's been miserable since Morgan left. Anything I can do to bring these two lovebirds back together, I'll do it."

Jane and Annie laughed as Jane wrote down Morgan's phone number and address. For the first time in two weeks, Shawn felt hopeful.

Chapter Twenty

Winter

Morgan had the bah humbugs. Thanksgiving came and went. She'd spent the holiday by herself watching holiday movies on the Hallmark Channel, scoffing at the happily ever afters celebrated around a Christmas tree. Her two dads had gone on holiday to Europe, she'd given her mother the obligatory holiday call that lasted less than five minutes, and her best friends spent the Thanksgiving holiday in Lake Tahoe. Morgan would never admit that she sat on the couch in her pajamas eating a whole pumpkin pie out of the tin.

She'd spent more than a few minutes wondering how Shawn was celebrating. Was she working hard in the diner? Was she having dinner with Jack and his wife? Or was she entertaining a fucking ski bunny in town for the weekend? The latter made Morgan want to throw up. Some blond-haired bimbo with big tits and even bigger lips in tight ski pants cuddling up to Shawn in front of a fire with hot toddies. She laughed evilly at the thought of Jameson baring his teeth at the bimbo.

Jane and Annie had only said they'd had pristine skiing conditions and that the weather was perfect. Good. Perfect skiing weather in Lake Tahoe. A place where just a month ago, Morgan imagined spending the weekend with Shawn. A mere four weeks ago, the thought of Lake Tahoe and Shawn brought a smile to Morgan's face. Now it left a gaping hole in Morgan's heart.

Work had been slow the past two weeks. Doctors were too busy getting in last-minute surgeries to meet one-on-one with her, but it wasn't for her lack of trying. Morgan had delivered some massive Christmas baskets to her most revered doctors, making an effort to keep her name in their minds when it came to needing the latest and greatest products.

The microwave beeped when her dinner was done, and she poured herself a glass of wine after she plated her food. Just because she was eating a microwave dinner didn't mean she had to eat like a savage out of the plastic tray. She carried her meal and her wine to the living room so she could watch that night's Hallmark movie. She was only a little ashamed for scoffing at the movie. It wasn't the screenwriter's fault that her love life was at the bottom of pig slop.

It was only six o'clock in the evening, but she hadn't done a thing that day. She hadn't showered, her hair wasn't brushed, and she was still in her flannel pajamas, the ones that kept her warm in the winter. The ones that reminded her of Shawn and her flannel shirts. She took a sip of wine after she'd finished her bite of food. The knock on her door interrupted her next sip. She'd considered not answering, but it was probably Jane and Annie. If she didn't answer, they'd just use their key. She might have to get that back from them if they would abuse that privilege by barging in on her without notice. She shuffled her slippered feet to the door, looked through the peephole, and cursed. What was she doing here? She opened the door just a few inches.

"What do you want?"

"I want to talk to you. Can I please come in?"

Morgan opened the door and stepped aside, not happy at all to see Jess. And looking really good while Morgan looked a mess.

"What is it, Jess? What do you possibly have to say to me after all this time?"

"Morgan, please. Can we sit?"

Morgan couldn't have a conversation with her ex looking the way she did.

"Go have a seat and I'll be right back."

Morgan went to her bedroom to change into something decent.

❖

Shawn checked the address one more time to be certain she had the right house. She'd been on the road for four hours, fighting the snow-covered highway and weekenders heading home from Tahoe. She should've taken the day off from the diner so she could have gotten an earlier start, but with winter here, the crowds picked up, especially on the weekends. She'd stopped to get flowers for Morgan, beautiful long-stemmed red roses that Shawn had hoped would help get her through the door. She exited her car, held her hand in front of her mouth to check her breath, then walked to the front door. When she knocked, she heard a woman's voice.

"I'll get it, baby."

A woman who wasn't Morgan opened the door.

"May I help you?"

Shawn peered around the woman's shoulder looking for Morgan. She rechecked the address numbers on the front of the house.

"Is Morgan here?"

"Who are you?"

"I'm Shawn. Who are you?"

"I'm Jess, Morgan's girlfriend. She's busy but I can give her a message."

So, this was the infamous ex. Or was it current now? Shawn hated that the woman was good-looking. She was shorter than Shawn by a few inches, athletic looking with red curly hair pulled back in a ponytail. The smug look on her face made her less attractive though. Shawn didn't know what to do. Should she ask to wait? Or should she just tuck her tail between her legs and get the hell out of Dodge? The pain in her chest made it difficult to breathe.

"Uh, no. I was in town and just wanted to stop by and say hi. I guess I'll just call her later."

Jess leaned against the doorframe with her arms crossed over her chest and looked Shawn up and down from head to toe as if she was sizing up the competition.

"I'll be sure to tell her you stopped by." Jess pushed off the doorframe and closed the door in Shawn's face. She threw the flowers under the hedge that lined Morgan's walkway and headed back to her car with a heavy feeling in the pit of her stomach.

❖

Morgan returned to the living room dressed in jeans, a cable-knit sweater, and her Ugg boots that kept her feet warm. While she'd been in the bedroom, she'd gone to the bathroom to wash her face and brush her hair, tying it up in a messy bun. At least she felt more human than before when she'd answered the door. She sat in her chair across the room from the couch Jess was sitting on.

"Okay, talk."

"I miss you, Morgan. I miss us. And I miss the woman I was when we were together."

"And what woman would that be? The cheater?" Morgan's words hit the desired mark when Jess dropped her head. Good. After all this time, Morgan still was pissed that Jess had cheated on her.

"I have no excuse for what happened, and if I could do anything to change what happened, I would. I made a huge mistake, and I promise if you take me back, I swear it'll never happen again."

Jess seemed sincere enough, but Morgan wouldn't be easily swayed.

"I appreciate your apology, but we can never go back. You hurt me. You brought a woman into our home. Into our bed. Do you have any idea how humiliated I was? I won't let you do that to me again. I won't let anyone hurt me like that." Morgan thought of Shawn and how quickly Shawn held that power. The grief she felt from Shawn hurting her was way more than she'd felt with Jess. Shawn hadn't used that power as a weapon though, at least Morgan didn't think so.

Morgan stood, done with this conversation, and done with Jess. "Thanks for coming over and apologizing, but we won't be getting back together."

Jess stood, her face red and stance aggressive, her fists clinched at her sides. "You think you can get better than me? Find someone who can give you what I can?"

Now Morgan was really pissed. How dare Jessica come in here to try and threaten her. "I know I can. I already did." Shawn was so much better than Jess. She was kind, romantic, funny, handsome. Morgan had always felt cared for by Shawn, even when they had just been friends.

Jess laughed. "You mean that big butch? What can she give you that I can't?"

What was Jess talking about? What big butch? The only one she could think of was Shawn, but how would Jess know about her?

"This is your last chance, Morgan. Once I walk out that door, I won't come back."

The relief Morgan felt from that statement was almost palpable, but she still wouldn't get her hopes up. "Promise? In that case, don't let the door hit you in the ass. Now get out of my house."

The door slamming startled Morgan, practically shaking the tears out of her eyes. She sat on the couch, gulping the rest of the forgotten wine. She quickly retrieved the bottle from the kitchen and refilled her glass. She was too amped up to sit still, and at every turn of her pacing, she took another drink. What big butch was Jess talking about? It couldn't be Shawn. Morgan hadn't talked to her in almost a month, and the only people who knew about Shawn were Jane and Annie. They hated Jess so they never would have told her so. She picked up her phone and called Jane.

"I have a crazy question. Have you seen Jess lately, and if so, did you tell her about Shawn?"

"Well, hello, Morgan. So nice to hear from you." Jane's sarcastic tone wasn't lost on Morgan.

"Yeah, yeah, hi. Now, answer the question."

"No and no. Even if I did see her, I'd never tell her about Shawn. Why? What happened?"

Morgan finished off her wine and she wished she had something stronger.

"Jess came here to ask me to get back together with her." Morgan told her the conversation they'd had. "She interrupted my lazy night, and I was pissed that she looked good." Morgan laughed as she told Jane about cleaning up and getting dressed.

"I just don't understand how she would know about Shawn, if she was even talking about her."

"Speaking of, have you heard from her at all?"

"No. I told her I didn't want to talk to her, so obviously she's obeying my wishes."

"Huh. Okay."

"What was that 'huh' for?"

"Nothing. Listen, Annie and I are about to eat. I'll talk to you later, okay? Love you."

Morgan looked at her phone wondering why Jane was acting weird. That woman was crazy sometimes, but Morgan loved her. She went to the living room window and looked out to the street, mostly to make sure Jess had left. The streets were wet from the falling rain that she could see from the streetlamp. She'd caught sight of something under her hedge, and she went to go check it out. She pulled out a bouquet of roses that looked fresh, and droplets of water adhered to the red velvety petals.

"What in the world?" Morgan continued to look around and found a small card facedown in the mud. She turned it over and gasped once she'd wiped the mud away. She'd recognize the small, all caps print that Shawn used.

Jameson misses you. But I miss you more.

Morgan clapped her hand over her mouth to stifle her cry. She stood and looked around for Shawn's Subaru. She hurried frantically up and down the block, desperate to see her, but Shawn was nowhere to be found. Her hair and clothes were soaked, her wet jeans weighing her down. Morgan went back inside and called Jane again, leaving a trail of water dripping from her clothes on the tile floor.

"She was here! Shawn was here!"

"What?"

"I was looking out the window to the street and I saw something, and I went to check and it turned out to be flowers. So, I looked some more, and I found a card in her writing." Morgan's words tumbled out of her mouth without taking a breath.

"What kind of flowers?"

Morgan squinted at her phone, wondering if her friend was some kind of stupid that night, then put it back to her ear.

"That's what you came away with? You want to know what kind of flowers they were? Red roses, by the way, but that's not the point."

"It kind of is. Red roses signify love. It would have been insulting if she'd brought you carnations or daisies."

"Jane! Listen to me. Shawn. Was. Here. Was that slow enough for you to understand? She was here. How did she get my address? Oh, shit! She must've come by when Jess was here and while I was changing. That's how Jess knew about Shawn. I have to call you back." Adrenaline coursed through Morgan's body, and along with being cold and wet, her body shook violently.

Morgan hung up and called Jess, the very last person she wanted to talk to. It actually surprised her that Jess picked up. Morgan put her on speaker as she went to her bedroom and stripped out of her wet clothes.

"Ready to take me back?" The egotistical tone made Morgan want to hang up, but she needed answers.

"Did someone come to my door when I was changing?" Morgan pulled on fleece sweatpants, a hoodie sweatshirt, and her fuzzy slippers.

"Maybe. Maybe no."

Fuck, she was infuriating. "Damn it, Jess. If you have a shred of decency left, tell me the truth." Morgan went back out to the kitchen, grabbed her wine, and sat on the couch, ignoring the water on her tile floor. She'd clean it later.

Morgan heard her sigh. "Yes. Some woman named Shawn. Is that what you're into now? Butch women?"

"Jess, focus. What did she say?"

"She just asked if you were home and I told her you were busy. She said she just stopped by to say hi then she left." Jess let out a frustrated sound. "I may have told her I was your girlfriend."

"You're unfuckingbelievable. Don't ever contact me again."

She called Jane again, jumped up from the couch, and started pacing again. She was too wound up to sit still.

"She *was* here. Fucking Jess answered the door and told Shawn she was my girlfriend."

"That bitch! Who the hell does she think she is?" Morgan couldn't remember the last time she'd heard Jane that angry.

"How did she know where I lived?" Morgan wondered out loud. The silence on the other line was deafening and telling. "Jane, how did Shawn know where I lived?"

"Well, um, we may have gone to see her over Thanksgiving."

"What? Are you serious right now?"

"Yep."

"Well, go on. Tell me your whole sordid story." Morgan emptied the rest of the wine into her glass and took a healthy swallow. The alcohol made her a little clumsy, and she used her hand to wipe some of the wine that dribbled to her chin.

Jane told her from beginning to end with Annie in the background confirming what Jane said.

"You've been so miserable, we just wanted to help. If it makes you feel any better, Shawn's been miserable too. Please don't be mad at us."

"Honey, I'm not mad. Strike that. I'm mad at Jess for doing and saying what she said to Shawn." Oh, God. Shawn came here looking for her, to tell her she missed her. "Are you telling me the truth about Paige, and that Shawn wasn't interested in anyone but me?"

"On my marriage, I swear I'm telling the truth. Morgan, she's been as miserable as you've been. She really cares for you and wants a relationship with you and only you. So, what are you going to do about it?"

What, indeed? Morgan had a lot to think about. That could be a life-changing decision, and she needed to figure out what was best for her.

Chapter Twenty-one

Shawn had been going through the motions for the past few weeks. When she'd left Morgan's, she grabbed a hotel room, not wanting to drive back to Tahoe late that night through the pouring rain on icy roads. She'd grabbed a small bottle of Scotch from a liquor store close to her hotel and drowned her sorrows in the amber liquid. She'd woke up hung over but sober, so she made the lonely trek home, listening to sad love songs that left her feeling hollower the farther she drove from Sacramento. The rain continued to fall, and the slapping of the wipers added to her headache. She'd picked up Jameson from Marcy's and spent the next couple of days in bed, heavy snowflakes falling from the gray sky, Shawn not wanting to face anyone. Not wanting to face the truth that she'd lost Morgan. She'd lost Morgan to fucking Jess, that smug bitch.

It was the day before Christmas Eve, and after they'd closed the diner, the crew had their own Christmas party. The diner had been festively decorated by Kerrie, Gina, and a few of her holiday staff that were home from college for the holidays, wanting to pick up a few extra shifts while they were home. Steve, Sophie, and Kaitlyn had worked for her over the summer, and they'd expressed their wishes to work when they were home. They were good kids and hard workers, so Shawn had no reservations hiring them back for the holidays. They'd all exchanged presents, feasted on ham, potatoes au gratin, salad, rolls, and pies. Once the kids left the party, Shawn handed envelopes to Kerrie, Melvin, Shorty, and Gina, her other full-time server and prep cook. They all ripped them open at the same time to find five hundred dollars in each one as their holiday bonus.

"Whoa, boss. This is way too much." Kerrie's eyes were wide as she pulled the five one-hundred-dollar bills out and fanned her face.

"Nonsense. This diner is as successful as it is because of you guys. It's just a small token of my appreciation for doing such a fantastic job and putting up with my grumpy ass for the past six weeks. I can't begin to tell you how much you all mean to me." Shawn looked at her employees, her friends, and didn't know how she'd been so blessed to have such a fine bunch working with her.

"Shorty, are you crying? You better not be crying, big guy."

Shorty wiped his eyes. "No, boss. My eyes are just sweating."

They all laughed and hugged each other. "Okay, enjoy the next couple of days, and we'll all be back here on December twenty-sixth ready to show off everything Santa brought us. Stay safe, my friends."

Shawn was the last one to leave, turning off the lights and locking up the diner for Christmas Eve and Christmas day. Typically, most restaurants were open those days to cater to those who didn't feel like cooking a big meal, but Shawn felt it was important for her staff to have the time with their families. The tourists and people of this town had plenty of other options to dine from the next two days.

By the time Shawn arrived home, it was almost dark. The only things she didn't like about winter was having to shovel the snow out of her driveway and that it was dark by five o'clock. Her house was dark, and for the third time this week, she'd reminded herself to reset the timer for her lamp in the living room to come on at four thirty. She opened the door to find Jameson wagging his tail and a rolled-up piece of paper in his mouth.

"What's this, doggo?" Shawn turned on the light just inside the door. She unrolled the paper and read the note.

My dear beloved hooman,

Please don't be mad. I called Morgan. I miss her. And she says she misses us too. Me more than you. But it still counts. Right? Can you please forgive her for leaving us? She said if you do, she'll never leave us again. She told me she loves you. And hopefully you can forgive her. Please, hooman mom. Forgive her.

The tears filling Shawn's eyes made it difficult for her to read the last few words.

"Morgan?" Shawn whispered reverently. Was she dreaming? She looked up from the note to find Morgan standing at the entrance of the kitchen.

"Are you really here?"

"I'm really here." Morgan took a step closer, uncertain if Shawn would accept her back in her life.

"How'd you get in?"

Morgan smiled. Shawn didn't sound upset which gave her the courage to take another step forward.

"You never lock your door, silly."

The laughter came through Shawn's tears. "I have so much to say to you. I can't believe you're actually here." Shawn swiped the tears away and Morgan yearned to go to her.

"All I need you to say is that you forgive me for ever doubting you. I was pigheaded. I blame that on being a Taurus, actually. I guess I still have a lot of work to do on myself, but I think with your help, I can be a better woman. A woman who is worthy of you and your love." Jameson barked and they both jumped. "I'm hoping I can be worthy of Jameson too."

Shawn laughed, and it was the sweetest sound to Morgan's ears. Shawn shook her head, quickly moved to Morgan, wrapping her arms around her and turning her in circles.

"I love you, Morgan. Please believe me that I love you so damn much. I don't want to be with anyone but you."

Morgan released her tears of joy, anxiety, and love. "I do believe you, Shawn. I love you so damn much too."

Shawn lowered Morgan so her feet were planted solidly on the ground although she was flying high at that moment.

"I came to your house, but Jess answered the door and she told me that you two were back together. Please tell me she was lying."

Morgan cupped Shawn's cheek with her hand. "She was. I want nothing to do with her, my love. You're the only one I want."

Jameson barked again, making them laugh with his tongue lolled out the side of his mouth, giving a big doggy smile. "And Jameson. I assume you're a package deal." Jameson barked again.

"If I'm dreaming, I don't ever want to wake up."

Morgan grabbed Shawn's face with both hands and kissed her like a sailor coming home after many years away. Their lips parted, Morgan's tongue wrestled with Shawn's, and when she broke the kiss, she pinched Shawn's ass.

"Ow!"

"That's how you know you're not dreaming."

Shawn laughed. "Please pinch me again. You know, just to be sure."

Morgan lowered her hands and squeezed Shawn's ass, filling her palms with Shawn's hard muscles, causing her to moan. That sound that had haunted Morgan's dreams for the past six weeks was reality now, and it made her clit hard and her sex wet.

"Shawn, please make love to me. I need to feel you. All of you."

Shawn said nothing but picked up Morgan and carried her to her room. Morgan wrapped her arms around Shawn's neck, finding comfort in Shawn's strong arms holding her tight, her scent of woods and diner bringing Morgan even more comfort.

Shawn set Morgan on her bed and slowly undressed her. When she pulled the last of Morgan's clothing away, Morgan scooted back on the bed while Shawn undressed herself. When she was completely naked, she crawled onto the bed, settling herself between Morgan's legs. At first touch of skin on skin, both of them moaned. Shawn propped herself up on straight arms and slowly moved her pelvis against Morgan's. Morgan wrapped her legs behind Shawn's and used her heels to pull Shawn deeper into her. The fire and intensity of Shawn's eyes as she thrust into her made Morgan hold on tighter.

"I've missed being under you, driving me crazy until I can't think straight." Morgan's words came out breathy. "I want you in me, baby. Fill me up with your fingers."

Shawn slid two fingers into Morgan's wet center, setting a deep and slow rhythm that was driving Morgan crazy and causing her hips to move, to take all of Shawn in. Shawn continued to look into Morgan's eyes, never breaking their connection.

"I love you so much, Shawn."

Shawn sped up her motion, going deeper, faster, hitting Morgan's clit with her palm with each stroke.

"You're going to make me come, baby."

"You're mine, love. Now, always, forever. Come for me. Let go, baby."

Morgan screamed out as she came. Shawn followed close behind, stroking her clit against the back of her hand that was buried deep in Morgan.

Shawn collapsed her entire weight onto Morgan, and she wrapped her arms around Shawn's waist, holding her close. Once they caught their breath, Shawn rolled off Morgan but kept her arm securely around her. Morgan turned on her side and ran her fingers through Shawn's damp hair. The lazy grin on Shawn's face lit a fire in Morgan. She crawled onto Shawn's back, kissing every inch of her from her neck to the small of her back. When Shawn raised her hips, Morgan slid two fingers into her from behind, continuing to nibble and bite her skin as she moved in and out of Shawn. Morgan loved how versatile Shawn was in bed. Every now and then, Morgan liked to take control, and she was very pleased that Shawn allowed her.

"I love you, and I want us to be together. Now and always."

"Always, baby." Shawn grunted as Morgan continued to fill her up. "I'm so close." Shawn cried out as the walls of her sex continued to spasm around Morgan's fingers. Morgan kissed the back of Shawn's shoulder then kissed her neck, sucking on the skin and marking her territory. Shawn yelped and Morgan laughed.

"I branded you, Evans. You are now the sole property of one Ms. Morgan Campbell."

"Consider me yours, love."

❖

Shawn woke Christmas Eve morning to an empty bed. She reached out and felt the cold sheets beneath her fingers. "No, please don't tell me that was a dream."

The door to her bedroom opened and Morgan walked in carrying a tray with two cups of coffee and homemade biscuits. The smell of hot dough and melted butter along with freshly brewed coffee made Shawn's stomach growl.

"Good morning, my love. I have breakfast, and Jameson has been fed and let outside."

"You're really here." Shawn felt like she could breathe again, realizing that Morgan was really there and not a mirage.

"I really am. For a few days at least, if you can stand me for that long."

Shawn sat up and accepted the steaming mug of coffee along with a kiss from Morgan's sweet lips. She could still taste herself on Morgan's mouth from when she went down on Shawn in the middle of the night. Last night's sleep consisted of short naps between bouts of making love, and Shawn's sore muscles were proof.

"I love that you're here, especially for Christmas. This will be the best holiday I've had in a long time."

"Ditto, baby. I know it's Christmas Eve, but I have something for you. Be right back."

Morgan returned with a thin box wrapped in red, gold, and green wrapping paper with a large silver bow.

"What is this?"

"Something I wanted to get you back in November, but never got around to. I figure better late than never."

Shawn unwrapped the box and pulled out an oil painting of a sunset from Sand Harbor.

"I saw this in Marcy's shop, and I thought it looked pretty similar to the sunset you took me to see. That was the night I started to fall for you."

Shawn wiped the tears from her eyes and sniffed. "You kissed me for the first time that night. That was when I knew I'd love you forever." Shawn pulled Morgan into her arms and held her tight. "I love it, and I love you."

Shawn frowned and Morgan traced her lips with her thumb. "Why the long face, love?"

Shawn looked away and Morgan grabbed her chin so she could see Shawn's face.

"I didn't get you anything. I didn't know you'd be here."

"Oh, Shawn. Don't you know that you've given me the best present I could ask for? It can't be wrapped and placed under the tree. You gave me the gift of forgiveness and your love. Nothing you could ever buy me could be better than that."

"I want to give you the world, Morgan."

Morgan placed her hand over Shawn's heart. "You have."

❖

"Are you sure I look okay? I should've packed something dressier."

Shawn kissed Morgan's forehead. "You look beautiful. You could be wearing a potato sack, and you'd still look gorgeous."

They stepped out of Shawn's car and the cold air hit Morgan like a slap in the face. Despite the heavy coat, Morgan shivered, but she wasn't sure if it was from the chilly temperature or the nerves she held in seeing Jack again. It had snowed all day, off and on, and this would be Morgan's first white Christmas.

Shawn knocked on the door and Jack answered, his surprise from seeing Morgan quickly broadened into a bright smile.

"Well, well, look who's here." Jack hugged Shawn then pushed her out of the way to welcome Morgan with a hug of her own. "I'm so happy to see you again, sweetheart. Welcome to our home." Jack introduced Morgan to his wife, Jeannie, who gave Morgan a warm hug, the kind of hug a grandparent gives their grandchild. Morgan handed her a gift from Shawn that she kindly signed Morgan's name to.

"Thank you for having us. You have a lovely home." It smelled of cinnamon and pine, and Morgan felt cozy and warm.

"I'm so happy to finally meet you." Jeannie took Morgan's hand and led her to the living room and introduced her to the wives of Bill, Dave, and Ernie. She was hugged by them all, including the men, who expressed their joy in seeing her again. They all sat in the living room in front of the fire, drinking their respective drinks, while Shawn and the men hung out in the kitchen drinking Scotch and bourbon. The living room was beautifully decorated, with garlands lining the mantel and a large tree in the corner adorned with lights and ornaments. Jeannie placed their gift under the tree to join the other beautifully wrapped presents.

"Morgan, honey, we're so happy to have you here. Our husbands have been going on and on about Shawny's new friend. What we really want to know, that our husbands are too dense to ask, is what are your intentions with our Shawny? Her grandparents are gone and her parents are in Texas, so we're essentially the only family she has here. We look after her like she was our own, and we don't want to see her hurt."

Morgan was impressed that Jeannie was able to say all that while a smile was plastered on her face. The other three women had similar smiles, but Morgan felt them sizing her up, and she had to be careful with her words. Morgan gave them the sweetest smile she had.

"I love how you all look after Shawn, and especially the way you love her. We've had some misunderstandings, but the one biggest lesson I've learned in all of this is that Shawn is a woman who loves with all her heart and is loyal to her friends. I love everything about her, and if she allows me, I'll continue to love her as long as she wants. Not only have I fallen in love with her, but her family as well." Morgan took a sip of her wine and thought of the words she wanted to say.

"When I left here, it wasn't just Shawn I was leaving. It was your husbands, Shawn's staff at the diner, and Jameson. All of those beautiful souls are what makes this town so special to me."

Jeannie and the other three wives looked at each other, then raised their glasses, waiting for Morgan to clink her glass against theirs. When the crystal came together, it made the most melodious sound.

"Welcome to our family, Morgan."

Later that night, cuddling under the covers, Shawn stroked the skin along Morgan's arms.

"You didn't have any trouble with the grandmothers, did you?"

Morgan chuckled. "Not at all. Once I told them my intentions for you were pure, they accepted me into the family."

Shawn laughed. "Good. So, Ms. Campbell, what *are* your intentions for me?"

Morgan crawled on top of Shawn and she reached her hands around Morgan and grabbed her ass. Morgan shivered at the feeling of her skin, her breasts, pressing into Shawn's.

"My intention is to love you and take care of you for as long as you want."

"Mmm." Shawn ran her hands up Morgan's back and around her front until she had them on Morgan's breasts. "I love how you think, Ms. Campbell." They welcomed in Christmas morning by making love and declaring once again their love for each other.

EPILOGUE

Spring

Winter had come and gone, and spring was in full bloom even though it was late May. There were still some patches of dirty snow on the ground, crystalized into near ice from the warm temperatures in the day and the colder temperature at night. The spring flowers were starting to sprout through the earth, thanks to a normal snowfall that winter, encouraged by the bright sun shining through the trees. The fiery red alpine paintbrush, the majestic purple lupine, and the red and yellow crimson columbine dotted the land. The colors were vibrant and brought joy to Shawn as she slowed down to savor the beauty of her town. Shawn had spent the warm afternoon mountain biking, trying to pass the time until Morgan arrived. Morgan had come up to the lake every other weekend, insisting she wanted to be up there, and that it made sense since Shawn had a diner to run. Shawn had gone to Sacramento for a few weekends, and they usually had dinner with Jane and Annie when Shawn was in town. Shawn felt like she'd owed them so much since they were instrumental in getting her and Morgan back together. Besides that, Shawn really liked them. She'd welcomed them to stay with her whenever they wanted to come to the lake.

Shawn rode her bike back to her house, ecstatic to see Morgan's car in the driveway, two hours earlier than expected. Shawn looked at her mud-spattered clothes and knew her face probably matched. That was the downside of spring mountain biking in the mountains.

She closed the front door behind her, calling for Morgan as she stripped her dirty clothes in the entry way. Morgan came out the kitchen holding a wooden spoon, her eyes wide. Shawn stood naked with the exception of her sports bra and underwear. Mud was splattered on her arms and legs that weren't covered by her mountain biking attire.

"Shawn Evans! What on earth were you doing?"

"I was mountain biking, and you're early, Ms. Campbell. Not that I'm complaining."

Shawn went to hug Morgan, but she stepped back. "You go shower before you get mud on me." Morgan stepped closer and leaned forward to give Shawn a kiss, but Shawn was too quick and grabbed her, lifting Morgan off the ground and kissing her senseless.

"Ack! You're getting me dirty."

Shawn laughed and despite Morgan acting upset, she wrapped her arms tight around Shawn's neck.

"I like you dirty, baby."

"You're right on that account. And I'll show you later just how dirty I can be. But dinner's almost ready, so go take a shower. I have something to talk to you about."

Shawn scrunched her eyebrows together, and Morgan smoothed out the wrinkles with her thumb.

"It's good news, love. Now, run along." Morgan smacked Shawn's bare ass with the wooden spoon, causing a loud crack.

When Shawn returned to the kitchen freshly showered, wet hair slicked back, and dressed in running pants and long sleeve T-shirt, Morgan let out a woof, causing Shawn to laugh. "Damn, baby. You clean up well."

They sat at the table, and before digging in, Shawn held Morgan's hand.

"What's the good news, Morgan?"

"Well, since we got back together, my time with you has been well spent, but short-lived. I hate it when I have to return back to Sacramento to go to work. And I hate it when you leave me to come back to the lake."

Shawn brought Morgan's hand to her lips and kissed it. "I hate that too. I want to have you with me every night and every morning."

"So, here's the thing. I told my boss that I was going to leave the company. My time with you and Jameson is much more important than my job."

Whoa! That was huge. Morgan loved her job and was really great at it. The fact that Morgan was willing to leave her job to be with Shawn made her soar, but also made her feel a little guilty. She didn't want to be the reason Morgan quit her job.

"He wouldn't accept my resignation, however he offered me a lateral transfer into inside/outside sales."

"I don't understand. What does that mean?"

"It means that working inside sales, I can work remotely, but he wants me in Sacramento for a day every other week to meet with the doctors."

Shawn didn't know what to say. "What are you saying?" Shawn was afraid to get her hopes up and needed to hear it from Morgan.

"It means, if you'll have me, I want to move up here and live with you. We'll be able to fall asleep and wake up next to each other every day. What do you think?"

Shawn just stared at Morgan, disbelieving how she'd been so lucky to have a woman like Morgan love her. Hearing those words from Morgan's mouth was a dream come true. Shawn stood and brought Morgan up with her. She held Morgan close and looked deep into her eyes, seeing the love and excitement she was sure mirrored her own.

"I think I've never loved you more than I do right this moment. You have no idea how happy you make me." Shawn kissed Morgan filled with promise and happily ever after. "Welcome home, my love."

Two Weeks Later

Shawn had taken a few days off work and joined Morgan in Sacramento to help pack her things. Since Shawn's house was fully furnished, Morgan had arranged for Habitat for Humanity to pick up her furniture in the living room and bedroom. Really, Morgan only needed to move her clothes and things that had sentimental value to her. Shawn had insisted she could bring whatever she wanted, and they could redecorate the cabin. All in all, they were able to pack everything in Shawn's SUV, Morgan's car, and Annie's truck. Morgan's house had only been on the market for a week before she had an offer for full price, and she took it.

The three vehicles arrived back to Shawn's with still a couple of hours of daylight left. It hardly took any time to unpack Morgan's things save for a few boxes they stored in the loft. With Jameson still at Marcy's, Shawn and Morgan took Annie and Jane to their favorite pizza place along the Truckee River. Once they'd finished their large combo pizza and a couple of pitchers of beer, they returned home. Morgan had gone into their bedroom to shower, leaving Shawn alone with Jane and Annie.

"I can't believe Morgan won't be living in Sacramento anymore." Jane's frown told Shawn how disappointed she was that Morgan had left.

"I know this change won't be easy for either of you, but we're only a two-hour drive away. We expect you both to celebrate the holidays with us, and with the new ski boat we just bought, we can go out on the lake whenever you want. I know how important you are to Morgan, but I want to tell you that you're important to me too. If it wasn't for you coming to see me over Thanksgiving, I might not have ever seen her again."

Jane reached over and took Shawn's hand in hers. "You're good for her, Shawn, and we love the way you love her. Just promise us that we'll be invited to the wedding."

Shawn laughed. "When we get to that point, you'll be the first to know."

Morgan joined them a few minutes later, sitting on the arm of the couch next to Shawn, skimming her fingers along the back of Shawn's neck, causing a shiver throughout Shawn's body.

Annie chuckled. "It might be sooner than you think."

Morgan continued to caress Shawn. "What will be sooner than she thinks?"

"That we'll be getting married someday, and that I promised they'd be the first to know."

Morgan leaned down and gave Shawn a short, sweet kiss, letting their lips linger for just a moment.

"Just so you know, when you're ready to pop the question, I'll be ready to say yes."

Shawn smiled as her lips met Morgan's again.

"Good to know, Ms. Campbell. I'll keep that in mind." Shawn grinned as she thought of the black velvet box hiding under her folded T-shirts in the bottom dresser drawer. She'd bought the two-carat princess cut diamond engagement ring shortly after Morgan told her she was moving in with her. Shawn was just waiting until September second. One year ago, on that day, was when Morgan walked into her diner, and Shawn's life had never been the same. Morgan had far exceeded Shawn's idea of her perfect love, and on September second, at Sand Harbor State Beach, as the sun sets, Shawn would get down on one knee and ask Morgan to be her wife for life.

About the Author

KC Richardson attended college on a basketball scholarship, and her numerous injuries in her various sports led her to a career in physical therapy. Her love for reading and writing allows her to create characters and tell their stories. She and her wife live in Southern California where they are trying to raise respectful fur kids.

When KC isn't torturing/fixing people, she loves spending time with her wonderful friends and family, reading, writing, kayaking, working out, and playing golf. She can be reached at kcrichardsonauthor@yahoo.com, on Twitter @KCRichardson7 and on Facebook.

Books Available from Bold Strokes Books

Flight SQA016 by Amanda Radley. Fastidious airline passenger Olivia Lewis is used to things being a certain way. When her routine is changed by a new, attractive member of the staff, sparks fly. (978-1-63679-045-9)

Home Is Where the Heart Is by Jenny Frame. Can Archie make the countryside her home and give Ash the fairytale romance she desires? Or will the countryside and small village life all be too much for her? (978-1-63555-922-4)

Moving Forward by PJ Trebelhorn. The last person Shelby Ryan expects to be attracted to is Iris Calhoun, the sister of the man who killed her wife four years and three thousand miles ago. (978-1-63555-953-8)

Poison Pen by Jean Copeland. Debut author Kendra Blake is finally living her best life until a nasty book review and exposed secrets threaten her promising new romance with aspiring journalist Alison Chatterley. (978-1-63555-849-4)

Seasons for Change by KC Richardson. Love, laughter, and trust develop for Shawn and Morgan throughout the changing seasons of Lake Tahoe. (978-1-63555-882-1)

Summer Lovin' by Julie Cannon. Three different women, three exotic locations, one unforgettable summer. What do you think will happen? (978-1-63555-920-0)

Unbridled by D. Jackson Leigh. A visit to a local stable turns into more than riding lessons between a novel writer and an equestrian with a taste for power play. (978-1-63555-847-0)

VIP by Jackie D. In a town where relationships are forged and shattered by perception, sometimes even love can't change who you really are. (978-1-63555-908-8)

Yearning by Gun Brooke. The sleepy town of Dennamore has an irresistible pull on those who've moved away. The mystery Darian Tennen and Samantha Pike uncover will change them forever, but the love they find along the way just might be the key to saving themselves. (978-1-63555-757-2)

A Turn of Fate by Ronica Black. Will Nev and Kinsley finally face their painful past and relent to their powerful, forbidden attraction? Or will facing their past be too much to fight through? (978-1-63555-930-9)

Desires After Dark by MJ Williamz. When her human lover falls deathly ill, Alex, a vampire, must decide which is worse, letting her go or condemning her to everlasting life. (978-1-63555-940-8)

Her Consigliere by Carsen Taite. FBI agent Royal Scott swore an oath to uphold the law, and criminal defense attorney Siobhan Collins pledged her loyalty to the only family she's ever known, but will their love be stronger than the bonds they've vowed to others, or will their competing allegiances tear them apart? (978-1-63555-924-8)

In Our Words: Queer Stories from Black, Indigenous, and People of Color Writers. Stories Selected by Anne Shade and Edited by Victoria Villaseñor. Comprising both the renowned and emerging voices of Black, Indigenous, and People of Color authors, this thoughtfully curated collection of short stories explores the intersection of racial and queer identity. (978-1-63555-936-1)

Measure of Devotion by CF Frizzell. Disguised as her late twin brother, Catherine Samson enters the Civil War to defend the Constitution as a Union soldier, never expecting her life to be altered by a Gettysburg farmer's daughter. (978-1-63555-951-4)

Not Guilty by Brit Ryder. Claire Weaver and Emery Pearson's day jobs clash, even as their desire for each other burns, and a discreet sex-only arrangement is the only option. (978-1-63555-896-8)

Opposites Attract: Butch/Femme Romances by Meghan O'Brien, Aurora Rey, Angie Williams. Sometimes opposites really do attract. Fall in love with these butch/femme romance novellas. (978-1-63555-784-8)

Swift Vengeance by Jean Copeland, Jackie D, Erin Zak. A journalist becomes the subject of her own investigation when sudden strange, violent visions summon her to a summer retreat and into the arms of a killer's possible next victim. (978-1-63555-880-7)

Under Her Influence by Amanda Radley. On their path to #truelove, will Beth and Jemma discover that reality is even better than illusion? (978-1-63555-963-7)

Wasteland by Kristin Keppler & Allisa Bahney. Danielle Clark is fighting against the National Armed Forces and finds peace as a scavenger, until the NAF general's daughter, Katelyn Turner, shows up on her doorstep and brings the fight right back to her. (978-1-63555-935-4)

When in Doubt by VK Powell. Police officer Jeri Wylder thinks she committed a crime in the line of duty but can't remember, until details emerge pointing to a cover-up by those close to her. (978-1-63555-955-2)

A Woman to Treasure by Ali Vali. An ancient scroll isn't the only treasure Levi Montbard finds as she starts her hunt for the truth—all she has to do is prove to Yasmine Hassani that there's more to her than an adventurous soul. (978-1-63555-890-6)

Before. After. Always. by Morgan Lee Miller. Still reeling from her tragic past, Eliza Walsh has sworn off taking risks, until Blake Navarro turns her world right-side up, making her question if falling in love again is worth it. (978-1-63555-845-6)

Bet the Farm by Fiona Riley. Lauren Calloway's luxury real estate sale of the century comes to a screeching halt when dairy farm heiress, and one-night stand, Thea Boudreaux calls her bluff. (978-1-63555-731-2)

Cowgirl by Nance Sparks. The last thing Aren expects is to fall for Carol. Sharing her home is one thing, but sharing her heart means sharing the demons in her past and risking everything to keep Carol safe. (978-1-63555-877-7)

Give In to Me by Elle Spencer. Gabriela Talbot never expected to sleep with her favorite author—certainly not after the scathing review she'd given Whitney Ainsworth's latest book. (978-1-63555-910-1)

Hidden Dreams by Shelley Thrasher. A lethal virus and its resulting vision send Texan Barbara Allan and her lovely guide, Dara, on a journey up Cambodia's Mekong River in search of Barbara's mother's mystifying past. (978-1-63555-856-2)

In the Spotlight by Lesley Davis. For actresses Cole Calder and Eris Whyte, their chance at love runs out fast when a fan's adoration turns to obsession. (978-1-63555-926-2)

Origins by Jen Jensen. Jamis Bachman is pulled into a dangerous mystery that becomes personal when she learns the truth of her origins as a ghost hunter. (978-1-63555-837-1)

Pursuit: A Victorian Entertainment by Felice Picano. An intelligent, handsome, ruthlessly ambitious young man who rose from the slums to become the right-hand man of the Lord Exchequer of England will stop at nothing as he pursues his Lord's vanished wife across Continental Europe. (978-1-63555-870-8)

Unrivaled by Radclyffe. Zoey Cohen will never accept second place in matters of the heart, even when her rival is a career, and Declan Black has nothing left to give of herself or her heart. (978-1-63679-013-8)

A Fae Tale by Genevieve McCluer. Dovana comes to terms with her changing feelings for her lifelong best friend and fae, Roze. (978-1-63555-918-7)

Accidental Desperados by Lee Lynch. Life is clobbering Berry, Jaudon, and their long romance. The arrival of directionless baby dyke MJ doesn't help. Can they find their passion again—and keep it? (978-1-63555-482-3)

Always Believe by Aimée. Greyson Walsden is pursuing ordination as an Anglican priest. Angela Arlingham doesn't believe in God. Do they follow their vocation or their hearts? (978-1-63555-912-5)

Best of the Wrong Reasons by Sander Santiago. For Fin Ness and Orion Starr, it takes a funeral to remind them that love is worth living for. (978-1-63555-867-8)

Courage by Jesse J. Thoma. No matter how often Natasha Parsons and Tommy Finch clash on the job, an undeniable attraction simmers just beneath the surface. Can they find the courage to change so love has room to grow? (978-1-63555-802-9)

I Am Chris by R Kent. There's one saving grace to losing everything and moving away. Nobody knows her as Chrissy Taylor. Now Chris can live who he truly is. (978-1-63555-904-0)

The Princess and the Odium by Sam Ledel. Jastyn and Princess Aurelia return to Venostes and join their families in a battle against the dark force to take back their homeland for a chance at a better tomorrow. (978-1-63555-894-4)

The Queen Has a Cold by Jane Kolven. What happens when the heir to the throne isn't a prince or a princess? (978-1-63555-878-4)

The Secret Poet by Georgia Beers. Agreeing to help her brother woo Zoe Blake seemed like a good idea to Morgan Thompson at first...until she realizes she's actually wooing Zoe for herself... (978-1-63555-858-6)

You Again by Aurora Rey. For high school sweethearts Kate Cormier and Sutton Guidry, the second chance might be the only one that matters. (978-1-63555-791-6)

Coming to Life on South High by Lee Patton. Twenty-one-year-old gay virgin Gabe Rafferty's first adult decade unfolds as an unpredictable journey into sex, love, and livelihood. (978-1-63555-906-4)

Love's Falling Star by B.D. Grayson. For country music megastar Lochlan Paige, can love conquer her fear of losing the one thing she's worked so hard to protect? (978-1-63555-873-9)

Love's Truth by C.A. Popovich. Can Lynette and Barb make love work when unhealed wounds of betrayed trust and a secret could change everything? (978-1-63555-755-8)

Next Exit Home by Dena Blake. Home may be where the heart is, but for Harper Sims and Addison Foster, is the journey back worth the pain? (978-1-63555-727-5)

Not Broken by Lyn Hemphill. Falling in love is hard enough—even more so for Rose who's carrying her ex's baby. (978-1-63555-869-2)

The Noble and the Nightingale by Barbara Ann Wright. Two women on opposite sides of empires at war risk all for a chance at love. (978-1-63555-812-8)

What a Tangled Web by Melissa Brayden. Clementine Monroe has the chance to buy the café she's managed for years, but Madison LeGrange swoops in and buys it first. Now Clementine is forced to work for the enemy and ignore her former crush. (978-1-63555-749-7)